"Was I so easy to forget?

Michael felt Blair's pain swirling inside him like a tornado, mixing with his own, confusing him, making it impossible for him to explain. How did he explain living a lie for ten years? How could he explain what he had done?

"Answer me, damn you!" she demanded in a strained whisper. "Why don't you answer?"

"You don't understand."

"No? Then make me understand! Make me understand how you could simply go away after what happened between us . . . what you said to me." Her lips began to tremble. "You got away without answering last time we were together, but not this time!"

Dear Reader,

One of your favorite authors is on tap for this month: Nora Roberts. It's been a while since she last appeared in the line, but I think you'll find *Unfinished Business* well worth the wait. I'm a particular fan of stories that reunite past lovers, so I was really rooting for Vanessa Sexton and Brady Tucker, and I think you will be, too.

The rest of this month is pretty exciting, as well. Ann Williams is back with *Without Warning,* a complex tale of greed, revenge and—of course!—passion. Hero Michael Baldwin was reported dead years ago, but as Blair Mallory discovers, the reports of his death were greatly exaggerated! In *True to the Fire,* Suzanne Carey uses her lush island setting to full effect as she spins a tale about a woman trying to carry on her father's legacy and the handsome revolutionary who wins her heart. Finally, welcome Blythe Stephens to Silhouette Intimate Moments. In *Wake to Darkness* she grabs your attention right on page one and never lets go. I found myself completely involved with heroine Yvonne Worthington's search to regain her memory—and find love.

In coming months, keep your eyes out for more great reading from Silhouette Intimate Moments. We'll be bringing you books from favorite authors such as Marilyn Pappano, Paula Detmer Riggs, Joyce McGill and—very soon!—Linda Howard. You won't want to miss a single one of the books we have scheduled for you.

Yours,
Leslie Wainger
Senior Editor and Editorial Coordinator

ANN WILLIAMS

Without Warning

SILHOUETTE·INTIMATE·MOMENTS®

Published by Silhouette Books New York

America's Publisher of Contemporary Romance

SILHOUETTE BOOKS
300 East 42nd St., New York, N.Y. 10017

WITHOUT WARNING

ISBN: 0-373-07436-0

First Silhouette Books printing June 1992

Printed in the U.S.A.

ANN WILLIAMS

gave up her career as a nurse, then as the owner and proprietor of a bookstore, in order to pursue her writing full-time. She was born and married in Indiana, and after a number of years in Texas, she now lives in Arizona with her husband of over twenty years and their four children.

Reading, writing, crocheting, classical music and a good romantic movie are among her diverse loves. Her dream is to one day move to a cabin in the Carolina mountains with her husband and "write to my heart's content."

To my long-suffering husband, Don

Chapter 1

Blair slipped the white nurse's shoes from her aching feet and dropped onto the chintz-covered wicker lover seat. Leaning back against the thick, colorful pillows with a tired sigh, she propped her feet on the wicker table before her and reached for the mail she'd stopped to collect a few minutes ago on her way into the house.

At first glance it didn't appear to be anything worth the trouble she'd taken to get it. Tossing aside a sheaf of leaf-lets advertising local sales, she found a utility bill, a missing child alert—and a small white envelope.

Blair held the envelope in one hand, staring curiously at her name and address printed across the front in small, neat, black letters. She didn't see a return address, only a post-mark near the upper right-hand corner.

Who would be writing to her from New Smyrna Beach? As far as she could recall, she didn't know anyone there. The town was situated about an hour's drive down the coast from Baywater, Florida, her own hometown. New Smyrna Beach was a well-known tourist town, noted for its eight-mile expanse of easily accessible beaches. But it had been years since she'd been there.

After ripping the end off the envelope curiously, she pulled a single folded sheet of paper from inside, glanced at her name at the top and then at the signature down near the bottom. Michael Baldwin. Michael . . . Baldwin?

A sudden shaft of pain made it difficult for her to breathe. No, it couldn't be. Michael Baldwin was dead! Was this someone's idea of a joke? She didn't find it funny in the least!

Blair angrily wadded the paper into a tight ball and held it over the wastebasket on the floor near her elbow. Who could be so cruel, so perverted? And why now? Why would someone wait ten years to play such a terrible joke?

And then a possible answer came to mind. The sale of the Baldwin estate was due to take place in about ten days. It was going up for public auction. Maybe this letter wasn't intended as a joke but as a forerunner to someone's coming forward to make a claim on the estate.

But who could it possibly be? A distant relative? No, she knew, after having lived next door to the family since birth, that Michael and his father had been the last of their family line.

Smoothing out the crumpled piece of paper, Blair began to read, thinking that perhaps the contents of the letter might give her a clue to the author's true identity and purpose.

Blair,
  I know this will come as a shock to you, but I'm alive. I didn't die ten years ago on Dad's boat, the *Lazy Daze*.
  I would like you to meet me at the Sunset Motel, five miles north of New Smyrna Beach. I'll be in room sixteen after nine each night. I'll be there for two days, from the sixteenth through the seventeenth.
  I know that at this moment you must have a lot of questions, and I'll explain everything when we meet.
  I hope you'll come, but if you decide against it, please don't mention *to anyone* that you've heard from me. Everyone in town thinks I'm dead—leave it that way.

It's a matter of life and death.

Michael Baldwin

"No," Blair muttered in protest. "It's impossible—Michael's dead!" Though the bodies had never been found, both men were presumed lost at sea. Hadn't she attended the memorial service for them over ten years ago? Hadn't she stood alongside Cheryl Prescott, her best friend and Michael's fiancé, supporting her through the awful ordeal?

Dropping her feet to the floor, she sat forward and stared at the paper clutched tightly in her hands as though it contained the answer to her bewilderment, if only she could see it.

What if he isn't dead? a voice somewhere at the back of her mind made itself heard above the confusion of her thoughts. *What if, somehow, he's really alive?*

"If that's so," she asked aloud, arguing with herself, "then why hasn't he come forward before now? Why has he waited so long to contact anyone? And why me?"

No, the letter was a fake. It had to be. Michael was dead.

Are you certain? that voice persisted. *Are you so willing to write him off?*

No, God, no, if Michael was alive... The thought caused her heart to pound, kindling a warm liquid feeling inside her. Michael...alive... After all this time, the thought was electrifying.

No, wait, she was getting all excited about something that in all likelihood wasn't true. The letter was almost certainly a hoax. Wishing for something didn't make it so.

Getting to her feet, she stared down at the small, finely printed black letters. Was this Michael's handwriting? She couldn't be certain after all these years. What she needed was a basis for comparison.

She hurried from the room and down the hall to her bedroom, which sat at the back of the two-story house facing the beach, and flew to her closet. On the top shelf she searched for and found a shoe box covered in youthfully printed paper and lace. Removing the lid, she lifted out a small bundle of cards and letters tied together with a pink satin ribbon.

From the bottom of the stack she withdrew a pale lavender envelope. Inside was a card wishing her a happy twenty-first birthday. Michael, she remembered, had had a quirk about his handwriting. He'd always maintained that no one, not even himself, could read it, so he'd printed everything in small, neat letters.

On the inside of the card was a short message penned in black ink and signed, Michael. With unsteady hands, stomach churning, Blair compared the two signatures, blinked, and looked again.

My God! Was it possible? The two signatures looked almost identical. There was a maturity to the penmanship in the letter that was lacking on the card, but the words appeared to have been written by the same hand.

Blair's knees became weak, and the card began to flutter violently between her fingers. She backed slowly toward the bed, then collapsed on the rose-printed coverlet, staring from the card in one hand to the letter in the other.

Michael...alive...after all this time... Her thoughts spun with the wonder of it. She whispered the words aloud, delighting in the sound of his name on her lips for the first time in years. "Michael. Alive!"

All this time she'd filed Michael away in the back of her mind along with her first grown-up party dress, her first date...her first kiss....

He was alive! Somewhere, at this very moment, he was sitting, standing, breathing, a real flesh-and-blood man, not the dark, hazy memory she kept hidden in her heart. At this very moment he could be thinking about her as she was thinking about him.

Blair glanced toward the mirror on her dressing table, saw her flushed face and overbright eyes, and raised both hands to hide her hot cheeks. Was she acting foolish to be so excited about a man from the past, a man she'd almost forgotten?

Don't lie to yourself. You never forgot him, not him or one single moment you spent with him over the years. You simply chose not to think about him. It was the only way you could deal with his loss.

But she didn't have to do that any longer. He was alive! Almost bouncing off the bed, forgetting that she was a mature woman of thirty-two years and not the twenty-two-year-old he'd last known, she turned toward the phone resting on the table nearby. She simply had to call Cheryl and tell her the wonderful news!

No—she couldn't! Michael had said to tell no one. He'd said it was a matter of life and death. Blair frowned. What did that mean? Was he in some sort of trouble? That didn't sound like the Michael she remembered from their youth.

That Michael had been soft-spoken, gentle, and just a little bit shy around people he didn't know very well. He'd been the kind of person you knew you could depend on in any situation, the kind you went to if you were in trouble, not the other way around. He'd been very special, and everyone, from small children to adults, had liked him.

A sudden thought popped into her mind, one she'd had a few minutes ago, but in her excitement had paid little attention. Why hadn't Michael contacted anyone in Baywater before now?

Obviously, whatever his reason for remaining silent all these years, something had changed. Could it be that he'd been injured in whatever catastrophe had befallen him and his father at sea and only now regained his memory? That seemed a bit farfetched.

If it wasn't injuries that had kept Michael silent, then what had? And why had he chosen to contact her, when Cheryl had been his fiancé at the time of his disappearance?

Blair covered her eyes with one hand and let the jumble of her thoughts drift into the distant past, seeing herself and Michael as children. Had his reason for writing to her and not Cheryl been the fact that as children and adolescents they'd practically been inseparable?

That must be it. But that still didn't answer the question of why he'd waited so long to come forward. Could it be that he'd read in the newspaper about Cheryl's upcoming marriage?

The brief moment of joy she'd experienced at the news of his return to the living began to dull, mired in questions and doubts concerning the reason for his long silence. Eventually her happiness seeped away altogether, leaving a hollow, empty space that slowly filled with a budding anger.

Why had Michael waited so long to write? Ten years—nearly a third of her lifetime.

And what about Michael's father? Was he alive, too? Had the whole incident—the boat trip, their disappearance, their supposed deaths—been nothing more than a ruse? To what end?

Dropping both the card and the letter into the shoe box, Blair moved around the large double bed that had belonged to her parents and stood at the window. Holding back the delicate, white lace curtain, she stared out at the gentle swell of the ocean.

It was late May, but the beach looked deserted, barren—just, if she was being honest with herself, as her life had been for the past ten years. Ever since the news of Michael's death had reached her ears.

Glancing back over her shoulder, she could see a corner of the letter sticking up over the edge of the shoe box. A dull ache began somewhere in the region of her heart, the same dull ache she'd felt every time she'd thought about Michael and remembered that last night...the night before the fishing trip.

What should she do? She gripped the curtain tightly. Maybe she should ignore the letter. That would be the simplest thing.

Why had he come back? Should she see him and find out?

Immediately upon the tail end of that question a stubborn, angry glint hardened her china-blue eyes. Maybe she should simply take the letter to John Saunders, despite the warning against it, and let *him* authenticate it.

No! She couldn't do that. What if the letter was for real and by showing it to someone else she caused something terrible to happen to Michael?

Besides, there was more to consider here than her own feelings. She couldn't hurt Cheryl again, not now. Cheryl had lost both Michael and the mother she'd dearly loved within a short span of time, and now her friend was getting married in two days. She deserved her chance at happiness without shadows from the past marring it.

The cry of a sea gull on the beach drew her attention to the scene beyond the window. The water was calm after days of high winds and rain. Calm...just like it had been on that night—the last night of Michael's life—so long ago....

Blair rolled onto her side and pulled the cover up over her head, but the sounds persisted. A soft, insistent clatter beating against her eardrums.

Lowering a corner of the sheet, she glared with one eye at the fluorescent dial of the alarm clock sitting beside her bed. Two a.m. Covering her head again, she snuggled down against the pillows, determined to ignore the bothersome noise.

The rattle of stones came again, harder this time, loud enough to wake the dead—or her parents. Groaning, she realized that no matter how long she ignored the sound, it—and Michael—wouldn't go away, not until she'd acknowledged his presence. And if she waited much longer, her parents would be awakened.

"Men!" she muttered in disgust, throwing back the covers and crawling from the bed, wishing she dared to yell at Michael Baldwin to go home and leave her alone.

Without bothering to turn on a light, Blair tugged her baggy nightshirt down to her knees and moved to lean against the cool glass of the window and glare at the tall figure standing below with his hands on his hips, staring up at her. She'd hardly seen him at all for the past couple of weeks, and now he'd chosen the middle of the night to remedy the situation.

Loosening the latch, Blair pushed the window back and called quietly, "What do you want? Can't a girl get a decent night's sleep without being disturbed by a hoodlum like you?"

Michael laughed softly, the sound causing gooseflesh to creep up her arms and legs. The reaction made her mad, because she couldn't account for the phenomenon. All she knew was that it had started about the time Michael's voice began to deepen and his muscles to develop and it had continued to this day.

Her reaction confused her, too. Until it began, Michael had always been like a brother to her, except for the fact that there was none of the sibling rivalry between them that occurred in most, if not all, families. And the anger she'd felt over his neglect these past two weeks went far beyond sisterly.

"Come on down, little girl. I've got something to tell you."

"Can't it wait until morning? And *don't* call me 'little girl'!" She knew he was referring to her stature and not her years, because they were within nine months of being the same age.

"No, it can't wait. You know Dad and I are leaving early in the morning on a fishing trip."

"Then tell me when you get back."

"Either you come down—right now," he demanded, "or I come up." He shrugged. "It's your decision."

Blair hesitated, saw him make a move in the direction of the trellis covered with her mother's passion flowers and roses, and answered hurriedly, "Okay, you win. I'll be down in a jiffy."

Her slight figure withdrew, then reappeared for an instant. "This had better be good!" she admonished shortly, then disappeared from sight.

She shimmied into a pair of shorts and fastened the snap. Running impatient fingers through her long, dark brown hair, she caught the ends and twisted them up on top of her head, where she fastened them with a comb. An instant later she dashed from the room.

In the hallway she slowed to a walk, moving cautiously down the staircase at the front of the house. Her parents' room was located on the ground floor at the back of the house, facing the beach. But she suspected that her father slept with one ear turned toward her bedroom, listening for even the slightest sound coming from overhead.

She was an only child born of middle-aged parents. She was their pride and joy, and at times they tended to smother her.

Blair figured that if she was very careful, and considerably lucky, they wouldn't hear her leaving the house by way of the kitchen door. She was sure her father wouldn't be very pleased at the idea of his single, twenty-two-year-old daughter going out at two a.m. to meet a man, even one she'd known practically from birth, dressed only in a nightshirt and shorts.

"Well, what have we here?" Without warning the words came at her from out of the dark.

Blair gave a tiny yelp and whirled quickly to find herself bumping unexpectedly against the solid warmth of Michael's chest. The only time they had been this close in years was on a crowded dance floor with dozens of friends around them. Their eyes met in the moonlight, and for a moment she couldn't seem to breathe—or to think....

"Don't do that!" she snapped angrily, coming to her senses and shoving him away with a halfhearted slap on his shoulder. "You know I hate it when you sneak up behind me that way." Turning back to the door, she fiddled with the lock.

"Yes, I do," Michael agreed as he bent closer, adding in a dangerously soft voice, "and that's *exactly* why I do it."

Blair trembled as his warm breath traveled over the bare sensitive skin at the back of her neck. What was wrong with her tonight? She was well past the awkward age, and being with Michael had never had that element of danger in it, anyway. Michael was...Michael, her soul mate, her very best friend. He understood her like no one else.

"Come on, quit stalling," Michael said impatiently. "That door is as closed as it's ever going to be."

Grabbing her arm, he pulled her along beside him. They moved away from the house through the flower garden, her mother's pride and joy, past the gazebo to the gate and down the embankment to the beach below, trudging along with the soft thick sand drifting between her toes.

"Where are we going?" Blair asked curiously.

"To the marina. Dad was tied up with our guests all evening, and I promised I'd make a few last-minute inspections on the boat for him, so we can get an early start in the morning. This is the first opportunity I've had to do it."

"Guests?" Blair asked in surprise. She gave his profile a quick glance in the bright moonlight.

"We had a small dinner party tonight." He hesitated. "A . . . kind of celebration . . ."

"Celebration?" Blair stopped dead in her tracks. "What kind of celebration?"

"That's what I wanted to talk to you about—"

"Who was invited?" Blair interrupted with a slight edge to her normally clear tones. There had been very few celebrations at the Baldwin house over the past twenty-two years from which she'd been excluded.

"Dr. Prescott and Cheryl—"

"I see," Blair interrupted again, a small catch in her voice. Head high, eyes focused straight ahead, she tried very hard not to be hurt. She understood about Michael and Cheryl. At least, she told herself she did.

"Hey." Michael grabbed her arm and swung her to face him. His dark eyes bored down into hers, seeing the wounded expression she was trying unsuccessfully to hide. All at once he found himself at a loss for words.

Blair wanted to assure him that she didn't mind not being invited to his party, but she couldn't seem to get the words past her stiff lips. Her gaze focused on the uncertain expression in his dark eyes and couldn't seem to move away.

Why was it that she'd never noticed how thick Michael's lashes were above his extraordinary eyes? Or how his brows formed an almost straight line across his forehead whenever he frowned?

Her glance shifted. And how long had his beard been so heavy it appeared as a dark shadow beneath the skin of his jaw and chin by the end of the day?

"Blair? Did you hear what I said?"

"W-what?" Giving her head a tiny shake to clear it of such capricious thoughts, feeling confused, wondering again what was wrong with her tonight, she asked, "What did you say?"

"I said I—"

His words were cut off in mid-sentence as Blair's dark pile of hair, held in place by a single comb, pulled loose and fell in a silken cascade around her slender white neck and narrow shoulders. Michael's eyes followed as the heavy mass slid over and beyond the tips of her small, taut breasts, clearly outlined beneath the pale pink nightshirt. He swallowed quickly and felt a sudden tightness in his chest.

The night, calm up till now, changed abruptly, as though reflecting the sudden tumult inside him. Wind began to stir, raising whitecaps on the waves behind them, lifting the long brown strands of Blair's hair, whipping them out in all directions.

Blair tore her glance from Michael as her hands flew toward the windblown strands, unconsciously drawing the flimsy shirt even more intimately against her small, enchanting frame. Michael couldn't seem to glance away from the sight of her budding curves straining at the thin material.

Struggling with the swirling mass of hair, Blair muttered, "Damn! I can't find my comb." Glad to have a reason for doing so, because the expression on his face was confusing her even more, Blair turned her back to him and asked quickly, "Michael, can you see it? Grab it before I lose the darned thing. I can never seem to keep one. I'm seriously considering getting this stuff hacked off." She gave the bunched hair a slight, irritated jerk, wondering why she was babbling like a fool.

Michael took an instinctive step forward in protest. If there was one thing about Blair he'd always consciously admired, it was the beauty of her thick, glossy mane of hair.

"Don't cut it," he protested impulsively, raising a hand toward her head. "It's too beautiful for that."

Blair turned slowly to face him, reacting to an odd, never before heard note in his voice. The move brought them close.

Michael could smell the fresh soap and powder scent of her skin. It was a scent he'd learned long ago to associate with Blair, but never had it affected him as it did now. His head began to swim, while a strange heat began to make itself known in his lower body and his knees began to feel weak. His eyes moved over her face, coming to rest on her full, pouting lips.

Had her mouth always looked this inviting? He could feel himself drowning in sensation, wondering what it would be like to...

All at once a loose strand of dark hair snaked out, slapping across his lower face, bringing him abruptly to his senses.

"W-what's wrong?" Blair asked uncertainly, wondering at the troubled look in his dark eyes. She hadn't missed his uncommonly personal remark about her hair. But she was uncomfortable with him in a way she'd never known, and she tried to ignore it as best she could.

Michael shook his head silently in answer to her question. At the moment speech was beyond him.

Blair interpreted the movement to mean nothing was wrong and bent her head to her original purpose. She needed time to get a perspective on the strange new sensations Michael had inspired tonight.

"Do you see the comb?" she asked a bit breathlessly.

"No," he answered without looking, still under the unexpected spell of her magic. "It's gone."

He didn't dare touch her, not even her hair, to find the missing comb, not while his mind and body were in such chaos. He was experiencing feelings he had no business feeling for Blair Mallory.

"Never mind, then," she said, accepting his answer without question. "We'll never find it now, and the tide will have taken it clear to China by morning."

Giving a mighty shiver, comprised mostly of emotion rather than cold, she complained all at once, "I'm freezing. Let's get to the boat before I turn into a block of ice."

Bunching her long hair in one hand, she whirled away, running quickly down the beach toward the lights of the marina visible in the distance. What she needed was action to occupy her body while her brain figured a way out of the maze of forbidden emotions.

Michael stood for a moment without moving, staring at her dim figure as she disappeared into the night. What was wrong with him? He was acting like—like he hadn't known Blair all his life. Feeling like he was fifteen all over again.

"Michael! Come on!"

"I'm coming," he muttered, feeling as though he'd done something indecent in noticing, really noticing, her innocent beauty just now.

"Michael! Will you come on?" Blair stopped, one hand twisted in her hair, the other motioning for him to hurry, the chill of the wind blowing against her bare legs causing her to shiver for real now.

Taking a fortifying breath, Michael muttered, "All right already, I'm coming."

He ran to catch up with her, caught her hand in his, and together they hurried toward the dock where the *Lazy Daze* stood waiting. Michael decided to forget what had just happened. Perhaps it was only the news he had yet to tell Blair that had produced the emotional roller coaster he felt trapped on tonight.

"Evening, Michael, Blair."

Just short of the steps leading down to the boat, they turned as one to confront the short, rotund man swinging a large black flashlight at his side as he approached them.

Blair spoke first. "Good evening, Mr. Wallace, how are you?"

"Fine, fine. How's your father, Blair? I heard he was ill."

"Much better. The doctor has adjusted his medication, and it seems to be helping."

"Good, good." He looked from one to the other. "You two aren't going out for a sail this time of night?" he asked, noting that they were headed for the *Lazy Daze*.

"No," Michael replied. "Just some last-minute things I need to do before the trip in the morning."

The older man nodded, scratched at a place on the side of his neck with the end of the flashlight, then waved it at them. "Haven't seen much of your father around lately, Michael. I know he must be real busy, but tell him, when he gets a chance, I'd like to talk with him."

"Will do, sir," Michael replied.

"Good. Well, you two be careful, and make sure you lock up after you're through," he admonished as he continued on his way.

An hour later, Blair lay in a deck chair waiting for Michael to join her. A cup of hot chocolate that he'd made in the galley below warmed her insides.

They'd made a thorough inspection of everything on the boat as specified by Michael's father. And in the interim Blair had forgotten her earlier upset at learning she'd been left off Michael's guest list that evening. Her questions about the reason for the dinner party could wait until later.

Besides, it had never been easy for her to stay mad at him. One way or another, he always managed to talk or tease her out of it. Their friendship went deep, in a totally different direction than the one she shared with Cheryl Prescott.

It was the advent of school that had caused the two of them to broaden their range of friends to include others. By that time Michael had been firmly entrenched in Blair's life as best friend, mentor and soul mate. Neither Cheryl's friendship, nor any other, ever quite attained that exalted stature.

When Michael and Cheryl had gravitated toward each other in their early teens, Blair had been upset for a while, had felt left out, but that feeling hadn't lasted. Michael had proved to her that their friendship continued to be a very important and necessary facet of his life, and Blair had learned to be satisfied with that. At least, she'd thought she had.

"Well, I see that, as usual whenever there's work to be done, you've managed to find a hiding place and make yourself comfortable while I do it." Michael dropped into the chair beside her.

Blair turned a solemn face to him and answered, "You're so strong and capable, I knew you didn't need my feeble efforts."

"Right." Michael drew the word out, pulling at a strand of her dark hair, a gesture he'd made countless times over the years.

With a self-satisfied grin, Blair snuggled down into the sweater of Michael's that she'd appropriated from the cabin below. Life was good. No, it was better than good—it was great!

She was so lucky. She had her parents, her two best friends, the sun, the ocean, everything she could ever want or need close at hand. She didn't want things to change—ever.

Wanting Michael to share what she was feeling, she blurted, "I love this, don't you? I mean, it's perfect, isn't it?" She hugged his sweater to her and stared around at the boats, the ocean and the night. "I could never live anywhere else on earth. I need the ocean close by me. Dad says I have salt water in my veins, instead of blood."

Drawing her knees up beneath her, making herself more comfortable, she glanced into his face and asked, "What about you?"

Michael's head lay back against the chair, his eyes closed. "I'd say there's probably enough salt in your veins to pickle you three or four times over."

"That's not what I mean, dummy." Leaning across the arm of the chair, she asked in a serious tone, "Would you ever consider leaving here?"

"You mean, move away?" he asked, opening his eyes and turning to look at her. "For good?"

"Yes. I don't think I could—could you?" She nodded in the direction from which they'd come earlier. "Remember the summers when we were kids and we practically lived on the beach?" A sudden grin spread across her mouth, crinkling her eyes at the corners. "Remember the night we sneaked out of our rooms to go looking for sea monsters and a storm blew up? The whole town was out looking for us, and your father found us the next morning asleep in the gazebo."

"Yes," Michael murmured wryly, sitting forward. "My backside also remembered it for a good long time."

"Mine, too," she said, laughing.

Michael reached automatically to remove a strand of hair blowing against her mouth, and at that instant the pink tip of Blair's tongue appeared to moisten her dry lips. The soft pad of his thumb came into brief but electrifying contact with its damp softness, and he almost jumped out of his chair.

Drawing back as far from her as possible, he derided, "Don't think you can kid me into believing your father raised a hand to you. I'll bet you never had a spanking in your entire life."

Blair tried to laugh. Her cheeks were flushed, and she hoped Michael would think the dampness in her eyes was caused by the sharp wind and not the hurt of his drawing away from her, as though she had something contagious.

"I guess you know me too well, don't you?" Lifting her eyes toward the night sky, she added seriously, "I think I'd die if I had to leave here. If I couldn't walk this stretch of beach anytime I wanted to, feel the wind on my face, hear the different sounds the ocean makes, or..." She paused and let her eyes slide toward his face "...see you every day."

Michael watched the changing expressions sweep over Blair's face and felt the same tightness in his chest that he'd experienced earlier. He understood what she meant about never wanting to leave Baywater, but instead of agreeing he found himself blurting, "I've asked Cheryl to marry me—I asked her two days ago, and she said yes. That's what the celebration tonight was all about."

For a moment there was only silence between them, broken by the slap of the waves against the hull of the boat, creating a gentle up-and-down movement. The tide still sighed against the shore, the wind still whistled around their ears, the full moon still rode high in the night sky, but Blair knew nothing would ever be quite the same in her world after this night.

"Michael," she found her voice at last, "that's—wonderful news. I'm so—happy for you—both of you."

Shielding her eyes quickly with half-lowered lids, she managed a bright smile. Never mind the choking sensation at the back of her throat, the feeling of nausea in the pit of her stomach. She'd known this was coming. She'd been expecting it since graduating from college last year.

Levering herself out of the chair, hugging the sweater around her thin figure like a drowning swimmer hugs a life preserver, Blair went to stand at the rail. She couldn't seem to stop shivering. The wind tugged at her hair, blowing it out behind her as she stood staring across the beach at the houses dimly outlined in the distance.

Which one was Cheryl's? After all these years she ought to be able to pick it out, even from this distance.

"Are you really happy for us?"

Michael had come to stand behind her, so close she could feel the warmth of his body all along the back of hers. It caused her to shiver harder.

"W-what a silly question. You're my best f-friends in the whole w-world, why wouldn't I be h-happy for you?"

Michael wished he could see her face, look into her eyes. She didn't sound happy; she sounded as though she were in pain, the same pain he was experiencing all at once at the thought of marriage to Cheryl.

Taking her by the shoulders, Michael turned her to face him. "What's this?" he asked, touching a fingertip to her wet cheek.

"Happiness?" She looked up at him from beneath damp lids and tried to smile. Michael quirked a brow at her, and she swallowed with difficulty and answered, "Foolish-ness . . . fear . . ."

"Fear?" He frowned.

"The fear of losing you—both of you."

"Losing us? Don't be ridiculous. We're the three mus-keteers, one for all and all for one."

"It won't be the same," Blair insisted, twisting her fin-gers in the front of Michael's shirt. "It won't be the three of us. It will be the two of you—*and me!*"

Michael started to protest, to reassure her that there would be no changes between them, but she didn't give him the chance.

Dropping her hands from his shirt, she twisted away from him. Michael made a move toward her, and she raised her hands in front of her, keeping him at bay. "I shouldn't have said that," she said quickly. "I'm sorry. You're right—of course you are. We'll all stay friends. Nothing will change."

She drew the back of one hand across both cheeks and smiled. She wished she could believe her own words, but knew she was only mouthing platitudes. There was no use, however, in making things harder for Michael. He had a right to choose the woman he wanted without consulting her about it.

"Do you truly believe that?" Michael murmured as he stepped closer. "Do you really think we'll all remain friends, be as close to one another in a few years as we are now?"

"Well, of course I do," Blair answered with false bravado, her eyes focused somewhere over his shoulder. When he didn't answer, she glanced back at his face and asked, "Don't you?"

"I believe..." His eyes traveled over the delicate lines of her forehead, cheek and chin, touched briefly on the luminous expression in her deep blue eyes, and faltered on the moist, trembling lips he'd never known.

"Y-yes? What do you believe?" Blair asked in a breathless voice, swaying toward him, drawn by some invisible force flowing from him.

"I believe... I'm going to kiss you," he whispered, suiting action to words as he bent her to his will.

Blair found herself trapped between the hard rail at her back and Michael's strong chest. She couldn't move, couldn't pull away, but after a few seconds she didn't want to.

It's been said that at the point of death a person's whole life flashes before his eyes. At that moment, with Michael's warm mouth pressed against hers, the whole of *their* lives, joined for so many years in friendship, passed before Blair's.

She'd always suspected there was something missing in her life that made her different from the other girls she'd known. It was the something that put a sparkle in their eyes when they discussed dating, their boyfriends, the senior prom.

As Michael's kiss grew feverish, his arms crushed her to him. She could feel his heart pounding against her breast, and suddenly she knew what had been missing in her life— Michael.

She'd always loved Michael, but now she knew she was also *in love* with Michael.

All the shared dreams and secrets of their youth floated through her mind's eye. She felt cast adrift on a warm cloud of sensation. This was Michael with his hands twisted in her hair, his lips devouring hers with mounting passion, sucking the sweet nectar of life directly out of her heart, making her feel like a woman for the first time in her life.

And then, slowly, like a movie reel coming to an end, the images faded to black, and a new reel took its place. Only this time they were pictures of Michael and Cheryl, together down through the years.

Blair stiffened.

What was she doing? What were *they* doing? Michael had just told her that he'd proposed to Cheryl and she'd accepted him. Why was he kissing her?

Why was she letting him?

Pulling out of his arms, lips swollen and throbbing from his passion, Blair rubbed at her mouth with one hand, backing slowly away, putting the expanse of the deck between them.

"Blair? What is it?" Michael felt bereft without her in his arms, now that he'd finally held her.

"Michael, how could you? How could *we?* You're marrying Cheryl, you've just told me so yourself."

Michael shook his head, his brown, almost black, hair falling in a boyish swath across his forehead. "You don't understand." He took a step toward her. "I'm not sure I understand it myself, but I ... Blair, I know this is going to sound crazy, but I can't marry Cheryl. Not now, not ever, because I ... think ... I love *you.*"

"Stop it!" Blair struck at the air between them with angry fists. "Don't say that! You can't just tell me you love me—not like this, not now! You can't hurt Cheryl! She loves you!"

"I think I've made a terrible mistake," Michael whispered. "I—"

"No! *I* made the mistake. I should never have come out here with you tonight."

"Blair—please—" Michael moved closer, trying to take her hands in his. He wanted only to soothe her. He knew she was confused, frightened of what had so suddenly erupted between them. He was confused, too, but not so confused that he didn't know it was Blair—not Cheryl—whom he loved.

How had he failed to realize it before now? How could he make the girl staring at him with huge, wounded blue eyes understand what he was feeling without sounding like a fool?

"Blair, I love you. No, don't pull away." He'd managed to take hold of her shoulders with unsteady hands. "Don't hide your face from me. I need to see what you're feeling."

He gave her a small shake. "Look at me! I'm as confused by this turn of events as you are. Why didn't I know it was you I loved all along? You feel the same—don't you?" He shook her again lightly when she closed her eyes and refused to look at him. "I know you do! Why didn't you hit me over the head years ago and make me see it?"

Blair kept her eyes stubbornly closed and her body held stiffly away from him. She would not be an active party in what was taking place between them. How could she look Cheryl in the face ever again if she allowed Michael to make love to her?

Michael tugged at her arms. "All right, then, tell me I only imagined what I felt in your kiss just now." His voice dropped almost to a whisper. "Tell me it wasn't love. Go on, tell me you don't love me."

Sensing a chink in the wall of her resistance, he drew her closer and whispered, "Look me full in the face and tell me to go away, to leave you alone . . . to marry Cheryl—"

"Don't!" Blair's eyes jerked open. She pulled her arms from his grasp and backed away, shaking her head from side to side. How could he hurt her this way?

"Why now?" she wailed. "It's too late for us! You can't hurt Cheryl—I can't hurt Cheryl! Why now, damn you?" she cried with tears streaming down her cheeks. "Why now?" Turning, she ran from the boat.

Michael caught up with her on the jetty. Grasping one shoulder, he spun her around and up against his chest in one swift movement.

"Let me go!" Blair pounded at his shoulders with ineffectual fists. "You're out of your mind! In the morning you'll come to your senses, you'll realize—"

"I've already come to my senses. And it's you I love."

"No." Shaking her head, Blair pushed herself to arm's length. "In the morning you'll realize you can't hurt Cheryl, and where will that leave me?"

Blinded by tears, she twisted and turned in his embrace until he relented and allowed her to break free. He watched sadly as she ran down the wooden jetty toward the beach and across the sand toward the pale, ghostly outlines of buildings in the distance.

As she was swallowed up by the darkness, Michael glanced down at the sweater he was holding. It was his sweater, the sweater she'd had around her shoulders when he kissed her. Crushing it to him, he buried his face in its folds and breathed in the scent clinging to it...Blair's scent.

He knew he could follow and try to reason with her, but in her present state of mind she wouldn't listen. Besides, he needed time to think, time to decide what to do about Cheryl. The announcement of their engagement was due to be placed in the newspaper shortly after his return from this weekend fishing trip with his father.

Michael dropped the sweater to his side and ran a weary hand over his forehead, slicking his hair back flat against his skull. "What a mess," he sighed, turning away. "What a god-awful mess I've made of things."

Blair was right, he didn't want to hurt Cheryl, but how could he marry her, knowing it was Blair he loved, had probably loved since the first time she shook a baby fist at him through the bars of her playpen?

What was he going to do?

Blair stumbled over the wet sand away from the marina, away from Michael, toward the seawall. Her feet knew the way, so it didn't matter that her eyes were filled with tears, or that the moon had plunged behind a cloud, leaving the beach in almost total darkness.

All at once she slammed up against something solid and felt the wind knocked from her. At first, when she got her breath back and could think, she thought she must have run up against a piling in the breakwater, but at that exact moment she felt strong hands fasten onto her upper arms, the nails biting into the tender skin just above each elbow.

A spurt of wind blew her hair across her face, obscuring her vision, hiding the figure's dark features from sight. She tried to pull away, but he held her fast in a steely grip.

Suddenly, without uttering a sound, her captor almost tossed her aside. Blair became aware of a sharp, piercing pain in her left arm as a result of the abrupt movement, and she cried out in protest.

The unidentified stranger quickly moved off into the night, leaving her once more alone. Blair didn't stop to try and figure out who the person might be but hurried with head bent toward home. She didn't want to know the stranger's identity; she didn't want to know who might have witnessed the total destruction of her future tonight. All she wanted was the security of home and family, the forgetfulness of sleep.

Two days later, the town of Baywater learned that Michael Baldwin and his father were missing. The coast guard reported that they hadn't checked in at the appointed time, and no one had heard from them since. The area where they were last known to have been was flooded at once with searchers.

For two weeks, once it was confirmed that they were indeed missing, ships and planes searched the area thoroughly, but nothing was ever found except for a few pieces of floating debris. Later the debris was identified as once having been a part of the *Lazy Daze*. Michael and his father were presumed dead.

Blair dropped the curtain and moved from the window toward the bed. She stood looking down at the letter without touching it. Was he really alive?

Awful as it was, she wondered for an instant whether Michael could have engineered his disappearance because he couldn't go through with his marriage to Cheryl and couldn't face the prospect of telling her. But it just didn't make sense.

And what about his father? Was Mark Baldwin alive? How could she not seek the answers to those questions?

She'd paid for the right to know what had happened ten years ago. Paid with guilt. Since Michael's death, her relationship with Cheryl had been altered. For weeks she'd been unable to look her friend in the face without remembering that last night, Michael's kiss, and wallowing in guilt over it.

All during the memorial service conducted on the Baldwins' behalf and the weeks following it, she'd held her own grief locked inside. She'd been too ashamed to admit, even to herself, that if Michael had returned, eventually she would have given in to her love for him and ended up hurting Cheryl.

Now the letter blurred before her eyes. Michael's letter had asked her to meet him at the Sunset Motel, room sixteen. He would be there the day of Cheryl's wedding and the next.

What should she do? Should she go to him—or not?

Chapter 2

The six-year-old Corvette skidded on the wet pavement, slewing toward the center line, forcing Blair to grip the steering wheel firmly in both hands to bring it back under control. As weather along the eastern seaboard was apt to do in the spring, a warm sunny day had become a chilling, rainy night.

The traffic on Interstate 95 was heavy even by weekend standards, and the rain-slickened pavement and limited vision made driving a definite hazard. She was a fool.

What else would you call someone on her way to meet a man who'd been dead for a decade? In the short time she'd been driving, she'd come full circle in her thinking, reaching the conclusion that she was a gullible idiot to be out on a night like this on a fool's errand.

No one back in Baywater even knew where she'd gone. This man she was going to meet, if anyone even showed up, could be a psycho. Blair swallowed tightly, thinking about the countless movies that had been made on such a theme.

Even with that thought in mind, she couldn't seem to make herself turn the car around and head back to the safety of her own home. Whatever fate awaited her at the Sunset Motel, she would meet it head-on.

Determined to put the ridiculous notion of a psycho killer out of her head, she filled her mind with less disturbing thoughts of the recent wedding.

Cheryl had made a beautiful bride. By now the happy couple would be on the plane taking them to Hawaii for their honeymoon. Blair couldn't help but wonder for an awful moment if that thought should bring with it a feeling of guilt, instead of the relief she was now feeling.

She admitted openly to herself that though she'd spent the better part of the past three days assuring herself she was keeping Michael's return a secret from Cheryl for her own good, down deep inside she'd known the truth of it. She hadn't wanted Cheryl to know about the letter.

Michael had written to *her,* and Blair didn't want to share that with anyone. Even though the guilt caused by her silence piled higher each day, creating a noticeable strain in her relationship with her friend, Blair kept her own counsel.

She knew Cheryl had sensed something different in her manner, though, and that she'd put it down to their coming separation. Blair allowed her to believe that, knowing she couldn't tell her the truth.

The wedding had gone off without a hitch, and no one had seemed to notice an air of strain in the maid of honor's manner. But the knowledge hidden deep in Blair's heart during the wedding ceremony and at the reception afterward kept her feeling slightly off balance.

The letter had created an emotional upheaval almost as great as the one she'd experienced at Michael's death ten years ago. She found it difficult to make a decision about its authenticity and stick with it.

One moment she was certain it was a fake, but later she would find herself filled with an overwhelming conviction that it was indeed genuine. She considered burning it one minute and counted the hours until the time of the proposed meeting the next.

And during every moment she spent in Cheryl's company, Blair felt an oppressive sense of guilt. Not only for what she was keeping hidden in the present, but for what had taken place between herself and Michael in the past.

How long, she asked herself bitterly, would her part in that last night's events continue to haunt her? She'd even wondered over the years if Michael's death had been a punishment for what they would have done to Cheryl if he had returned.

Then she would go to sleep at night and he would be there. Michael, alive again in her dreams, his dark eyes flashing with laughter as he teased her, trying to appear stern as he chided her for not taking a stand on something important to her, or brimming with tenderness and passion as they had that last night.

In her dreams no one existed except the two of them. Time stood still, keeping them forever young, no older than on that night when he'd first declared his love. And in her dreams nothing stood in the way of their happiness together.

But that was true only in dreams. In reality, time hadn't stood still. Cheryl had found a new love. Dr. David Brennon, the man her father had hired to help him in his practice, was now her new husband. It had taken awhile, but it looked as though Cheryl had put Michael out of her heart at last.

And Blair? Well, she was the first to admit that life for her had never fulfilled that youthful promise of great things to come. Over the last decade she'd lost what little impulsiveness she'd developed under Michael's tutelage and became warily cautious in her emotional dealings with others. Unbridled sentiment played no part in her life, and it hadn't since that night so long ago.

And that was why, in the end, she had waited until the very last day to make the decision to see the man who called himself Michael Baldwin.

The rain became a heavy sheet, and driving conditions worsened, forcing Blair's mind off reflections of the past and onto the present. She was glad, under the present circumstances, that she'd given in to that small dissenting voice at the back of her mind and decided to arrive at the motel ahead of the scheduled time of the meeting. She planned to get a look at the man claiming to be Michael, if he truly existed, before he saw her.

At seven-fifteen Blair left the interstate and followed the access road to the red-and-yellow neon sign in the shape of a sunset. She parked outside the motel office and sat for a time, butterflies fluttering in her stomach as she glanced down the row of white-painted doors trimmed in blue.

Was there a man calling himself Michael Baldwin waiting for her behind one of them? Was he feeling as nervous and uncertain as she was at this very moment?

Ten minutes later, her overnight case stowed in room eight, the room she'd reserved for one night only, Blair stood outside the door, arms hanging at her sides, staring at the unit directly across from her own. The letter had said he wouldn't be in his room until nine. That was over an hour and a half away.

He might be there anyway.

If she wanted to get a look at him, now was the time to do it. The rain had stopped, leaving the cool air thick with mist. Stepping away from the door to her unit, Blair zipped her windbreaker up to her chin.

With her stomach twisted in a tight, hard knot, hands clenched inside the pockets of the windbreaker, she made her decision. Stepping off the walkway, skirting a puddle of rainwater, she moved across the few yards separating her from the door marked Sixteen.

Despite her determination, however, once she stood before it, she couldn't seem to get her limbs to respond to her will. Neither hand wanted to leave the security of her jacket pocket to rap at the door. After a few moments of telling herself that this was what she had come here for and she might as well get on with it, she managed to lift a closed fist and strike the door panel.

The damp wind buffeted her stiff body as she rapped again, more loudly this time. It didn't take long for her to realize it was useless.

He wasn't there.

Blair didn't know if it was relief she felt or bitter disappointment as she turned away. Expelling her breath on a long sigh, she stood looking around her. After a moment she began walking toward the street, and the bar and grill next door. The motel manager has said the food there was palatable. She wasn't really hungry, but she couldn't stand the thought of sitting in her room, alone with her memories, for the next hour and a half, either.

Her shoes made little sound as she moved over the rough concrete, splashing through puddles of rainwater without noticing. Skirting the fenced-in pool, concealed beneath a heavy black cover, she rounded a corner and came face-to-face with a couple walking arm in arm.

The tiny, dark-haired woman, hanging on to a man at least a foot taller, giggled drunkenly as Blair sidestepped and the pair moved in the same direction. The man gave Blair a devilish wink and a broad, inviting grin.

Blair's eyes frosted over as she glared back at him, and his attention quickly returned to the agreeable brunette hugging his hips. The couple moved past without a word being spoken and disappeared into the night.

Blair continued on to the lighted door of the Sunken Inn. At the door she paused; this wasn't the type of place she normally chose to frequent, but the low murmur of country and western music coming from inside somehow attracted rather than repelled her. Opening the door without further consideration, she stepped over the threshold and inside.

A waitress, wearing an almost nonexistent pirate outfit, arrived at once to show her to a seat in a dim recess in a far corner of the room, then hurried away, promising to return shortly for her order. Blair perched on the padded bench and leaned carefully back against the wall, scanning the room with a critical eye.

She guessed the place was supposed to look like the inside of a sunken ship. The walls were made of what appeared to be wooden planks that looked as though they'd been submerged in salt water for a number of years. Candles enclosed in hurricane lamps provided the only light, except for a couple of lamps situated above the bar. Conch shells and fishnets filled with colored glass balls decorated the walls and hung from the ceiling.

In one corner of the room the tentacles of an octopus—rubber, she supposed—dangled from one of the nets affixed to the wall and caught her eye. Her glance drifted down toward the table placed directly beneath and the lone figure occupying it, facing the door.

Candlelight played over the man's features, making them appear gaunt and eerie in the flickering light. It was impossible, with the distance separating them, for her to see the color or expression in his deep-set eyes. The sockets appeared empty, giving his face the aspect of a death's-head, adding to the macabre illusion he presented.

Blair glanced at the bottle of whiskey sitting on the small table in front of him, felt a chill run down her spine and looked away. But something about him, as he sat with his elbows propped on the table, his shoulders hunched and his head slightly bent forward, nothing but a bottle of whiskey for company in a room filled with people, had gotten to her. She found her glance drifting back to him again and again, drawn by his air of isolation.

For the umpteenth time her eyes shifted determinedly away from him, then glided slowly back, drawn this time by a question taking shape at the back of her mind. Was there something familiar about him? Something in the way he held his head?

The object of her scrutiny looked up, and the hand holding the glass of whiskey tilted toward his waiting lips, halting abruptly in midair.

Blair caught her breath. Was he looking at her? She couldn't be certain in the dim light, but he remained frozen in place, staring at something across the room.

A creeping uneasiness began to steal over her. No...it couldn't be! Her eyes focused on the glass in the man's hand. Impossible! He didn't drink! His mother had died an alcoholic before he'd reached his teens.

The moment of tension shattered precipitously when the man jerked the glass of amber liquid to his lips and downed it in one long gulp.

Blair wasn't quite certain why, but she felt outraged by the deliberate act. This man, *this stranger,* couldn't possibly be Michael Baldwin. And if his intention was to try and pass himself off as her dead friend in order to take control of the family fortune, she was determined to put a stop to it at once.

Climbing to her feet, shaking her head at the waitress coming to take her order, Blair wound her way across the wooden floor sprinkled with sand. She ignored the groups of people talking loudly above the rumble of music in the background, shook her head at an invitation for her to join one of them and made her way steadily toward the secluded figure sitting alone in the corner.

When she halted beside the table at last, it was with both fists planted firmly on her hips. She stood there silently, staring down at the top of the man's dark head, waiting for him to acknowledge her presence.

Even up close she could see nothing the least bit familiar about his features. From the black, close-cropped hair styled longer on top to the scar severing his left eyebrow, she gave his face a thorough examination. True, it had been ten years since she'd last seen Michael, but surely...

"Sit down," the man whispered roughly, his glance leveled on the whiskey bottle sitting before him.

Blair remained standing. "Who are you?" she demanded curtly.

He didn't answer.

"Are you the man trying to pass yourself off as Michael Baldwin?" she continued, getting right to the heart of the matter. "If you are, then let me assure you, it won't work. I know—knew—the family well, and you don't stand a chance in hell—"

"Shut up!" The long fingers lying next to the empty shot glass clenched spasmodically. "Sit down and keep your voice quiet. Do you want every ear in this place to be a party to this conversation?"

"I won't sit," Blair answered huffily. Just who did he think he was? "Who are—"

He looked up, and his dark eyes—*Michael's eyes*—shot like a blow from a powerful fist directly to her face.

"You! B-but—" It couldn't be! "I don't understand... your face..."

"Lower your voice!" The stranger with Michael's eyes glanced from beneath half-lowered lids at the interested faces of the people sitting around them who'd heard her opening gambit.

A feeling of intense anger swept through Blair. She couldn't believe—wouldn't believe—that this imposter was Michael. Yes, his eyes were uncannily like Michael's, but there had to be another explanation. He didn't look like Michael, he didn't act like Michael, and he certainly didn't treat her the way Michael would have done.

She'd been afraid all along that this was a hoax and she would find a stranger, a con-artist, trying to cash in on Michael's birthright. Yet at the same time, deep inside, she'd been hoping that by some miracle of fate the Michael she had known and loved was about to be miraculously restored to her intact.

"Don't you tell me what to do!" Bending to place her hands flat against the table's scarred surface, she looked deeply into his eyes and, against her will, felt a flicker of recognition click into place somewhere in her memory.

"Is it really you?" she couldn't help but ask. "What's happened to you? Why do you look . . . so different?"

"Lower your voice," he ordered again in that same cold, rough tone. "I don't want my business known by everyone in this place."

He reached for the bottle of whiskey and poured the glass full, then raised it toward his lips. He didn't see the sudden spasm of pain in Blair's eyes, changing them from clear blue to a dark, stormy gray. This man acted as though he were doing her a favor by simply being here, when it was she who'd come to meet him at his request.

Who was this man? Michael would never have spoken to her in such a manner, nor would he have consumed the amount of alcohol this man had drunk since she'd first spotted him.

For someone who'd sent for her, he was acting very strangely indeed. If he'd had a reason for asking her to meet with him, why wasn't he telling her? In his letter he'd said that he would answer all her questions. So far, he'd answered none.

And there was one question that, above all the others, burned a hole in her brain. If he *was* Michael, why had he kept silent about his being alive until now?

Confused by such hostile treatment, battling a sense of denial that this obnoxious person could be Michael, Blair glared angrily at the top of his dark head. Torn by a deep feeling of disappointment at the total dissimilarity between what she'd expected to find and the reality of what now sat before her, she felt as though she might explode if she didn't do something to release some of the pain.

Her eyes alighted on the whiskey glass being slowly lifted toward the firm, somber mouth, and without conscious thought her hand flew through the air, sweeping the amber liquid from his hand.

She didn't even bother glancing at his face to see his reaction to her impulsive act. There was only one thing she wanted to see at that moment, and that was how fast she could leave this terrible place.

She didn't know this man. And if, by some misbegotten stroke of fate, he really was Michael and his character had changed as drastically as his appearance, transforming him from the gentle, caring young man who thought more of others than of himself into this monster, then she didn't want to know him, either.

"Go back to wherever you've been all these years," she told him shortly without looking at him. "Forget you knew me—if you ever did. That shouldn't be too hard," she couldn't resist adding. "You've had ten years practice."

Whirling about, she hurried around the tables, bumping into a figure here and there as she made her way hastily toward the entrance.

Why had she come? Had she really expected to find the lost companion of her youth? What a joke, and this time the joke was positively on her.

With quick, angry strides she made her way across the motel parking lot, through the puddle of water, to the door of her room. By that time her hands were shaking so badly with reaction that she could hardly get the key into the lock.

It slid home at last, and she gave it an abrupt twist, pushing against the door and almost collapsing inside as it burst suddenly inward. But before she could close it securely, a heavy weight shoved against it from outside.

She hadn't heard him, but it seemed the man calling himself Michael had followed.

"Get out!"

He shoved her wordlessly inside, closing the door firmly behind him. He clicked the dead bolt into place, turned and leaned back against the door with crossed arms, staring at her with dark, unfathomable eyes.

"What do you want?" she demanded. He didn't answer, just kept staring at her intently. "All right, say whatever it is you have to say, then get out."

She turned toward her overnight case lying near the foot of the bed so she wouldn't have to look at him and remember the past. In a couple of hours she could be home, safe in her own house, safe from this stranger who mocked her with Michael's soulful eyes.

But still he didn't speak, and the silence stretched between them. Like a time capsule, it sealed the room and its occupants from the rest of the world. After a few moments the strain became more than Blair could stand, and she faced him defiantly. "What do you want from me?"

She tried to read his intentions in his dark eyes; they were the only truly familiar thing about him, but they remained shuttered against her. Knowing she should never have come here, she folded her arms in a protective gesture across her chest and knew, too, that the past was indisputably dead and she should have left it that way.

That was when she knew she had to get out of the room and away from him. Dropping her arms, she reached for the handle of her overnight bag, at the same time slinging her purse over the other shoulder.

"Where do you think you're going?" he bit out.

So, the sphinx could speak. "Home, back to Baywater," she answered, taking a step in his direction, toward the door at his back.

"Running away—again?" he mocked her.

Stung despite herself by the unfairness of the remark, Blair stopped dead in her tracks. It was true that in her youth she'd been more inclined to run away from an unpleasant situation than stay and face it. And she knew without a doubt that he was referring to one situation in particular. But in this instance it was indeed the pot calling the kettle black.

Letting the overnight bag slide from her fingers to the floor, she met his challenging stare with one of her own and demanded, "*I* ran away? What about you? I was confused that night," she admitted. "I needed some time to get used to what had happened between us. But I only ran home. You knew where I was. All you had to do was pick up a phone and call me.

"But you—" She pointed an accusing finger at him. "You ran out of my life—let me believe you were dead—for over ten years. Tell me, who's the *real* coward here?"

He looked away, but not before Blair understood that it really *was* Michael. Not before she caught a glimpse of the raw pain moving over his face. When he looked back, there was a new aloofness in his eyes.

"I had no choice in the matter. And I wasn't running away from you," he answered without inflection.

"No? Who then? Cheryl?"

A muscle flexed tautly in his jaw, but he answered flatly, "From the man who murdered my father—who thought he'd murdered me, too."

"W-what?" Blair felt her knees suddenly go weak. "You mean, your father really is dead?"

Michael made an abrupt movement in her direction. "Of course he's dead," he answered harshly, pushing a hand through his hair, pressing the dark strands flat against his scalp in a sign of impatience.

Blair's eyes were caught and held by the familiar gesture. But his next words threw her even further off guard.

"Did you honestly think the two of us would have stayed away for ten years, falsified our own deaths, just because I was engaged to one girl and in love with another?"

Blair's glance flew to his face, a flutter of remembered passion springing to life in her breast before she could beat it down with reality. If he'd loved her, then why hadn't he come back to her?

Michael met her look without expression, and the passion died, killed by the tight, hard knot growing in the pit of her stomach.

"Where have you been all this time? Why are you so...why is your appearance so—altered?"

Michael raised a hand to his face, touching the fine thread of scars at his hairline, beneath his chin, crisscrossing his larynx. "It takes some getting used to, doesn't it? I still get a shock every time I look in the mirror."

"I didn't mean it—you—looked bad," she whispered haltingly. "Just...different."

"I know what I look like. I know the scars are there. I just don't see them much myself, anymore. And I've gotten used to sounding like a frog whenever I speak."

"Are you going to tell me where you've been? What happened to you?" she asked again, needing to know what had changed the man she'd known into the man standing before her.

Michael rubbed a hand over the back of his neck and gave his head a slight shake. "I'm not really certain I know myself."

Blair frowned. "What do you mean?"

Michael stared at the wall above Blair's right shoulder for a long moment without answering.

"Dad and I were on the boat," he answered finally, shifting his attention back to her face. "Everything was fine—then all hell broke loose."

His voice took on an even rougher edge, a look of confusion clouding his face. "Dad was standing there one minute...and the next he was gone...vanished in a wall of flame." He broke off, swallowing tightly.

"Oh, God." Blair hadn't known what to expect, but hearing Michael's flat explanation of how his father had died, the horror of the picture he painted made her momentarily forget her anger with him. She backed toward the bed and dropped onto it, tears pooling in her eyes at the memory of a man she'd loved almost as much as she'd loved her own parents.

Michael's father had been the kind of man everyone liked and respected. As president of the town's leading bank, he'd made friends instead of enemies, because he cared more about people than about money. He'd bent over backward to help the townspeople with their financial needs, and because of that, it was to him they came with their savings and investments.

Who would want to kill such a man? Why?

"What makes you think your father's death was—" she couldn't bring herself to say the word "murder" "—not an accident?"

"Think?"

Blair was unprepared for the way he rounded on her. She jumped at the sudden vehemence in his voice and stared with wide eyes at the taut lines of anger on his dark face. He looked as though he hated her.

"I don't *think* it was murder! I *know* it was!"

"What made you come back now?" she asked abruptly.

"Revenge!" he bit out harshly, taking her breath away.

Blair managed not to cringe away from him. "I—I don't understand."

"No, I don't suppose you do."

Michael took a seat on the bed beside her, a part of him wishing now that he'd never written the letter. With shoulders slumped, hands lying flat on his thighs, he studied the toe of one boot while he contemplated exactly what to tell her.

This was proving to be more difficult than he'd expected. He was fighting more than the pain of remembering how his father had died; he was having to fight the loss of his past all over again.

"Tell me what happened," Blair whispered softly, wishing she could give comfort to this stranger who, in his pain, showed some evidence of being the man she remembered.

"Please, tell me where you've been, what happened to you after the accident."

"You really want to know?" The dark brows lifted, and Michael's eyes glinted up at her. "You sure you don't just want to get your things and run away from this mess?" he mocked her.

Blair's fingers knotted themselves on her lap, but she only repeated, "Tell me."

Michael's glance roamed her face, feeling the unwelcome stirrings of a past long dead. She was even more beautiful in maturity than he remembered her in youth.

He should never have contacted her; that had been a mistake. He hoped it wasn't the first of many.

Blair pushed a damp curl off her forehead and waited for him to begin speaking.

"I was wrong," he commented obliquely, knowing he should keep the thought to himself. He hadn't contacted her for personal reasons.

"Wrong?" she asked in confusion.

"About your hair. You're even lovelier with it short." It framed her face, bringing out the delicate lines of her cheekbones, the sparkle in her large, wide-set eyes, and the full, generous curve of her lower lip.

Blair tried to deny the hot breathless sensation racing through her at the unexpected compliment and concentrated on maintaining an air of detachment. He had a lot to answer for, and she wouldn't let him get around her with slick compliments.

Michael cleared his throat and began to speak. "Dad and I left Baywater as planned just after six on Saturday morning."

He didn't mention that at five-thirty, knowing Blair's parents were early risers, he'd gone to her house to give her mother a message for Blair. He'd wanted her to meet him at the marina on his return Sunday evening. He wondered if she'd ever gotten the message. She hadn't said anything, so maybe her mother—who had never been happy about their friendship—had simply "forgotten" to deliver it.

"We were somewhere off the coast of Florida, south of here, when he said he had something important to tell me. He said it was the real reason for our trip.

"I couldn't imagine what he was talking about, but I kept silent and waited for him to explain. And then he told me someone had threatened his life—"

"What? Who?"

Michael shook his head. "It seems there had been several veiled threats made against him over a period of weeks, but he didn't take them seriously until someone tried to poison him."

"Poison him?" Blair sat forward, her eyes fastened on Michael's face.

"That's right. He had what I thought was a bout of stomach flu a couple of months before the fishing trip, but he told me he'd been poisoned."

"But surely Dr. Prescott—"

"Roger Prescott wasn't taking care of Dad by then. He was going to a specialist in Saint Augustine, because of his high blood pressure."

"What kind of poison was it?"

"Something used in weed killer."

"But... couldn't that have been an accident?"

"No. The man admitted what he'd done. He told Dad it was only a warning, and he threatened my life, too."

"You! Why didn't your father go to the police?"

Michael shrugged. "I asked Dad that question myself. He said no one would believe him. He said he'd come out looking like a fool, because the man was prominent in the community. And he had no proof to substantiate his claims against the man. Dad never even told me who it was. I guess he thought I would be safer that way."

"What did the man want from your father?" Blair asked curiously.

"Land."

"Land," Blair repeated blankly. "Someone threatened your father's life—your life—over a piece of property? What property?"

Michael shrugged.

"Well, why didn't your father just sell the man what he wanted?"

"I don't know. Maybe if I knew the answer to that, then I'd know who murdered him."

"Michael," she began hesitantly, "are you certain it was murder and not an accident?"

Apparently she didn't realize she'd called him by name, but Michael did, and something tense inside of him relaxed in relief. "It was murder, all right. Dad said the man had been putting pressure on him to make him change his mind for some time. He didn't say so, but I got the feeling there was more involved than the land."

"What?"

"I don't know." He paused, gave a shrug and added, "I could be wrong about that. I don't know.

"Anyway, after the poisoning, Dad said he realized the guy wasn't fooling around. You knew Dad, he could be pretty stubborn when he wanted to. Apparently he dug his heels in and decided he wasn't about to knuckle under, whatever the cost. Except my life.

"And that's where the idea for the fishing trip came from. He said he wanted me out of the way, so he could get whatever proof he needed without worrying about my safety. He intended to send the man to jail.

"While he was talking, Dad took a chain with a key on it from around his neck and handed it to me. He told me to put it on. He said the key was to a safe-deposit box with new identification and enough money in it for me to start life all over again someplace far away from Baywater, someplace where I'd be safe."

With the memories crowding his head, Michael couldn't sit still any longer. He stood and wandered around the room. "I couldn't believe what he was saying. He expected me to run like a dog with its tail tucked between its legs and leave him to face this man all alone, as though I didn't care at all about what happened to him.

"I didn't know what to say. I was trying to think of something when the explosion came."

"Oh, Michael!" Blair was on her feet, reaching out to him.

"The concussion threw me off the boat and into the water. I must have hit my head or been knocked out by the concussion from the explosion, because I don't remember anything past the first explosion. If Dad hadn't insisted I wear my life jacket, I would have drowned."

"Wasn't your father wearing his life jacket, too?" Blair asked, dropping her hands without touching him.

"Dad didn't always abide by his own rules."

"What happened then?"

"That's all I can remember . . . until I came to in the hospital. Weeks passed before I even remembered the explosion and our conversation. That was when I started asking questions and finally learned what had happened to me after I hit the water. It seems some people came by in a boat and found me unconscious, floating in the water. It must have been hours after the explosion, because according to them, there was very little debris around."

He gave her a humorless grin. "From what I understand, they thought at first that I'd been pushed off a boat and maybe drugs were involved. They didn't want any part of me. But I'm here." He shrugged. "So I guess they changed their minds about that."

"Why didn't the authorities identify you?"

"I don't know. I was really out of it for a long time and I couldn't give them any help. So I suppose they must have figured I was just another bozo who'd gone out in a boat without knowing the first thing about water safety and gotten into trouble."

"But what about the news reports?" Blair asked. "Why didn't someone see a broadcast about you and your father being missing and put the facts together?"

"People disappear every day. After a while, without anything to go on, I guess my case simply got lost in the pile. I suppose the people in Baywater must have figured Dad and I were the victims of a tragic accident at sea." He turned a questioning glance toward her troubled face.

Blair hesitated before nodding. It hadn't been that cut-and-dried for her—or for Cheryl. "Why didn't you let ... us ... know you were alive?"

Michael glanced down at his left hand, at the faint white line that was still visible. It would be easier to give her an evasion than the truth. But he wouldn't let himself take the easy way out. "I couldn't."

"Couldn't? Why not?"

"In those first few months I was in and out of consciousness and in and out of surgery a lot of the time. My face required major reconstruction, and since they didn't have a picture of me to show how I looked before the accident..."

He lifted one side of his mouth in a wry grin. "I don't know what hit me, but whatever it was, it did a pretty thorough job of destroying my face." He raised a hand to his throat and added, "My larynx, too."

After a moment of silence he continued in an uneven tone, "Besides, by then I'd met . . . Mary."

Blair's breath got lost somewhere in her chest. "Mary?"

Michael rubbed his thumb against the pale line on the ring finger on his left hand. "She was the nurse who took care of me. She specialized in trauma cases like mine. She worked days, but she used to come back at night, after she'd had dinner and a few hours rest, and stay with me. The hospital was short-staffed, so they didn't mind.

"I needed a lot of attention in those days," he recalled, adding tightly, "I couldn't do much for myself."

He remembered all too vividly what it had been like, swathed in dressings like a mummy, having to ask a stranger to help with the most personal needs.

"For a while even my eyes were bandaged. The doctors weren't certain whether I'd be able to see again. Mary—" his voice wavered over the name "—became my eyes as well as my hands. She did everything for me that I couldn't do for myself."

That was but a small part of the truth he didn't want to explain to the woman standing before him with her hands clenched so tightly that the knuckles showed white. How could he expect her to understand the confusion, fear and hopeless frustration he'd faced during that time?

His days had been spent in a raging battle with everyone, doctors and nurses alike, as he fought against whatever treatment they prescribed. He'd been secretly terrified his case was hopeless and he would end up a useless hulk, lying in a hospital bed for the rest of his life.

During that time he'd prayed every night for death to put an end to his physical suffering and emotional anguish at losing his father. But eventually his resistance wore down and he got used to Mary being there, helping him, giving him subtle encouragement, day after day. It took time, but in the end she gave him back his will to live.

Once he'd stopped hating her, Mary had earned his undying gratitude for her devotion to making him well again. It took a whole lot longer for him to admit how deeply he'd come to care for the quiet, strong-willed young nurse as a woman. He had even loved her. He just hadn't loved her enough.

It wasn't until months after the accident that he even considered getting in touch with anyone in Baywater, only to discover that everyone there believed he was dead. He knew that no matter how badly he wanted to, he would never be able to recapture the past. Things would never be the same for him. He wasn't the same.

He'd contemplated getting in touch with Blair. That was about the time he saw himself for the first time in a mirror and rejected what he saw with horror. There was no way in hell he would have let her see him in that condition.

His appearance made it easier for him to justify his decision to remain dead. There were still Cheryl and his engagement to her to contend with if he made himself known, as well. Though he didn't love her, he didn't want to hurt her. She, too, would be better off with him out of her life.

It hurt, knowing the people you loved, those who loved you, thought you were dead. He'd struggled against the thought of keeping silent, but in the end it had seemed the best way.

How could he have asked Blair to put up with a man who could barely see his own hand in front of his face, who couldn't speak at all, a man whose face looked like something from a horror movie? Blair, his sweet Blair, had been lost to him forever.

The anger, the desire for revenge against the man who'd done all that to him, hadn't started at that point. He'd still been attempting to deal with all that had happened, still reeling under the blow of his new, distasteful self.

Those were all the things he could have told Blair, but he didn't. What would be the use? The past was just that, and he still couldn't see a future for them.

Blair tried to keep jealousy out of her feelings as she listened to his story, surprised to realize she could feel so much emotion for this man. She tried to imagine how it must have been for him, all alone, terribly injured, his father so suddenly, horribly, dead. How confused he must have felt, how afraid to trust others. Especially those in Baywater.

Perhaps, just perhaps, she might be able to understand his silence. Besides, he was back now.

"I came to depend on Mary," Michael continued after a long silence. "And once I was well enough . . . we were married."

All at once Blair couldn't seem to get enough air to breathe. The room began to close in around her. She moved instinctively, like a swimmer in trouble, toward fresh air, toward the door.

"Where are you going?" Michael barked abruptly.

"Outside. I need to walk on the beach and breathe the salt air." She needed to get away from the pain shredding her insides, away from this man who had caused it.

The ocean always calmed her. Unlike people, she could count on its always being there. It didn't grow up, grow old and die, or leave you. It stayed in the same place, year after year, always there whenever you needed a friend.

Blair grasped the door handle and fumbled with the lock, desperate to get away.

Hard fingers came down over hers, stilling her inept fumbling. Blair's eyes were drawn to his hand. Where was his wedding ring? Where was his wife? Her heart gave a flutter and began to race. But he only lifted her cold fingers and placed them on the dead bolt, giving it a turn. His other hand covered hers on the doorknob and gave it a twist.

The door stood open, but Blair couldn't seem to move. Michael lifted his hands and stepped back abruptly, releasing her from the spell of his nearness.

"Do you mind if I walk with you?" he rasped in the whispery voice she was becoming used to.

"N-no, I guess not," she answered, though what she really wanted was to be alone to sort out her confused thoughts.

The motel claimed as its right a stretch of sand fronting the ocean. Blair followed the wood-planked walkway leading to steps that climbed over the breakwater and down to the beach on the other side.

Lights had been placed at intervals around cabanas the motel had constructed for the comfort of its guests. They created patches of illumination in the misty darkness.

With her hands in her pockets, Blair skirted the lights and made for the water's edge. After a while the familiar roar of the surf pounding in her ears, blotting out every other sound, brought a feeling of peace as nothing else ever could.

She looked up and found Michael watching her.

"Feel better?" He raised his voice to be heard over the waves.

Blair nodded without speaking. In the dark, she could almost believe this man was Michael, unchanged from the past.

But to believe that was to believe in a lie. Nothing would ever be the same between them again.

"What made you write to me, M—Michael," she stumbled over his name, "after all these years?"

"I need you."

Blair gave a soft gasp and took a step back from him, slanting a quick glance at his face.

"I need your help," he amended, going on to explain. "I intend to find the man who killed my father. I need your help to do that."

"My help? What can I do?"

His expression became visible as moonlight sifted through a break in the clouds overhead. "Whoever the man is, he lived in Baywater ten years ago, and I'm confident he still lives there today. You'll know who has moved and who's still there."

"The town is full of people," she protested. "Are we going to go through everyone who's living there now, who lived there then, too?"

"There's also the fact that he knew Dad," Michael added, taking little note of her protest.

"A-are you saying you think this m-man was a friend of your father's?"

"Well, what do you think? It stands to reason it had to be someone who knew Dad pretty well or he wouldn't have been able to poison him so easily. And Dad must have trusted him in the beginning, or he'd have taken the man's threats more seriously."

"What are you planning to do when—if—you find him?"

"Make him pay!"

There was only one construction Blair could put on the ominous tone of his voice. "I can't help you. I won't be a party to murder."

Michael drew his brows together in a straight line reminiscent of the old days, except now, with the addition of the scar, there were three segments instead of two.

"Did I mention murder?" He hadn't thought that far ahead himself, at least not in specific terms. All he wanted was to learn the man's identity, then, well, he wasn't certain what course of action he would take.

"It's been ten years. What makes you so sure this man, whoever he might be, is still in Baywater?"

"What happened to Dad's will?"

"A will was never found," she admitted slowly.

Michael grinned without humor. "That's what I figured."

Blair was almost frightened by this stranger looking at her with flat, hard, passionless eyes. "What do you mean?"

"If my father was murdered and whoever did it thinks I'm dead, too, then naturally a will couldn't turn up."

"I don't understand."

"A will would only complicate matters. My guess is it must have disposed of the property in such a manner that it would have pointed the finger of guilt at someone."

"Finger of guilt?" Blair asked haltingly.

"That's right," Michael answered. His father probably hadn't had time to take the man's name out of his will.

John Saunders, the family lawyer, would know what was in the will. Michael wanted that information. But he didn't dare go to the man and ask for it himself. John was not the kind of man to give out information to a stranger, and revealing his own identity too early in the game would be tantamount to issuing his own death warrant.

"What is it you want from me?" Blair asked, uncomfortable in the strained silence.

"Do you agree, in light of what I've told you tonight, that Dad was murdered?" he responded with a studied glance at her pale face.

"Maybe it was an accident."

"Murder," Michael insisted. "I've waited ten years, just like the killer, to get what I want." He took a threatening step in her direction. "I won't let *anyone* stand in my way," he added by way of a warning.

"Why ten years?"

"The state holds intestate land—abandoned property, as it's called—for ten years before it goes to public auction. I read the notice in the newspaper last week. I am right, aren't I, all our property is going up for public auction?"

"Yes, but..."

He nodded. "That's how I had it figured." He gave her a dark penetrating stare. "How many of Dad's friends still live in Baywater?"

"Are you really suggesting that one of his friends is a cold-blooded murderer?" she asked incredulously.

"I told you before, that's exactly what I'm suggesting," he answered without inflection. "And I need your help to find out which one."

"You want me to spy on my friends and neighbors?" Blair asked shortly, drawing farther away from him. "You want me to snoop on people I've known for as long as I can remember? So that you, in your infinite wisdom, can play God and point the finger of guilt at one of them?"

She shook her head slowly back and forth. "I won't do it. I won't spy on people I've known all my life. I don't believe someone in Baywater killed your father, and I won't help you to try to prove otherwise."

"Look," he said, grinding his teeth against the anger seething inside him, trying to keep a lid on it. Shouting at her wouldn't get the results he wanted. "Someone killed my father in cold blood, probably the same person who stole Dad's will—" He broke off, slamming a closed fist against his thigh in anger. "If I only knew what was in the will, I might be able to figure out who the killer—"

"That doesn't make sense," Blair interrupted. "If the killer was named in the will, why steal it? Why not just wait and inherit? No one could prove your death—your father's death—was anything other than an accident. No one knows what actually took place on the boat that day."

"Then maybe the will left the property to someone else," Michael reasoned out loud. "And that's why it had to disappear, so that now he can *buy* what he wants with no questions asked."

"Michael, what you're saying just doesn't make any sense. How can this hypothetical killer be certain he'll be the one to get the land he wants? What is to stop someone else from purchasing the land at auction? And why wouldn't this person simply buy another piece of property?"

"That's what I need your help to find out. And as far as the auction goes, money talks, or haven't you learned that over the years? Don't you think this man, considering he was willing to kill for the property, will be willing to outbid everyone, pay whatever it takes, to get what he wants?"

Blair stared at him in silence.

"Will you help me?" he asked again. Then he increased the pressure by adding, "You owe me that, if for no other reason than because of our past... friendship."

"I don't owe you anything," Blair answered coolly.

She was right, he thought. She didn't owe him anything, but he couldn't let her walk away. He needed her. He'd thought that she, of all people, would understand this thing he needed to do.

"You'd let the man who killed Dad get away with it?"

The thought that Mark Baldwin's death was anything other than an accident made her feel ill, but still she didn't put much faith in Michael's conviction that it was murder. In her opinion, he was looking for a reason, an answer he could understand, for his father's senseless death and the guilt he was probably feeling over the fact that he himself had survived the accident.

She tried reasoning with him. "Michael, listen to yourself. You're condemning someone—some unknown man—on speculation. What proof do you have? Your father's suspicions because he somehow ingested weed killer? Your father did his own gardening, the poisoning could have been an accident. And as sad as it is, explosions happen on boats all the time, but that doesn't mean someone sabotaged them. I'm sorry your father's dead. I loved him, too, but I won't help you try to prove some innocent man guilty of a crime he didn't commit.''

"Innocent!" Michael exclaimed. "The bastard is as guilty as sin! Dad's death was not an accident!"

"Okay, what if you're right? What if someone did kill your father? He's been clever enough to keep his secret all these years, and you think you and I are going to bring him down?" She shook her head. "If you truly believe someone killed your father, go to the police. Let them decide if it warrants a murder investigation."

Angered by her stubborn refusal to help him, and disappointed in her lack of belief in the facts, Michael could only stand in silence as she marched away.

He'd spent more than one sleepless night before contacting her, worrying about involving her in danger, but he'd never once seriously considered the possibility that she would refuse to help him. He needed her, and there was no way he was going to let her walk away so easily.

Chapter 3

Michael knew he had to convince Blair to change her mind. His father's killer must not be allowed to go free forever.

He caught up with her a few yards down the beach beneath the glow of a light near one of the cabanas. Capturing her shoulder in one hand, he swung her toward him.

Blair pulled away from his touch but continued to face him, waiting. She hadn't really expected to get away from him so easily, not this new Michael.

He stared at her, unable to think of a single reason why she should change her mind and do as he'd asked. In the weeks before he'd written to her, he'd thought of many reasons to convince her, but not one of them came to mind as he stood trapped within her blue glare.

"What about our past relationship?" he managed at last. "Doesn't that qualify as grounds for your trust?"

A shaft of pain darted through her, causing her to catch her breath to keep from crying out. Her hands, hidden in the pockets of her jacket, clenched tightly against the pain.

"How can you even ask me that?" she whispered to keep from screaming at him. She'd kept her anger under control up till now, but it was beginning to boil over, and she was inclined to let it.

"I trusted you ten years ago. I trusted you when I went with you to your father's boat. I trusted you when you...kissed me." Tears pooled in her eyes, but they were caused more by anger than by pain. "I trusted you to come back to me...after you said you loved me."

Michael opened his mouth to protest, but she raised her voice over what he might have to say and continued. "Oh, yes, you came back, all right." Drawing her clenched fists from her pockets, she held them up in front of her as though she wanted to pound him. "You came back, all right! Ten years too late!

"I hate you! God, how I hate you! You think you suffered after the accident? Well, what about us, the people who loved you? Don't you think we suffered? What about Cheryl? You were engaged to her. Did you ever think about how she might feel, knowing you were missing and presumed dead?

"You're selfish, Michael, selfish! You didn't used to be. But here you are, after all this time, showing up out of the blue, asking me to help you, playing on my emotions to get me to do what you want. Don't you have any feelings? One of the last things you said to me before you left was that you loved me, and now you tell me you're married. How can you do this?"

Brushing at the tears on her face with an impatient fist, she sniffed and turned away. "No, I won't help you. Go away and leave me alone. I don't ever want to see you again."

"I'm sorry." Michael stepped up behind her, took hold of her shoulders and attempted to draw her resistant figure back against him.

"Let me go," she whimpered, trying to pull away from him. "I don't know you anymore. And I don't want to know you. You don't know me. It's too late for us...."

"I know you like I know the back of my hand," Michael whispered. "And I know you don't mean what you're saying—"

Blair jerked free and whirled to face him, the words "Yes, I do" dying on her lips as she found herself trapped against his broad chest—much in the same way as she'd been trapped on a bright moonlit night so long ago.

The silence between them grew taut as Michael wrapped his arms around her shoulders and drew her closer. Blair felt a tingling start in the pit of her stomach, and her whole body became filled with a kind of breathless waiting.

He was going to do it, Michael thought. The thing he'd told himself he must not under any circumstances do. He was going to make love to her.

Blair felt his body ripple with sudden tension and couldn't control her own spasmodic trembling as Michael's face drew slowly near. And then he spoke.

"You're all I have," he whispered, as though continuing the argument of a few minutes earlier. "The only hope I have of seeing this thing through to the end, of seeing my father's killer caught and punished."

His fingers flexed on her shoulders. "You can't let me down, not now, not when I need you . . . so badly. . . ."

The words ripped at her heart, tearing at the fragile shield she'd been constructing in the short time since she'd begun to accept this man as Michael.

A part of her wanted desperately to give in to him. But her motives were unclear. Would she be agreeing to help him because she believed the story he'd told? Or because she wanted him to make love to her?

The sane, sensible, part of her knew the answer to both questions, and it was that part that made her pull out of his arms. "I'm sorry, but I can't do what you want."

The people of Baywater were her friends. They'd stood by her when her parents had died, leaving her all alone in the world. She couldn't equate any one of them with such a cold-blooded act as murder.

No matter how she'd once felt about him, and despite the attraction she was beginning to feel toward this new Michael, ten years was a long time. Her Michael had been noted for his strength of character and fine manners. She didn't know this man. And there was another important fact she must not forget, this Michael was married. How did his wife figure into his plans?

The new Michael gave a snort of irritation and shook his dark head. "How can you refuse me?"

"How could you walk away and forget all about me?"

"You don't understand!" He dragged a hand through his hair in frustration.

"*You* don't understand."

"Damn it, I need you!"

This was getting them nowhere. Blair asked abruptly, "What if you're recognized?"

"Recognized? Is that what's bothering you?" He almost laughed. "Well, take a good look at this face." Leaning closer, he turned it to the light. "Would you recognize it from ten years ago? *Did* you recognize it?"

At her quick gulp of air his head turned sharply, and he found that his face was only a scant few inches from hers. Her breath blew sweet against his lips and chin. Something clutched at his insides.

"How can you refuse me?" he whispered again, his glance on her mouth. He could almost taste her sweet lips.

"It wouldn't be right," Blair protested quickly, uncertain which she was protesting against, helping him, or the desire she saw moving over his face.

"I can take care of myself, believe me, and I can take care of you, too." The glow in his dark eyes as they met hers lent a deeper meaning to his words. "I won't let anything happen to you, I promise. If you'll only trust me," he whispered, bending closer, but not quite touching her.

The air around them shimmered and grew still. Not even the sound of the ocean could penetrate the wall separating them from the rest of the world.

Blair felt trapped within the blaze from Michael's eyes, felt the shock of his body as it drifted warmly, insistently, against her, could almost taste his lips hovering so near to her own. She wanted to refute what she saw in his face, but she was mesmerized by the aura of strength and raw masculinity this new Michael exuded.

Could he feel the erratic beat of her heart? She licked her dry lips and felt her pulse give a little kick as Michael's eyes followed the movement closely.

He lowered his head, and Blair couldn't help it, she rose on her toes to meet him. Michael's lips closed warmly over hers, and Blair tasted whiskey an instant before she caved in to his demands by answering his kiss with a store of passion she'd been saving up for ten years.

Despite his resolve against it, Michael felt the memories come crowding back. He wanted to make love to her. He'd spent weeks—months—of his recovery thinking about making love to her.

Not even Mary's sweet presence had been able to penetrate the fantasy world he'd lived in during that stage of his convalescence. Though he was ashamed to admit it even to himself, there had been times even after his marriage when dreams of this woman had become almost more than he could bear.

Nights when he'd awakened bathed in sweat, torn apart by the memory of Blair and all he'd lost, too ashamed to lie beside the woman who was his wife, and spent the rest of the night on the couch in the den. He knew Mary thought it was nightmares about the accident that drove him to leave her, and he'd never disabused her of the idea. He could never have hurt her by telling her it was love of another woman driving him from her bed.

He'd married Mary in a moment of despair, knowing she loved him, knowing he could never go back to the woman he loved. Blair had loved the handsome, laughing companion of her youth. The man he'd once been but was no more. How could he have asked her to accept this scarred, broken hulk in that man's place?

In an agony of memory, he held Blair's face tenderly between the palms of his hands as he kissed her again and again, drawing from her the sweetness he'd missed all these years. He could no more stop what was about to take place then he could stop his own heart from beating.

A warning sounded from somewhere inside, but Michael denied it; this moment was fated to happen, and he'd waited a long time for it. Closing his mouth over hers, he took her lips in a kiss that seemed to last forever, spanning both the present and the past, tying them together for all time.

Blair was disarmed by the hunger in his kiss and responded with a need that shocked him. He felt her lips open beneath his, drawing his tongue inside her mouth. He felt her hands crawl up his chest and fasten themselves around his neck, felt her body warm against his as she stretched on her toes to accommodate his greater height.

The sensation of her breasts jutting against his chest, her hips sliding against his, quickly pushed him past the brink of control. His fingers clenched in her hair, and his kisses became feverish. He hardly gave her time to breathe as he literally swept her off her feet, clutching her against his throbbing body.

It had been so long... so long....

As his need for her grew, one hand moved beneath her jacket and sweater to caress the smooth satiny hollow at the base of her spine, sliding to cup her derriere tautly, pressing her to him as he moved urgently against her. His lips stroked hers, his tongue pressed against her lips, slipped between them and touched her tongue, while his other hand found its way beneath the tail of her shirt and moved up around her rib cage to close over one small breast.

Blair couldn't withhold a soft moan of pleasure that intensified as Michael slipped one leg between hers, rocking her against him. The fingers playing against her spine found the clasp of her bra and began to work it loose as questing fingers slipped beneath a lacy cup and freed one small globe into his palm.

All at once Blair gave a convulsive shiver and froze. What was she doing? Had she forgotten the last ten years so easily?

Pulling her arms from around his neck, she wedged them between their bodies and pressed her elbows against his chest, trying at the same time to turn her face away from his kiss.

"No," Michael protested in a gruff, uneven tone, following her movements. "Don't pull away," he pleaded.

His fingers captured her head, his elbows locking her against him as he tried to turn her face back to his straining mouth. "Don't fight me. No, please..." he panted. "Don't fight!"

But the voice of Blair's conscience was too loud for her to ignore. Held captive within his viselike grip, she took the only recourse left to her. Swinging one foot back, she kicked at his shin, hard enough to get his attention.

"Ow! What the—" Michael released her abruptly, quickly taking a step back before she could let fly again. Bending to rub at his aching shin, his eyes glittered up at her angrily in the moonlight. "Why did you do that?"

"What is it with you?" Blair forced herself to speak in an angry, accusing tone, hiding her own pain. "Isn't one woman *ever* going to be enough for you?"

Michael shook his head and asked, "What are you talking about?"

"Have you forgotten your wife," she asked angrily, "as easily as you forgot your fiancée a decade ago?"

Michael's whole body turned to a solid block of ice, and then he was blazingly angry. Straightening to his full height, he drew one hand back in a reflex action.

Blair caught her breath but lifted her face defiantly and challenged, "Go ahead—hit me if it will make you feel better. But it won't change the fact that you're a married man, and I think more of myself than to fool around with married men."

"It isn't like that," he protested.

"No? Then what's it like?" she asked, unable to mask the pain in her voice. No matter how she tried, she just couldn't seem to let go of the past. "You were engaged to Cheryl. We'd never—you'd never—looked at me like you did that night." The thought made her throat ache with remorse. "And then you kissed me... and I never saw you again."

Swallowing back the tears that were suddenly too near the surface, Blair continued in a stronger voice edged with contempt. "Well, it doesn't matter now. You're married, and Cheryl is married too, and I'm—"

"I don't want Cheryl," he growled, grabbing her shoulders and hauling her up against him. "I want you!"

"No!" Blair put a hand against his chest, holding him off. "You have a wife!"

"She has nothing to do with this—with us," he muttered.

In the next moment he lifted a stunned Blair off her feet, into his arms, and moved toward one of the cabanas. Inside its shelter he sat on the bench running along the back and folded her onto his lap, wrapping his arms around her to hold her in place.

"Let me go, Michael." Blair found her voice again to whisper sadly, "This isn't right. I can't make love to you now, while you're another woman's husband, any more than I could have ten years ago, when you were engaged to Cheryl." Her soft voice quivered with the strain of keeping it firm. "I'm just not made that way," she explained hesitantly. "Please, let me go. I wish I'd never come...."

The hollow sound of her voice affected him far more than her words. Michael released her, damping his own ardor with the memory of his wife. Getting to his feet, he turned toward the open side of the small structure and went to lean against one of the poles supporting the wall in an attempt to gain control of his emotions.

She was right; this shouldn't be happening between them. When he'd written that letter, it had been for the sole purpose of appealing to her for help, nothing more.

After a few minutes Blair managed to get herself in hand. Looking up at his tall figure silhouetted in the moonlight, arms hanging loosely at his sides, she noted again that air of isolation that had seemed to surround him earlier in the bar.

She tried telling herself it was nothing more than her own emotion, colored by the terrible account of what had happened to him and his father. There had been nothing dark or mysterious about the Michael of her youth.

But he's gone, a part of her insisted, and in his place is this stranger. A man who's older, tougher, scarred, both physically and mentally. Admit it, you're intrigued by him.

That had nothing to do with it!

Michael's gaze drifted from the ocean to Blair's indistinct figure huddled on the bench. She looked so small, sitting where he'd literally dropped her.

What was he doing? Why was he trying to force his way back into her life? Why was he denying her the truth? That wasn't what he wanted, not what he wanted at all.

Taking a seat beside her, Michael lifted the hand closest to him and placed it on his palm. Sliding a thumb over its back, he tested the softness of her fingers against his own rougher, callused ones. Inside, his emotions were in utter turmoil, but outwardly he appeared quite calm.

"My wife died over a year ago." Blair was ashamed of the leap of joy she quickly repressed. Michael hesitated, then continued with difficulty. "I invited you here to ask for your help, nothing more."

Blair glanced into his face, straining to see his expression in the dark. "I wish I could give you what you want." Pulling her fingers from his, she added, "But I can't."

"Then that's that," he answered, heaving a sigh of finality. Was there a part of him that was relieved by her refusal? "Come on, I'll walk you back to your room."

They moved in single file, Blair walking in front, over the sand toward the lights of the motel in the distance. It was nearly midnight, and in the misty darkness it felt as though they were walking in another world, another time.

Blair felt a chill sweep over her and dropped back to walk at Michael's side, giving his stern profile a quick, sidelong glance. Was she making a mistake by refusing to help him? Could his father really have been murdered by someone in Baywater?

Or was it only bitterness, caused by his father's death and his own inability to prevent it, that had sent him to her? Was he seeking other answers for what had happened because he couldn't face reality, couldn't face the fact that he'd survived when his father hadn't?

She'd seen it happen before to the survivors of a catastrophe. They felt guilt for being alive when their loved ones weren't, and had to find some reason for it. Had Michael found a murderer to explain his father's death?

At the entrance to her room, Blair used her key, then stood with her back against the door, denying him admittance. She didn't want to prolong the goodbyes, because she had no intention of spending the night after he'd gone.

She realized now that her life had been put on hold, while everyone she knew, including Michael, had gone on. It was time she took up the reins and shaped her own future, instead of allowing it to be shaped by images from the past.

Let her go! The command rang in Michael's brain as his eyes studied her face. What was it about her that had haunted him all these years?

"I guess this is goodbye," Blair murmured, holding out an awkward hand.

Michael glanced down at the unsteady fingers without touching them, then looked directly into her eyes. He should have made love to her when they were both fifteen and he'd felt the first stirring of manhood and desire for her.

"It isn't going to work," he murmured gruffly, knowing they'd both been headed toward this moment all their lives. Blair's breath became trapped in her lungs at his next words. "I can't let you go." Touching a fingertip to her quivering lips, he added, "Whatever sprang to life between us in the past is still there." He pressed closer.

"No," she protested weakly, fighting the eager way her heart leaped at his words. Michael's finger moved from her lower lip down the side of her cheek to the sensitive underside of her chin, and Blair whispered weakly, "We're different people."

"Yes, we are," he agreed, bending his knees, fusing his hips to hers, feeling a rush of hot desire course through him at the intimate contact. She'd been a fever in his blood for too long. Perhaps all it would take was one time, one night in her arms, to break the spell she'd held over him for at least half of his entire life.

With a breathless murmur of protest, Blair swallowed tightly and felt the hand beneath her chin move slowly down across the front of her sweater. When it slipped beneath the waistband of her slacks, her voice became almost inaudible. "Things have changed.... This is wrong."

Her insides were quivering like jelly, and every time his hand progressed an inch farther her breath caught on a tiny gasp of anticipation. "No...don't do this...." She swallowed back a moan, knowing that even while she objected, she wanted him to make love to her. She'd been waiting all her life for him.

"I want you," he breathed hotly against the side of her neck, pressing the palm of his hand flat against the taut flesh of her belly. "And you want me, too."

His hand delved past the hard ridge of her pelvis to the soft, warm flesh at the apex of her thighs.

Blair gave a slight jerk and licked her lips. "No," she whimpered, suddenly afraid, straining away from him. She didn't know this man who held her so intimately in his hand. He wasn't the Michael she knew and loved but rather a fearsome stranger she'd just met. She couldn't....

Michael pushed the fingers of his free hand into her hair and lifted her face to his.

"What—" Blair began, eyelids fluttering, swallowing a moan as the hard fingers at her thigh moved gently but insistently against her. "What are you doing?"

Michael reached for one of her clenched fists, drew it to his chest and pressed it open above his heart. "Feel that?" he panted. "It started when I looked up a little while ago and saw you sitting across that bar, staring at me as though you'd just seen a ghost."

Blair's fingers curled beneath his, digging into his chest, her breath coming in short, sharp gasps. What was he doing to her?

She wanted him. How she wanted him. This time when he made love to her, it wouldn't be a dream. This time she would feel him, flesh and blood, muscle and bone, beneath her, inside her.

Michael pressed his hard length against her, flattening her against the door. "Put your arms around me," he panted into her ear. "Touch me—touch me...."

When she didn't do as he commanded, in frustration he agonized, "I've dreamed of making love to you all my life. Put your arms around me, please!"

His mouth fastened hotly over hers, and Blair gave a moan and was lost. She wrapped her arms around his shoulders and tilted her face hungrily to his kiss.

This was Michael, holding her, kissing her, burning her skin wherever he touched, setting her on fire with need for him. This was the Michael of her dreams, the man she'd thought she would never see again in this lifetime. And he wanted her! Not Cheryl, not even the woman who'd been his wife. He wanted her!

Michael drank from her lips like a dying man offered a last sweet taste of life. Capturing them between his, he kissed each one separately, drawing his closed lips over them slowly, rubbing his tongue wetly along the lower one, opening his mouth over hers and drawing the sweet nectar that was Blair into his starved body.

The hand in her hair strained her head back as he rained kisses down her neck to her shoulders to the edge of her sweater. He began to work the slacks down her hips, so caught up in what was happening that he'd forgotten where they were.

Blair pulled her lips from his long enough to whisper, "No—not here—inside."

Michael found the door handle behind her with one hand and gave it a twist, keeping her pressed tightly to him, afraid to let her go in case she changed her mind and told him to leave. They fell back into the room, stumbling over the threshold, holding each other up to keep from tumbling to the floor.

Michael slammed the door shut and twisted the dead bolt into place with Blair locked in one arm. A small stream of light from the bathroom, where Blair had turned on a light when she'd first arrived, gave them enough light to see each other clearly.

In a flurry of impatience Michael stripped the jacket from Blair's shoulders, pulled the sweater over her head and put his hands at her waist to slip the slacks down over her shapely hips. He was brought up short when the slacks wouldn't slip over the bulk of her shoes.

"Wait," Blair murmured softly, touching him on the shoulder to get his attention. He looked up from where he was trying to work the gray slacks over her sneaker. "Let me do it."

With one hand on his shoulder to steady herself, Blair pushed the slacks and shoe from her foot. Changing hands, she did the same with the other leg and found herself standing before him in two scraps of pale, lavender lace—and a pair of heavy, white sweat socks.

"You're beautiful," he whispered gruffly, his eyes moving over the slender curves of her body.

Bending forward, he removed first one sock and then the other, taking his time about it, touching her slender ankles and delicate feet with gentle fingers.

Blair reached behind her to unsnap the fastening of her bra and removed it slowly, slipping her arms first from one strap and then the other, holding the lacy cups against her.

From his place at her feet Michael reached up and removed her fingers, taking the bra from her body. His eyes darkened, his breath becoming a solid lump in his throat as he sat back on his heels and studied the beauty of mauve-tipped breasts, slender waist and narrow, curved hips.

He took only a quick moment to enjoy the picture she made, and then he was anxiously slipping the lace from her hips, down past her shapely thighs to lie against her trim ankles. The last barrier was gone.

Blair stepped out of the lacy briefs and stood before him, feeling as though she should cover herself from his bold stare. But before she could make a move, he rose to his feet and began to unfasten the buttons on his navy shirt. And then, as his chest was laid bare, it was she who couldn't get her fill of watching him.

With the release of each button a broader expanse of bare chest was revealed, and the hot, liquid heat running rampant through her veins began to pool low in her body. She could hardly breathe and wouldn't have been able to speak if her life had depended on it.

Michael shrugged one shoulder from the shirt and then Blair's hands were there helping him to remove it. He paused as his eyes found hers, gave a slight smile and let her take over.

Blair had undressed, or helped to undress, numerous people as a nurse. Many of them had been male, and some of them had been young and good-looking, but none had affected her as she was now affected. The sight of Michael's muscled shoulders and broad, hair-roughened chest, warm beneath her hands, made her want to curl against him and beg him to make love to her, quickly, before either one of them could change their mind.

Biting her lip, her glance sliding up over his and then down to his chest again, Blair lifted shaky fingers toward his belt buckle. Goose bumps ruffled the skin on the backs of her legs and buttocks. She gave a slight shiver and stood still, her fingers still inches from the metal buckle.

Understanding her sudden shyness, Michael leaned down and planted a light kiss against the soft skin where her shoulder met her neck; then, taking her cold fingers in his warm clasp, he placed them on the buckle. He gave them a reassuring squeeze, released them and held his breath, taming the white-hot passion raging through him, barely under control.

Blair managed after several false attempts to get the belt unfastened, but froze as her fingers touched the snap on his jeans. She stared at it, the image blurring before her eyes.

"I can't," she whispered finally. "You . . . do . . . it."

Turning away, she stood with lowered head, hands clasped at her waist. What was she doing here, planning to make love to a stranger? And then Michael touched her, took her by the shoulders and drew her back against his naked chest, and Blair knew what she was doing. She was fulfilling a lifelong fantasy.

"Do it, Michael." She turned in a rush and lifted her arms around his neck. "Do it now before I change my mind. Make love to me!"

"I'm going to," he answered in a harshly tender voice, his hands on her shoulders, smoothing down to her forearms and back, pressing her up against him, against the whole naked, pulsating length of him. "Oh, I'm going to!"

His mouth captured hers, enflaming it with repeated assaults. His tongue prodded her lips, tasting them, gliding between them, touching her gums, her teeth, the tip of her tongue. He'd wanted this for so long.

A few months after his wife's death, he'd awakened in the small hours of the night, bathed in a cold sweat and aching with guilt. Night after night he dreamed of making love to a young nurse who took care of him after his accident. But the young woman hadn't worn blond hair pulled up beneath a white nurse's cap as his wife had done. Her long dark tresses had hung uncovered down the center of her back, swaying gracefully from side to side as she glided toward where he lay helpless in a hospital bed.

Michael's hands ranged up and down her back, the slender, shapely back of the young woman he could only dream about—until now. Grasping her hips in both hands, pulling her against him, he held her, just held her, letting the tide of feelings wash over him.

This was Blair, no dream, the real flesh and blood woman he craved. She was a woman now, not the frightened, half-grown child-woman he'd blurted out his love to that last night.

For ten long years he'd yearned for her in moments of weakness, moments of soul-destroying guilt during his brief marriage, and now she was his for the taking.

He'd loved his wife, differently from the way he loved Blair, but he'd loved her all the same. And the feelings he couldn't kill for Blair had taken nothing away from the other woman, because his love for Blair was unconsummated and would remain so for the rest of his life. Or so he had told himself, night after night, day after day, as the hours stretched, turning into weeks, months and finally years.

When his wife became ill, he'd put Blair's face out of his mind. But when his wife died, he used those secret longings for Blair as a means of punishment, telling himself his wife's death was a judgment against him for ignoring his father's murder, for thinking of another woman while married to Mary. He floundered, mired in guilt, unable to see the world around him for the world he'd lost.

In the end he'd come to terms with his feelings and learned to exist on hate. Somehow his guilt about his wife and the death of his father became all mixed up in his mind. And he decided that retribution on his father's behalf would win him some small measure of forgiveness for marrying one woman while loving another. All he had lived for during the next year was revenge as he waited until the right moment to strike.

And then he'd looked up and seen Blair. She wasn't the Blair of his youthful dreams, and at first he'd thought he could get away with his plan, the plan he'd had in mind when he'd written to her.

He would be cool, distant, all business, and there would be nothing personal in their new relationship, a relationship founded on past friendship. Michael drew back and looked down into Blair's passion-flushed features.

He'd been a fool! How had he ever hoped to get away with something like that? Whatever his reasons for contacting her, he needed her now more than ever, needed her as he'd never needed anyone else in his whole life.

Michael knew he was heading down an uncharted road that might lead him straight to hell. He didn't know what tomorrow might bring, probably sorrow and regret for what he was about to do. But tonight he had Blair, and nothing else mattered.

Blair was with him every step of the way. With her arms around his neck, mouth opened to his, matching stroke for stroke, they made love.

Michael groaned softly, grasped her hips in both hands and lifted her legs around his waist. Her moist heat closed over him, and he clutched her to him, easing her gently into place. His hands massaged her hips rhythmically in time to the movement of their bodies, while their tongues dueled, parodying the act of love.

"Blair," Michael whispered hoarsely as his knees began to weaken, sweat standing out on his shoulders and back. "Blair," he murmured again, between pants, feeling as though the woman clinging to him, matching him thrust for thrust, was draining every ounce of life from his soul.

Blair felt a ripping sensation tear through her, stripping away everything she'd ever known, or thought she knew, about fulfillment, and a new tide of enchantment began to build. Grasping Michael's hair in both hands, pressing her lips to his, she rode her passion to the end.

Michael took a couple of steps forward, and the two of them fell back on the bed still locked in passion's grip. For several minutes all that could be heard was the ragged sound of their harsh breathing. Exhaustion made the muscles of Michael's calves and thighs quiver, caused his chest to burn.

Blair couldn't move except for the rapid rising and falling of her chest as she tried to gasp enough oxygen into her lungs to satisfy her pounding heart. Her mind was a total blank, except for one thought.

So, this was how it felt to "know" the man you loved.

Blair felt Michael stir against her. Her head rolled in his direction. Rising up on one elbow, he reached out to smooth one dark curl back behind her ear.

Passion flared quickly in the dark eyes flecked with gold, and an answering spark was ignited in the blue eyes locked with them.

"This time," Michael mouthed against her lips, "let's take it slow." His kisses trailed fire down her neck across her shoulder to her breast.

Blair closed her eyes, her hands pressing him to her as his lips fastened over a puckered nipple, and murmured, "Yes, oh, yes, let's...."

Blair felt Michael move in the bed beside her. She'd thought he was asleep. She would have been asleep herself if thoughts about what came next hadn't kept her awake. They'd made love twice after that first time. She felt like a newlywed on her wedding night—only she and Michael weren't married. And she didn't know if they would ever see each other again after tonight.

She still hadn't agreed to help him find the man responsible for his father's death, and he hadn't mentioned it again. She wasn't certain, based on what Michael had said, if she even believed in this anonymous killer.

On the other hand, if what Michael had said was true, could she live with herself, knowing she'd refused to help him bring such a man to justice?

Blair closed her eyes, telling herself she couldn't deal with that at the moment. They popped open again when she felt Michael slip silently from the bed. She watched as he moved on careful feet toward his clothes lying strewn about the floor.

Just for an instant he stood tall in the shaft of light from the bathroom, and Blair felt her insides turn to mush at the sight of his sleek, naked body, as though she hadn't just made love to him throughout the long night.

She couldn't seem to take her eyes off his lean flanks and watched shamelessly as muscles rippled beneath smooth skin when he bent to retrieve his jeans and shirt.

With his shirt hanging open down the front, socks and boots in one hand, Michael turned to throw a quick glance over one shoulder toward the bed where Blair lay. He hesitated for one breathless instant, then turned toward the door and let himself out.

As the door closed softly behind him, Blair raised herself up on one elbow and took a deep breath. She wanted to call out to him, ask if he was coming back, if she would see him again. But the words died on her lips.

Gone like a thief in the night. The phrase echoed inside her head. And she was letting him go.

Would he show up in Baywater, despite her refusal of help? And how would they meet if he did? As old friends . . . lovers . . . or strangers?

Chapter 4

"Are you going to the auction on Saturday?"

"Auction? What auction?" Dr. Roger Prescott, Blair's employer, laid his fork down on his salad plate and turned startlingly blue eyes, set in a deeply tanned face, to the young woman sitting across from him.

"The Baldwin estate," Blair answered softly, meeting his glance.

After a moment of silence he asked, "Has it been that long?"

"Ten years," Blair responded with a slight catch in her voice. But only three days since she'd last seen Michael. She wished she dared tell this man that, because those three days had been filled with unrest and confusion.

She kept asking herself if Michael had only made love to her in order to get her to help him and, when she showed no sign of agreeing, cut his losses and disappeared.

Roger's glance centered on her face. "Are you going?"

Blair focused her attention reluctantly on what her dining companion was saying and answered, "I might. I probably will," she amended after a slight hesitation. "I've been acting as unofficial caretaker of the house and all the things in it for so long, I feel as though I should."

"I suppose right at this moment all your care must seem as though it was for nothing," he responded gently.

Blair smiled self-consciously, pushed a piece of lettuce around on her plate with her fork and nodded. "I guess I have become sort of overly attached to the place." She met the man's sympathetic gaze. "I know it sounds silly, but I started looking after the place because . . ." She paused, uncertain how to continue.

"Because," he took up her words, "since neither Michael nor his father's bodies were found, you thought, hoped, someday they might just suddenly come walking through the door."

Blair's eyes widened. "Oh—I didn't—I never really believed that could happen, but—"

"You've never accepted their deaths, have you?" he asked abruptly, startling her.

"I—"

"It's all right," he interrupted. "I understand." Roger reached over and covered her hand warmly with one of his own. "I dare say most of us who knew Mark and his son have looked at that house more than once over the years and had much the same thought."

"You, too?"

Sadness crept into the man's eyes, dulling their sparkle. "I confess that, when they first came up missing, I used to drive by the street and wonder if I might see a light burning in the window of Mark's study."

"It's just so inconclusive," Blair said, "their disappearing that way. Everyone around town has speculated on what might have occurred. What do you think happened?"

Roger studied her for a moment before replying. "I don't know. Maybe a sudden storm came up and the waves swept them overboard."

"Yes, but wouldn't the coast guard have found the . . . bodies?"

"No." He shook his head. "Not unless they managed to get onto a piece of the debris from the wreckage, before the ship broke up. If there was a lightning storm, fire could have destroyed the boat, or an explosion— What is it, my dear?" he asked, seeing the abrupt change come over her face.

She'd turned as white as the cloth on the table before them. "Are you feeling ill?"

"I'm fine. It's only the thought of an explosion at sea, with no one around to come to their aid." She shuddered.

His words came too near the facts as Michael had revealed them to her such a short time ago, and hearing them again, even as speculation from this man, brought the horror too close.

"I know, my dear, it's an appalling picture. I realize how close you and Michael were to each other, more like brother and sister than friends."

"You and his father were good friends, too," Blair interjected swiftly, hoping to change the course of the conversation. Guilt, caused by her knowledge of Michael's return, was making her uncomfortable beneath his compassionate stare.

This was something new for her. In the five years she'd worked for him, she'd never once felt guilt in his presence, despite his being Cheryl's father. But since returning from her meeting with Michael, she felt as though the words *Michael Baldwin is alive and I slept with him* were written across her forehead for everyone to see.

"You know," Roger was speaking again, "Mark grew up in that very house where Michael was born. We were neighbors, too, at the time. The house where I was born, a little farther along the beach, is no longer there. Your house stands only a few yards from where it stood." Roger smiled to himself and shook his dark blond head sadly.

Blair's voice recalled him from a memory of the past. "It will seem strange, knowing the house doesn't belong to the Baldwins anymore. I don't know how I'll feel about strangers living there." Her eyes dropped to the table; she hated herself for her duplicity and couldn't look him in the face.

Misinterpreting her feelings, Roger said softly, "You have to let them go and get on with your life. Don't think I don't know how you've clung to their memories," he admonished, drawing her eyes. "But it's time to put them to rest. I know it's hard to let go of someone you cared a great deal about. Hard even," he added with a wry grin, "for someone like me, who remembers a friend from his youth, a hundred years or so ago.''

''You aren't anywhere near that old,'' Blair protested. ''You forget, I work with you every day. I've seen the way the women flock to your office with little or no excuse for an appointment.''

''You're good for my ego.'' He smiled into her eyes. ''You know, we make a good pair, you and I.''

''You're right.'' She smiled serenely. ''And that's why your office runs so smoothly.''

''You aren't fooling me,'' he murmured seriously.

Blair gave a start she tried to cover by shifting her napkin on her lap and stared at him from beneath half-lowered lids.

''I'm a doctor, remember?'' he continued. ''Losing the Baldwin men must have punched a great hole in your life. But, just as you had to let your parents go when they passed on, you have to let Mark and his son go, too.'' He searched her face before adding, ''I prescribe a man in your life, someone to wine you and dine you and whisper sweet nothings in your lovely ears.''

Blair felt her cheeks grow warm with embarrassment. She wished she could tell him there was already a man in her life.

Something at the corner of her vision drew her attention. She glanced up—directly into a pair of dark, gold-flecked eyes—and all at once Blair couldn't seem to draw enough air into her lungs.

Michael!

He wasn't alone. A tall, elegant blonde walked at his side with her hand in the crook of his elbow, smiling up into his face. Michael bent his head toward the attractive young woman, though his eyes were still locked with Blair's. He murmured something in her ear, causing her to laugh briefly, and disengaged his glance from Blair's as the blonde gave his arm a little pat. They followed the waiter single file as he led them across the crowded dining room in Blair's direction.

Michael's eyes found Blair's again as he drew within a few feet of their table, slid over Roger's hand covering hers on the white tablecloth, and moved back to her face. Blair withdrew her hand and clasped it with the other one, placing them both out of sight on her lap.

Michael's glance burned into her. His steps slowed; then, as though a shutter had clicked into place, he gave her an impersonal nod, swept her companion a disinterested glance and moved quickly past.

Roger glanced up in time to see Blair's eyes fastened on the man's retreating back. His own glance swung in the man's direction, following the attractive couple across the crowded floor.

"Is anything wrong?" he asked curiously, turning toward the silent woman sitting across from him.

"W-what?" Blair straightened and focused her glance on his face.

"Do you know that couple?" Roger asked with a slight furrowing of his elegant brow.

"K-know them?" She thought frantically. "No—that is, not exactly. I met the, uh, man a few days ago, over the weekend, while I was gone. We stayed at the same place."

Roger twisted in his seat to give the man's strong face a keen stare, watched as he assisted his companion into her chair.

"You don't suppose he followed you here, do you?" he asked with a frown.

"F-followed me?" She laughed weakly, turning it into disdain. "Of course he didn't follow me. It wasn't that kind of an acquaintance."

Her glance found the couple across the room engaged in conversation, and she continued, "As you can see, he's much more interested in his dining companion than he is in renewing what was at best only a nodding acquaintance with me."

Roger gave the blonde a moment's scrutiny before turning back to Blair. His mustache twitched upward in a smile as his attractive eyes twinkled at her. "I find your good breeding and quiet beauty much more attractive than the somewhat conspicuous charms of his dining companion. The man obviously has no taste." He dismissed the incident and the other couple with a wave of his hand.

Their meal arrived, and the conversation resumed along the lines of what was taking place in the office that afternoon. No more was said about the Baldwin auction or whether Roger was planning to attend.

Nor was the couple across the room mentioned again. But more than once during that awkward luncheon Blair found her glance straying to the two people with so much to say to each other that they seemed oblivious to the rest of the room, and for the first time since she'd begun eating in that restaurant, she found the food there unpalatable.

Had Michael found someone more willing to accede to his demands?

Back at work, the afternoon crept slowly by. Blair gave a mental start every time the phone rang, expecting to hear Michael's newly coarse voice coming down the line to her.

By five-thirty Blair was a nervous wreck. Office hours ended at five, but she always stayed half an hour later to make certain she'd filed all the patients' charts correctly and added any notations that might have had been made that day.

Normally Dr. Prescott was gone by five-fifteen, but this afternoon he was still in his office, making notes on his last patient, when Blair was ready to leave. She was just about to see if there was anything else she could do for him before leaving when someone knocked at the outer door.

For a moment she couldn't move. Was it *him?* He'd told her he needed to investigate his father's friends and business acquaintances in his search for the killer. Was Michael about to start with Roger Prescott?

The very idea was crazy. The knock came again.

What should she do? Should she answer the door, or should she warn Roger?

"Blair?" Roger spoke from his office doorway behind her. "Are you going to answer that? I know office hours are over, but we can at least make certain it isn't an emergency."

"Oh, yes," she replied, moving swiftly toward the door, "of course." Reversing the bolt with nervous fingers, she pulled the door slowly back and peered around the edge.

"Blair? Hello, child, how are you? I know it's late, but I need to talk to your boss for a moment. I saw his car on the lot, so I know he's still here."

"Mr. Welborn." She grinned in relief. "Come in. I'll tell him—"

"No need, Blair. I'm here." Roger moved into the room, holding out his hand to the other man. "Well, you're back early, Marvin. I thought you were going to be out of town until the weekend."

"I finished my business early and saw no reason to delay getting home," the other man answered, shaking the doctor's hand warmly.

They headed toward Roger's office, making small talk. At the door Roger paused to turn back and ask, "Are you leaving?"

"Yes, unless you have something else you need me to do."

"No, no, go ahead. Anything else can wait until morning. We've had a busy day, and I know you must be tired."

Blair smiled at his thoughtfulness. "See you in the morning." She reached for her purse and keys.

"Blair?" Roger closed his office door and came a few steps into the room.

"Yes?" She looked up.

"I enjoyed lunch with you today. I can't imagine why we haven't done it before." He paused before adding in a more serious tone, "I meant what I said about getting on with your life."

"I'll give it some thought," she answered, not knowing what else to say.

"Fine." He turned away and went to join the man waiting for him in his office.

Blair drove home with the top down on her convertible, hoping to blow the uncertainties from her mind. What was she going to do about Michael if he contacted her again? If he didn't?

She parked in the garage and walked through the side door and up the steps to her house. Pausing there for a moment, she gave the house next door a long appraising glance, wondering if Michael might be inside.

The Baldwin mansion and her own more modest home were the only two houses on the street. It dead-ended at the beach a few yards past Michael's house. She hadn't known until today that at one time there had been three houses on the street.

Why had Michael looked right through her at the restaurant? No, that wasn't exactly how it had been; for a moment he'd looked as though he hated her, and *then* he'd looked through her.

Blair shivered, hurried down the walk to the side door, unlocked it and stumbled over the doorstep in her anxiety to get inside. Michael was a stranger, and she kept thinking of him as though he were a friend. No, not a friend, a man, a very attractive, rather mysterious man.

What was happening to her? Nothing seemed to make sense anymore—*she* didn't make sense anymore.

She'd gone to see a man she had believed to be dead for a decade. He'd told her some bizarre story of murder and betrayal, and despite her disbelief in what he'd said, despite her anger and confusion at his long silence, despite the fact that he'd married someone else during his long period of silence, she had allowed herself to be seduced, had actually made love with him.

And now she was upset because he'd ignored her in a restaurant. She was too young to be having a mid-life crisis!

Kicking off her nurse's shoes, ripping open the snaps along the front of her uniform, Blair marched in stocking-feet to her bedroom, threw her purse down on the bed and stood undecided. Maybe a hot shower, followed by a cold one, would clear up the mess of her mind.

She had a decision to make. Did she simply ignore Michael's presence in town? Go on pretending she didn't know him? She slipped out of her underthings and stepped into the shower. Or did she get in touch with him? Call all the motels in town if she had to until she found him and offered her help?

What if he was right? What if there was a killer hiding in their midst? What if he should decide to strike again? Anyone could be a victim—even herself. Living all alone in this big house made her a prime target for...

Now look at what she was doing, building fantasies again, only this time to scare herself. It was time she stopped living in daydreams and began living in the real world. She was thirty-two years old, not a kid anymore.

Roger Prescott and Michael had both been right about that. It was time she took charge of her own life.

Helping Michael find out the truth—whatever it turned out to be—would be a start in the right direction. Coming to terms with her feelings for him would be another.

Soaping her short hair, she rubbed at her scalp with her nails, wishing the answer to all her problems could be taken care of as simply as washing away unwanted hair spray.

She stood beneath the shower with closed eyes and turned her face up to it, feeling the water against her eyelids. Thoughts of Michael and the night they'd spent together just three short days ago pounded against the walls of her subconscious, forcing their way into her conscious mind.

Lifting her hands, she smoothed her fingers through the short strands of hair, removing the shampoo, remembering the way Michael had threaded his fingers in her hair just so, grasped it and held her head back for his kiss. And while his lips had caressed hers, his strong hands had moved down her face to her shoulders and breasts, touching, testing, massaging her soft flesh.

Her own hands drifted down the sides of her face to her neck, over her shoulders, across the slopes of her breasts. She shivered, consumed by the memory. . . .

All at once the water turned cold. She gave a start and jerked her hands from her body. What was the matter with her? For a moment it had almost seemed as though he were there in the shower stall with her.

Twisting the water off, Blair jerked the shower door open—and fell back against the wall, gasping in shock.

"W-what are you doing here? How did you get in!"

Michael's dark, insolent gaze slid from her face to her shoulders, moving slowly and seductively downward. Blair felt her insides quicken, her flesh prickle, as though he were actually touching her. She knew she should cover herself, but she couldn't seem to move.

By the time his glance had plundered her secrets and returned to her face, his eyes were smoldering with dark, barely contained fires. Holding her gaze, he lifted a hand and touched a fingertip to one swollen nipple.

Blair bit her lip and closed her eyes. Her breath caught in her throat as he circled the puckered flesh with his finger, then drew it slowly down between both breasts, trailing over the silky skin past her trim waist to her navel. There he hesitated as she gave a short, quick gasp, tightening her stomach muscles. After a slight pause he moved on, feeling her shudder as his finger inched steadily downward.

When his hand paused and remained stationary, Blair opened her eyes. He was staring at her. Their glances became tangled, and she couldn't look away. Slowly and deliberately, he lifted the finger still damp from her body and placed it against his lips, licking the moisture from its tip.

Blair swallowed back a whimper, her body vibrating with each movement of his tongue, yearning for a more intimate touch.

Michael bent forward, and Blair's heart plunged to her toes as she felt his breath blow warm against her thighs, a ripple of gooseflesh dancing up her spine in anticipation. An instant later he straightened, handed her the towel that had fallen from the handrail to the floor and, without a word, turned and left the steamy bathroom.

Blair's limbs were trembling so hard she could barely stand. Stepping from the shower stall she dropped the lid on the toilet and sat, clutching the towel to her breasts, shivering uncontrollably.

What was he doing to her? Why had he come here? What did he want from her?

She knew the answer to that last question. He wanted her help. And she had a feeling he would stop at nothing until he got it.

Fifteen minutes later, dressed and once more composed, Blair went to find Michael. At first she thought he'd left as silently and unexpectedly as he'd come, but a moment later she found him on the patio. Enclosed on two sides, one open side faced the ocean, the other the back of the house next door. Michael stood with his hands in his pockets staring at his former home.

At her entrance he turned, motioned toward the house and said, "It doesn't look any different. Somehow I thought it would."

"How did you get in?" she asked curtly, knowing both her doors had been locked when she went to take her shower.

"A window was unlocked in the laundry room." He was staring at the house next door again. "I did knock. Several times, as a matter of fact. I even called you, but you didn't answer. I saw you drive up, so I knew you were home." He shrugged and turned to face her. "I thought something might have happened, so I crawled in the—"

"Why did you come?" she cut him off, angry at his intrusion into her life after the way he'd left the motel without a word, and the three succeeding days of silence. "I didn't expect to see you again. And I don't appreciate being...disturbed in my bath. Don't think you can simply come and go in my life, climb through my window, sneak into my house, anytime you like. This isn't ten years ago, and I don't like being treated as though I'm something you can pick up and put down at will."

"You're angry." It wasn't a question but a statement of fact, and he appeared puzzled by it. He took a step toward her, stopping abruptly, realizing all at once why she was upset.

"I couldn't speak to you in the restaurant. You were with Roger Prescott."

"Yes."

"You seemed very...friendly."

"I work for him," she replied stonily.

"Work for him?"

"Yes, I'm—" She hesitated, remembering that he'd told her his wife had been a nurse. "I'm a nurse."

Michael expelled his breath on a note of surprise. "Nurse? You?"

"Yes."

He almost laughed out loud at the irony of it. "As I recall, your burning ambition was to be a marine biologist—or a nursery school teacher."

She'd never been able to make up her mind between the two. Even in college her courses had been haphazardly chosen, with no clear goal in sight.

"I went back to college," she explained, "and studied nursing. I did it because by then, both mother and father were in poor health. I wanted to be able to take care of them with the love and skill they'd shown in taking care of me while I was growing up."

"They spoiled you rotten," Michael muttered, "and kept you from growing up."

"Michael!" she cried, hurt to the quick. In the past, he'd never been so blunt in his opinion of her parents.

"It's true, Blair, face up to it. You allowed them to make every decision for you, and you know it. The first time I ever heard you voice an opinion that differed from theirs was that last night, when you said you were going to cut your hair."

Blair put a hand to her head, recalling not only her parents' insistence on its remaining uncut, but this man's remark about it when they'd met again for the first time a few days ago.

"That isn't true. Not entirely," she qualified, adding with an air of defiance, "I sneaked out at night and met you. You know what my father would have said about that."

"Yes, you did," Michael agreed, giving her a keen glance. "So maybe there's hope for me yet."

Blair turned away, taking a seat in one of the comfortable chairs placed about the patio. It was a relatively small area, but it had an air of spaciousness, created by allowing the flowers, bushes and trees her mother had so loved to spill out on the broad pathway leading to a Victorian-style gazebo and on down toward the seawall.

Resting back against a red-and-black-flowered cushion, Blair crossed her legs and looked up at him. "What do you mean?"

"You know what I mean." His eyes caught and held hers, a question in their depths.

"You don't need my help," Blair answered his unspoken question, tearing her gaze from his to stare down at the fingers clenched together on her lap. "Why don't you ask your... friend to help you?"

"I thought I was," Michael answered as he seated himself in the chair beside her.

Oh, no, he wasn't going to get to her that way. "I mean your new... friend."

"If you mean the woman you saw me with at lunch, I met her at the tax assessor's office. She's the clerk who helped me find the information I was looking for. Time slipped by, and the next thing I knew it was lunchtime." He shrugged. "She'd given me a great deal of her time, so I invited her to lunch."

Blair couldn't help the thought that slid through her mind at his words. What else had she given him?

"I wouldn't be any help to you," she maintained. "I work all day, and I don't get out much in the evenings. Perhaps, someone like your new friend would be of more use to you."

"Her help was invaluable, I admit," he replied. "But I doubt she'll be of much use in the future. She's new in town and doesn't know the people I'm after."

Was that what it was all about? How much use everyone could be to him? What about when her usefulness to him was at an end?

"I came here tonight to see if you'd changed your mind."

"Really? I thought perhaps you were here to tell me you'd come to your senses and decided to claim what's rightfully yours before it's too late." A wistful light entered the blue eyes as Blair leaned slightly toward him. "You can still identify yourself to the authorities, Michael, and make a claim against your father's estate."

"And wind up dead for my trouble?"

"Oh, Michael..." She shook her head in dismay.

"Are you going to help me?" he asked with deceptive calm.

"What can you possibly hope to learn?" she asked in exasperation. "Do you think the killer is going to admit to what he's done? And if he did, then what? What would you do?"

Michael pounced on her words. "You said 'the killer.' Does that mean you believe me at last?"

Blair met his probing stare for a brief moment, then looked away. Did she believe him?

Without waiting for an answer, Michael took one of her hands in both of his and threaded his fingers between hers as he spoke. "You can talk to John Saunders for me and see if you can find out what he thinks happened to Dad's will."

Blair pulled her hand from his and got to her feet. Did he think he could get around her so easily? Was this how he'd gotten the blonde to go to lunch with him?

"I can't simply go up to John and ask him something like that. He'd tell me it was none of my business." She whirled to face him. "The man's a lawyer, for God's sake. Don't you think he'd be curious as to why I was asking questions about the will so long after the fact?"

Michael stood and ran a hand through his dark hair, spiking it. "I don't expect you to just walk up and start asking him questions. Work up to it."

"Work up to it? How?"

"I don't know, damn it! Invite him to lunch." He motioned toward her slender body, encased in the colorful sarong. "Use your feminine wiles—"

"What? John Saunders is old enough to be my father!" She glared at him with burning, reproachful eyes.

"So is Roger Prescott, but that didn't seem to matter at lunch today." He'd hated the sight of the two of them together, looking so friendly with each other. And now, to learn she was with him every day...

Clenching her hands at her sides, Blair muttered, "That was not what it appeared. I mean, Roger and I never have lunch—today was the first time." Realizing that she sounded as though she were apologizing, she straightened her shoulders, tilted her head at a defiant angle and said, "I don't have to explain myself to you." Her mood veered sharply to anger. "What about your motives?" She threw the words at him like stones. "Are they so pure?"

Taking an abrupt step toward him, she asked, "Why didn't you let me know you were alive—if you were too ill to contact me after the accident, why didn't you have someone do it for you? What kept you from calling me when you were well?"

Her questions took the wind out of his sails. "We have to put the past behind us."

"Why?" she asked coldly.

"It's the only way we'll be able to keep from...wounding each other."

"I don't think I've wounded you, Michael!" She drew herself up sharply. "It's the other way around." Emotion made her voice brittle. "And you haven't answered my questions. You had to know my parents and I weren't involved in what happened to you and your father. Why didn't you let us know you were alive?" Raising her chin, assuming all the dignity she could muster, she asked, "Was I so easy to forget?"

Michael felt her pain swirling inside him like a tornado, mixing with his own, confusing him, making it impossible for him to explain. How did he explain living a lie for ten years? How did he explain what he'd done to Mary?

It was said you could never go home again. Perhaps that should read, you *should* never go home again.

Blair raised a fist toward him, demanding in a strained whisper, "Answer me, damn you! Why don't you answer?"

"You don't understand." Michael stood and pushed his hands deep into his pockets.

"No? Then make me understand! Make me understand how you could simply go away after what happened between us on the boat...what you said to me." Her lips began to tremble. "You got away without answering the last time we were together, but not this time!"

Clenching her jaw, swallowing back tears, determined he wouldn't see her cry, she took a deep breath and added, "Tell me how easy it was for you to come back into my life *ten years later,* make love to me and ask for my help."

"I think I should go." He strode toward her, toward the open side of the patio, but as he started past her, one of Blair's hands touched his thigh. Michael stilled instantly.

"You left me with nothing, Michael," she whispered in a tortured voice, her eyes on the house in the distance, once a place of laughter and warmth, now a place of silence, echoes of the past and tears. "Don't you understand? Cheryl had her memories. She had the solace of knowing you loved her…and she had me…her good friend." Her fingers dug painfully into the muscle of his leg, but nothing showed in his expression as he stared down at her white face and somber profile. "What did *I* have, Michael? What did you leave *me?*"

Twisting her head toward him, eyes shimmering with unshed tears, she stared at him for a long, silent moment. When she spoke next, all emotion had been wiped from her voice. "Cheryl came to me the night she learned you were being officially listed as dead. She needed someone who could empathize with her pain…someone to hold her while she cried…someone with whom she could relive your most intimate moments together."

She felt the muscle beneath her fingers grow rigid and knew he was about to withdraw from her, but she couldn't let him go. There was too much pain—too much bitterness—inside her to let him walk away this time. This time he had to stand and face it with her.

"There was no one for me, no one to whom I could cry out *my* pain. I had to keep it locked up inside me. But it was there. All the time I was being strong for Cheryl, it was there, eating away at me.

"Night after night, I'd sneak out of the house, just as I used to sneak away to meet you, and walk the beach." Emotion edged her voice, but she beat it back. "I cried for you until there were no more tears left inside me…and then I cursed you. I hated you for dying and leaving everyone to believe it was Cheryl you loved . . . and not me.

"In pubic I kept up the pretense of our friendship, until, finally, I was even beginning to believe it myself. Then your letter came. Why? Why did you wait ten years for your… revenge?"

"I had to," he answered gruffly. "I had a family I couldn't put in danger."

Blair loosened her hand and turned away. "Yes, of course. I'd forgotten your wife." How could she have forgotten that in the interim he'd taken a wife? Blair stood with her back to him, staring at the ocean. "What exactly happened to her?"

"I told you, she died."

"How?"

"Pneumonia."

"Was she ill a long time?"

"No, it was...unexpected."

"Did you love her very much?" He couldn't know what the question cost her, but she couldn't hold it back.

"Why are you doing this?" Michael asked in a low, tense tone, moving to stand in front of her.

"That isn't an answer." She felt him compelling her to look at him, but she resisted.

"She gave me back my sanity," he responded roughly. "Restored my will to live. How could I not have loved her?"

A suffocating sensation of jealousy rose at the back of Blair's throat. It made her angry with herself and with him, but it also made it possible for her to continue. "What did your wife look like?"

"Why are you doing this?" he asked again, taking her by the shoulders, the warmth of her naked skin beneath his hands making him want to pull her close.

"What did she look like? Did she have long hair or short? Was she a blonde, a brunette, a redhead?" The nails of the hands curled at her sides bit into her palms.

"Blond—she was blond," Michael answered, hoping to silence her. He felt her tremble beneath his hands.

She knew she should stop, but couldn't. "Was she tall—"

"Stop this, Blair!" He pushed her away from him and strode across the patio, returning his hands to his pockets. It was the only safe place for them, otherwise he would wrap them around her throat and throttle her.

"What was she like—"

Michael whirled abruptly to face her, replying in a cold, furious voice, "She was five foot nine in her stocking-feet, and weighed one hundred and ten pounds. Her hair was shoulder-length, naturally blond, and she had green eyes. There, are you satisfied?"

"Was she very beautiful?"

"Yes," Michael muttered. "She was very beautiful."

"Is that why you married her?"

"I told you why I married her." He worked to get his emotions under control before adding, "Look, I know you must be ... curious, and I ... think I understand."

Did he? She doubted it. She herself didn't understand this compulsion to learn everything she could about the woman who had usurped her place in his life, so how could he?

"Do you?" she asked, feeling consumed by an anger she had no clear place to aim. With whom was she angry? Herself? Michael? His dead wife? The blonde in the restaurant? Or the unkind fate that had brought them all to this point?

And then she didn't care. She only wished she could make Michael feel a small fraction of the pain she was now experiencing, that she'd experienced over the years.

"The woman you were with at lunch today was blond and very beautiful. Does she remind you of your wife?" The tension in the air became so thick that Blair felt as though it would choke her. "Why aren't you with her tonight?"

Michael stared at her with clenched jaw and narrowed eyes, his mouth twisted into a threat. She thought he was about to blast her with anger, but all at once his expression turned enigmatic.

Stalking closer, until he left her no room at all, he asked in a deceptively calm voice, "Have you lived here in this big house all alone since your parents passed on?"

Blair tilted her head to stare up at him and nodded.

"You never married?"

"No."

"Ever been engaged? Do you date? Is there a man in your life right now?"

Blair frowned. "No, I've never been engaged—"

"But there have been men," he interrupted, drawing closer, smothering her with his nearness. "You aren't going to tell me," he chided cynically, "that you don't date. You weren't a virgin," he added pithily.

Blair flinched and retreated a step, feeling the rough stones of the patio wall against her bare back. "I fail to see how that has anything to do with what we were discussing."

"Tit for tat," he replied softly.

"Excuse me?" she asked haughtily, managing to step around him without touching him.

He turned and followed her movement, staying between her and any exit. "You've been trying to find out all evening if I went to bed with Janey."

Janey? She wrinkled her nose in distaste at the juvenile-sounding name. "I have not!" she denied, though that was exactly what had been in her mind.

Stomping past him, pushing against his shoulder with an angry fist, she jeered, "Why should I give a damn who you go to bed with?"

Michael grabbed her arm above the elbow and held her despite her struggles to get free. "You shouldn't," he admonished hoarsely, giving the arm a slight shake for emphasis. "That's my whole point." If only he could find the right words to make her understand. "Things change—people change—"

"What's inside you, Michael?" she interrupted him impatiently. "What's here?" She pointed a shaky finger at his chest.

"Emptiness," he responded gruffly. "Nothing but emptiness."

She didn't believe that. Hadn't she experienced his passion? Pulling loose, she turned to him, flattening a hand against his chest. "That isn't emptiness but a heart I feel pounding against my hand. That makes you alive, Michael, a flesh and blood man, with feelings like everyone else."

Her hand began to slide down the front of his shirt, over the solid wall of muscle, the heat from his body making her palm tingle. Her blue eyes locked on his face, and her heart lurched madly at the changes she saw taking place there.

The rigid planes softened, and a tremor touched the marble hardness of his lips. The flat, passionless expression in his dark eyes disappeared as the gold flecks began to shimmer and glow.

The downward sweep of Blair's hand took on an unconscious caressing quality as she neared the wide belt of his jeans. She could feel his breathing escalate, his stomach muscles contract sharply.

Michael caught her hand in rigid fingers, holding it still beneath his own.

"If you're so willing to let the past go," she muttered in frustration, "then why must you find this man you *think* killed your father?"

"That's different. It takes a different kind of emotion. Don't you understand?" He squeezed her fingers until they felt numb. "I have plenty of hate left in me—passion, if you will. It fills me to the exclusion of everything else." Cupping her chin roughly, he asked, "Is that what you want from me?"

"No," she whispered huskily. She wanted his love.

"It's all I have to give!" His fingers tightened for an instant, and then he let her go.

"What am I to you?" she asked as he thrust her aside. Somewhere inside him there must be a spark of what he'd once felt for her. And if there was a spark, then all she needed was to find what it would take to fan it into flame.

"You're my friend," Michael replied. "The only real friend I've ever had."

His words deflated her. "What about the future?" she managed. "What about when your... work is done?"

Michael realized she still didn't understand the point he'd been trying to make. There could be no future for the two of them.

If he stayed in her life, he would only destroy her, as he'd destroyed his father and Mary. It seemed he was cursed to kill those he loved. First his father had died trying to save him from a killer, and then Mary, loving him, taking care of him, had died from exhaustion. If she hadn't been so rundown, so tired from all the extra work, she wouldn't have succumbed so easily to her illness. He wouldn't make Blair his third victim.

"I can't look that far ahead," he hedged. He knew she would never accept the truth.

"Michael..."

"It's getting late."

"Yes," Blair murmured, hearing the obstinate finality in his voice and knowing it would do no good to press him further. She'd learned something of value in her dealings with Michael this evening. She'd learned he was hiding something from her, and she knew that until she discovered what it was, they didn't have a chance in hell of reconciling the past with the present.

She'd been naive enough to think that having him back in her life would be all that mattered. But that wasn't so. Somehow she had to gain his trust.

The only way she knew to accomplish that was to spend time with him, to try and make sense out of what had happened on the boat ten years ago.

After a long moment Michael asked, "Can I count on you?"

"What do you want me to do?"

"Be my eyes and ears. Find out how my father's death affected the people here, especially the people who knew him best."

"Your father wasn't a fool, Michael. If he trusted men like John Saunders and Roger Prescott, why don't you? You were engaged to marry Roger's daughter. What about that?"

He didn't want to discuss Cheryl. "Dad was smart, that's true enough, but he had a soft spot inside him as big as the ocean. It would have taken a lot to get him to distrust someone he knew, but he did. I just don't know who it was." Returning anger at the thought of a friend murdering his father thinned his lips and made the faint scars on his face and neck turn a dark pink. "Well, I'm going to find out who it is, if it takes the rest of my life. And I'll do it with or without your help!"

Michael stormed toward the patio exit, with Blair following closely on his heels.

"I didn't say I wouldn't help you."

Her words halted him beneath the broad leaves of a magnolia tree, the sweet scent from its white blooms filling the air.

"What?" He turned to face her.

"I said—" She clasped her hands together at her waist. "I said . . . I'll help you."

Chapter 5

Michael stared at her without speaking, afraid that if he questioned her further she would change her mind. Some small part of him wished that was true, because then he would be forced to leave her alone.

Despite what he'd said to her just now about there being nothing inside him, he knew he'd lied. Whether it was strictly passion or something more, there was a bond between them that he couldn't break with logic or guilt. But she must never know that; it would only make it harder for her when the time came for him to leave.

But nonetheless his feelings for her were strong, strong enough to have made him frantic when she hadn't answered the door a little while ago. It was that same feeling that had held him in thrall when he'd caught a glimpse of her naked silhouette through the frosted glass in the shower stall and had kept his feet rooted to the spot as she threw the door open, revealing all her beauty to his hungry eyes.

It had been a mistake to make love to her that night in the motel. He knew that now. Before that he hadn't touched a woman in over a year, not since his wife's death. He hadn't wanted to... not until Blair had reentered his life.

That night, in the haven of her arms, he'd learned what peace was like. Something told him that she could heal him in a way none of the doctors, their treatments and medicine, even Mary, had been able to.

Michael stared at Blair's pale face and reached deep inside him for the blackness, the hate, he kept caged for the man who'd killed his father and destroyed his own life in the process by removing all that he knew and held dear.

Hate was all that had kept him going for the past ten years. And he knew he couldn't let anything, anyone, interfere with his purpose in returning to Baywater.

Michael gave his head a slight shake. He didn't want to think about that right now.

He hadn't bargained on any of this. From the moment he'd spotted her across the room in that dive, where he'd been trying to find enough artificial courage to face her, to the time they'd spent making love, thoughts of Blair had taken up the larger part of his waking hours.

When he'd written her the letter, in his arrogance he'd been confident of his ability to keep the past under control. This new, ruthless man he'd become was impervious to such frail emotions as love and desire.

An hour with Blair had proved him wrong. But it wouldn't happen again.

"Did you hear?" Blair asked, stepping closer. "I said I'll help you."

After a slight hesitation he nodded. From now on he would strive to keep personalities out of what went on between them.

"Good," he answered with relish. "I've waited a long time for this."

Blair led the way to the house and into the living room. There she moved to the love seat, where she'd opened his letter less than a week earlier. She waited, expecting him to sit, but he remained standing.

Settling back against the cushions, folding her hands together on her lap in a false pose of serenity, she felt his eyes on her face and tried to find the courage for what she was about to say.

"Michael...I..." She glanced up and said in a rush, "I'm not convinced the man you're looking for really exists."

She paused, expecting him to immediately contradict her, but he remained rigidly silent, his glance fixed on her face.

Her hands fluttered nervously as she explained. "I don't know the extent of your father's wealth, nor do I want to," she added hurriedly. "But I don't want to believe that someone in Baywater murdered him for any part of it. John Saunders, Marvin Welborn and Roger Prescott were men your father trusted." Her eyes pleaded with him for understanding. "They were his friends. So when you say someone close to him killed him, then I have to assume you mean one of them.

"We've known those men all our lives. Your father grew up with them, did business with them, had them in his home. I just can't picture any one of them as a cold-blooded killer."

"Someone is," Michael insisted tautly, breaking his self-imposed silence. "And it could very well be one of them, *because* of their closeness to Dad," he emphasized.

Blair shook her head. "Those men are wealthy in their own right. They don't need your father's money or property—"

"Haven't you ever heard of the word 'greed'?" he interjected tersely.

"Of course I have."

"Then you know it can be a very potent motive. Look," he added, before she could make any further protests, "I didn't tell you everything. I didn't want to put you in danger."

"Go on." Blair waved aside his concern with an impatient hand.

"What I'm about to tell you, Dad said almost as though he were talking to himself, as though he didn't understand how this turn of events could have come about." Michael's scratchy voice died, his glance turning inward.

"What did he say, Michael?"

He looked at her without really seeing her, seeing instead his father, the wind ruffling his silver-threaded dark hair, a look of pain around his dark eyes. "He said, 'I trusted him with everything I hold dear, but it wasn't enough. He wanted my very soul.' "

"But I don't see—"

Drawing his thoughts from the past with difficulty, Michael added, "If you've decided to give me the benefit of the doubt, let's just get on with it."

"That isn't...exactly why I agreed to help you." She met his quick glance with a slight air of defiance and explained. "I think you're wrong—I hope you're wrong. While you're looking for evidence with which to...hang someone, I warn you, I'll be looking just as hard for proof that he's innocent."

Michael's jaw clamped down tight on his anger. He couldn't alienate her; he needed her. But at that moment he would have liked nothing better than to stalk angrily from the room without a backward glance. She was telling him that she would be working against him the whole time.

Blair took note of his pinched look, his tight lips, and sought in her mind for something to say to pacify the mounting fury she sensed he was barely holding in check. It hadn't been her purpose to make him angry, only to acquaint him with her true motives. She wanted to deal with him honestly.

The question of his own honesty regarding his dealings with her continued to bother her. At the back of her mind a voice nagged at her, whispering that he'd made love to her for his own purpose and that there was none of the love he had once professed to have for her left in his stony heart.

"I don't want to hurt you, Michael." She hesitated. "I just think...it's been a long time since your father died—"

"Was murdered!"

"Time has a way of clouding the issue."

"Are you telling me you think I made this up? That I dreamed it up while I was in the hospital, fighting for my life?"

Blair took a quelling breath and tried to explain her thoughts. "Sometimes, in retrospect, the memory of an event can take on aspects not altogether in keeping with the reality. I'm not saying you made this up. I'm only saying...perhaps seeing your father die that way, right before your eyes, and not being able to help him..." Again she hesitated, taking stock of the inflexible expression on Michael's face. "Guilt may be playing a part in your interpretation of what happened that night."

"Guilt? Are you saying I'm responsible for my father's death?" he asked murderously.

"No!" Blair jumped to her feet and reached toward him. "I'm not saying that at all. It's just that...I've worked with patients who survived accidents that killed members of their family. They felt guilty because they were still alive, while their loved ones were gone."

"I don't need a lesson in psychology," Michael muttered, stepping away from her.

Blair could see it was no use trying to talk to him. It would take cold, hard facts to make him change his mind.

"All right," she gave in. "You know what I'm about and I know how you feel, let's just leave it at that."

"As long as you agree to keep an open mind."

Blair looked at him askance. She wasn't the one insisting, on the flimsiest of evidence, that there was a murderer in their midst! No, wait, she calmed herself. There was no sense in getting riled up again. They were at an impasse. One of them had to give a little or they would never be able to go on from here.

"I agree," she answered calmly. "What about you?"

He studied her coolly without answering, and then all at once he gave a short nod and turned away.

Blair allowed herself a fleeting smile of victory before asking abruptly, "Have you had dinner?"

Michael shook his head without speaking.

"I could fix us something—"

"I don't think that would be wise," he cut her off in midsentence, facing her. "We've discussed what I came here to discuss, and I think I should leave now. I really shouldn't spend too much time with you."

Blair gave him a searching glance and managed to ask, "Why not?"

Several reasons came to mind, but Michael answered, "What if someone should come by and find me here? I'm a stranger in town. I don't want people questioning you about me. I know I don't look like the Michael Baldwin anyone would readily remember, but we're going to be stirring up people's thought processes in the next few days with questions. I don't want anyone concentrating too hard on any similarities they might find between me and the dead Michael.''

''I don't have many visitors,'' Blair said, mentally wincing over the phrase, ''the dead Michael.''

''What about Prescott?''

''I told you, Roger Prescott and I don't have that kind of relationship,'' she answered tightly. ''He's my employer, nothing more.''

''All right, I'll stay,'' he placated her, telling himself he was only staying to keep her sweet. ''I'm really not hungry, but coffee sounds good.''

''No,'' she replied shortly, miffed at his continued, ridiculous, implication that there was something between herself and Roger Prescott. ''You don't have to stay.''

She hadn't realized he'd moved until she felt the finger he pressed against her lips. It was an automatic gesture he'd employed more than once in the distant past to shut her up. She gave a slight jerk, eyelids fluttering, and stared up at him in surprise.

''I said I'll stay for coffee,'' he repeated gruffly.

Blair's lips trembled beneath the warmth of his touch. She smelled tobacco on his skin, felt the harshness of a callus rough against the sensitive skin of her lips, and her legs turned to water. Her hands went to his waist for support. His glance found hers—and then he was moving away. He stopped on the far side of the room.

''Coffee,'' Blair murmured on a sudden intake of breath. ''I'll start the coffee.'' She turned toward the kitchen, licked her lips and tasted the essence of Michael.

If he didn't want her, why had he made love to her, and why had he played that cruel game with her in the bathroom a short while ago?

She didn't understand this new Michael, but that didn't stop her from wanting him. She was ashamed to admit just how badly she wanted him. Their brief night of love had only whetted her appetite. She was surprised to learn that when she compared the youth she'd known with this more mature, more complex man, it was the man who made her heart beat faster and her blood surge like liquid fire through her veins.

Michael waited a few moments after Blair had left, collecting himself before following her. His mind was telling him to cool it, too many things, too many people, stood between them. But his body was finding it hard to accept that decision.

In the kitchen, which seemed to have changed very little in ten years, Michael took care to keep a safe distance between them as he automatically began to help prepare the food. Though he'd specified coffee only, he made no protest as Blair removed a plate of roast beef from the refrigerator and set about making sandwiches.

He began to realize that with a little imagination, this could almost be ten years ago, with the two of them preparing a meal together. They'd done it countless times in the past.

For years he and Blair had lived in each other's pockets, like brother and sister. That, he decided, was how he would think of her in the present, because that was the part of his past with which he could live.

The silence between them stretched, and Michael found his gaze returning more and more often to her face. She didn't look like the little girl with the flyaway hair who'd chased him down the beach day after day in a skimpy swimsuit, all elbows and knees, her eyes the biggest thing in her thin face.

She walked past him, leaving a trail of light perfume. She didn't smell of sunscreen and antiseptic like that child had, either.

For a moment he watched without moving as she stretched to reach the cabinet above the sink. The muscles in the calves of her legs tightened as she stood on her toes and leaned forward, raising the hem of the short flowered skirt to the tops of her thighs. But her fingertips made only brief contact with the plastic wrap of the bread she was trying to get.

Michael moved up behind her, lifting the bread from the shelf. Their fingers met as he passed it to her, and he knew with certainty that his plan wasn't going to work. He wasn't twelve years old anymore, and Blair was all woman.

Blair accepted the loaf, smiling up at him, words of thanks on her lips, but the words died unspoken as her smile was met with cool reserve.

It seemed Michael had learned to get what he wanted but didn't waste time on charm when there was nothing in the offing for him. She felt chilled to the bone by the thought and tried to keep her own heart cold and still, promising herself that she wouldn't be the first to break the awful silence between them.

But she found it impossible to keep that promise. How could she maintain a guise of indifference with the tough, virile, reality of Michael standing so temptingly within reach? How was she supposed to keep at bay the ambivalent feelings he aroused in her?

One minute she wanted to slap his arrogant face, tell him to get out of her life and quit complicating it. Life might have been mundane before his return, but at least she'd found a measure of peace.

And then all she had to do was glance sideways, catch a glimpse of powerful muscles rippling in sinewy forearms sprinkled with black, silky hair below the rolled up sleeves of the white shirt Michael wore, and her knees turned to jelly.

It was no longer the past holding her in its grip but the presence of this giant of a man with scars on his heart ten times the size of those on his face. He attracted her as no other man ever could—not even his younger self.

She became breathlessly aware of the flexing of his powerful thighs each time he shifted his weight, and it was all she could do to keep the hand nearest him from reaching out to feel the surge of power and strength encased in those tight-fitting jeans. Swallowing nervously, she wondered what Michael would do if he knew what she was thinking.

She fantasized that this was their home, their kitchen, and this was how it would have been if Michael had returned and they'd gotten married....

Blair cast a furtive glance at his profile and wondered at the somberness there. Was he recalling times like this... spent with his wife?

The thought shattered the fantasy into a million sharp, hurting pieces. She tried, but found she couldn't maintain the detached silence any longer. She had to speak—or scream—to relieve the tension.

"A lot of people have come and gone since you lived here. A lot of things have changed." With unsteady fingers she placed a thin slice of ripe, red tomato on the open face of the sandwich she was preparing, wondering if he would answer.

"I noticed there's a new high school built on the spot where ours used to stand," Michael answered, clearing away some of the debris from their efforts. He was glad she'd spoken. The silence had been getting on his nerves.

"The old school became too crowded. It couldn't accommodate the influx of people that have moved to the area in the past few years. The town has almost doubled in size."

"The old baseball diamond is gone, too," Michael commented. "I drove past there when I arrived. We had some good games there when we were young. I saw there's a shopping mall where it used to be."

Blair finished making the sandwich and put it on a plate. "A lot of new businesses have sprung up, almost overnight, it seems. Marvin Welborn's real estate and development company has been booming."

"Welborn, huh?" Michael stopped pouring lemonade to stare at her reflectively. "He still a bachelor?" When Blair nodded, he said, "He used to spend a lot of time at our house a few years before the accident."

"Is he your prime suspect, then?" she asked sharply. Did he do it deliberately? Every time they tried to have a normal conversation, he brought up his almost paranoid suspicions.

Michael gave her an irritated glance, wiped his hands on a towel and threw it on the counter. "I suspect everyone, and I will until Dad's killer is found."

They didn't talk much after that. Blair carried the food to the table with Michael's help, and they ate in silence.

The impromptu meal was finished and she'd poured them both coffee and returned to her seat when she said in as normal a voice as she could muster under the circumstances, "So, tell me, what did you learn today?"

"The land on either side of Dad's has been owned by the same corporation for the past fifteen years," Michael responded, relieved to have the uncomfortable meal at an end. "I didn't learn anything about the company except its name, Unico Corporation. You ever heard of it?"

Blair shook her head.

"Well, it seems they don't have offices here in town. I have to go to Saint Augustine to look them up. I'm planning on making a trip there tomorrow."

"Did you learn anything that would explain why someone wanted your father dead?" There, she'd sounded perfectly normal—for someone who felt completely out of sync with everything around her.

"No. But I've been thinking about it, and I'm convinced the land the killer wanted is that parcel at the edge of town, the one Dad bought a couple of years before he died. It's the single largest piece of undeveloped property he owned within the boundaries of the county. I figured that if someone was buying the land beside Dad's, it just might be the same person who'd engineered his death. It was a long shot, but I had nothing else to go on."

Blair stood and moved to the sink to scrape the plates into the garbage disposal. She heard the rumble of Michael's voice in the background of her thoughts, while in her mind's eye she was seeing the blonde Michael had lunched with that day.

Blair wondered what he'd found to talk about with her. She recalled how he'd made her laugh, then grinned in response.

He never smiled or grinned whenever he was with her.

"Did you hear what I said?"

From her place at the sink Blair looked back over her shoulder.

"Can't you leave that for now?" Michael asked impatiently.

Blair moved to the table and resumed her seat.

"I asked if you were sure you'd never heard of Unico."

"The man you should talk to about that is Marvin Welborn."

"Him again," Michael murmured thoughtfully.

"What are you implying?"

"I'm not implying anything, except that I need more information before I can figure this whole mess out."

"Well, I think you should talk to Welborn. Ask him about the Unico Corporation. If there's anything going on around here that has to do with land or investments, he'll know about it."

"Let me see what I find out in Saint Augustine first. And then there's the auction to look forward to." The hand lying beside Blair's tightened reflexively. "One way or another, I'm going to find this man, whoever he is," Michael rasped from between clenched jaws, "and see him rot in hell for what he's done."

At the underlying anger behind Michael's words Blair felt a chill cross her skin. She still didn't know what he had in mind for the man when—if—he found him, and that was what frightened her.

"What about that doctor you said your father was seeing in Saint Augustine?" she asked, trying to shake the awful feeling his words had inspired. "The one treating him for high blood pressure. Have you talked to him yet?"

"What about?"

"To find out if there were any other instances when your father suffered from other . . . accidents, such as the poisoning."

"That's a mighty long shot—besides, do you know how many doctors there are in Saint Augustine?"

"Do you know if Dr. Prescott referred your father to him?" A note of repressed excitement had crept into her voice.

"I have no idea." He looked at her curiously, wondering what she was getting at.

"He must have. He was your father's doctor. I could tell him—" Blair began tentatively.

"No!" Michael thundered, slapping a balled-up fist against the table's surface, rattling the china and knocking over the saltshaker. "I don't want *anyone* to know I'm alive."

"Michael, you don't seriously suspect him?" she asked incredulously. "He was at your house that night. He was going to be your father-in-law."

"Dad said *no one* would believe this man was capable of murder. Doesn't that fit Prescott? In fact, as we've already established, that fits all Dad's good friends, the closest of whom were Prescott, Welborn and Saunders. And I think those are the three we should concentrate on first."

"If you'd just let me speak to Roger—"

"No!" He grasped her hand and squeezed her fingers. "Don't tell anyone *anything*, do you understand? Not unless you want to be responsible for my death—and just possibly your own."

Blair gasped and withdrew her numb fingers. "Aren't you being melodramatic?"

"I don't know," he lashed at her. "Why don't you ask my father if he was being melodramatic when he made his accusation? If you can find anything left of him, that is."

Blair jumped up from the table, stung by the cruelty in his voice, and hurried toward the door. Michael caught her from behind. She resisted his efforts to turn her around, but still he drew her back against him, holding her there with his arms wrapped around her waist.

"I'm sorry if that sounded unfeeling." He spoke the words against the top of her head. "But this isn't a game, Blair. The bad guys are real. And both our lives may depend on your keeping my secret." His hold on her tightened for a brief instant. "I won't—I can't—take the responsibility for anything happening to you."

Just as suddenly as he'd grabbed hold of her, he released her.

Blair shuddered, wrapped her arms around her naked shoulders and whispered, "I don't know how you can stand it, suspecting everyone you've ever trusted of deceit and . . . murder."

"I've lived with this for a long time now. I've had time to get used to the idea."

"But I haven't," she protested in a stronger voice, turning to face him.

Michael's glance rested on her troubled face. "Life was far less complicated when we were children, wasn't it?"

"We're not children anymore, Michael."

"I know," he answered regretfully. "More's the pity."

He left the kitchen by the back door.

Blair followed him through her mother's flower garden to the Victorian-style gazebo situated on a slight rise overlooking the ocean. From there you could see where the ocean met the sky. The air was heavy with the perfume from the azalea bushes lining the walk.

She saw him pause in the waning light, his eyes turned toward the ocean. How were they ever going to work together when all it took was a word, a look, for the memories to come flooding back and swamp them both in pain and bitterness?

Blair thought the ocean's roar muffled her approach, but as she entered the small enclosure Michael began to speak.

"Can we do it?" he asked without preamble. "Can we shelve the past long enough to find a killer?"

"I'll try."

"That's all I ask."

"Michael, what, besides what your father told you, makes you so certain the killer is among your father's friends?"

"The marina was patrolled at night, as you well know." He was referring to the fact Tom Wallace had stopped them as they'd headed for the *Lazy Daze* that last night. "Only someone who was known around the area would have had access to Dad's boat. A stranger messing about would have been spotted and stopped for questioning. Was such a report made?"

"Not that I know about, but that isn't conclusive. Have you spoken to Tom Wallace—" She broke off. "No," she answered her own question, "of course you haven't. But I can—"

"Be careful, Blair," he reminded her. "Be very careful of what you say and to whom you say it."

"Don't you want me to speak to Tom? *He* was a friend of your father's, too. Do you suspect him, as well?"

"Of course I don't. He didn't do business with Dad." He shrugged. "It might not be a bad idea to talk to him. But I think that if he'd seen anything suspicious, knowing how meticulous he was in his work and with his background as a cop, he would have made some kind of report at the time. Is he still at the same address?"

"No, he's in a nursing home on the north edge of town. Tom's . . . forgetful, that's why he's living in the home. But he might have forgotten something, in the shock of learning about the accident that night, that a little prodding might help him to remember."

"I'll go see him."

Blair had thought more along the lines of seeing him herself, but she only murmured, "Be careful."

"Just you be careful," he replied, disappearing into the night. Blair wasn't certain if it was said in concern or meant as a warning.

After a moment she moved toward the house. It wasn't really late, but she felt exhausted.

Tonight she would go to bed early and get a good night's sleep, because she had a full day planned for tomorrow. Because, whether Michael liked it or not, she was going to carry out a little detective work of her own.

She would help Michael put his demons to rest, even find a killer if it turned out that way, because once that was done, Michael would be free to make a new life. And she was determined to be a part of that new life whether Michael knew it or not.

The thought of having him all to herself for the rest of her life helped negate the fear she felt when contemplating the prospect of coming face-to-face with a killer.

Chapter 6

The next morning Blair arrived at work earlier than usual. Office hours started at eight-thirty, so she gave herself half an hour to see what she could find.

She hadn't given up the idea of trying to get the name of the doctor Michael's father had been seeing in Saint Augustine before his death. It stood to reason that since Roger had been his doctor at the time the disease developed, he would have been the one to make the referral to this other doctor.

She wanted to know more about the poisoning Michael's father had told him about, too.

Unlike many doctors, Roger hadn't entered the computer age. He still kept his patients' records on paper and stored them in filing cabinets.

All of the current patients' files were kept in a locked cabinet behind Blair's desk. But the files of deceased patients, or those whom Roger no longer treated for one reason or another, were kept in a small room behind his office.

Blair didn't handle the paperwork on those patients, because Roger preferred to do it himself. He had his own filing system that worked quite well for him, so he said, though no one else seemed to understand it.

Blair knew the room was kept locked, but she tried the door just the same, hoping for a minor miracle. No miracle this time. The door wouldn't budge. But she was determined not to be thwarted in her first effort to gather information for Michael. Leaning back against the corner of the doctor's desk, she crossed her arms and contemplated the problem. Perhaps the magic of a hairpin...

Fat chance! She didn't use hairpins. A small wire or a screwdriver might work. Glancing around the elegant office she doubted she would find either of those things here. She had them at home, but—

"Well, what's this?" Roger spoke from the doorway, startling Blair so badly that she almost fell.

Pulling herself upright just in time to keep from making a complete fool of herself by falling on the floor at his feet, she smoothed the skirt of her uniform and turned slowly to face him. She opened her mouth to explain what she was doing and couldn't think of a single thing to say. Not one explanation came to mind for her being in his office, leaning against the desk, glaring at his file closet.

"Is something wrong?" Roger asked as he took off his suit jacket and hung it on the coat tree behind the door.

"N-no, of course not. I—just—I came in early to—" Her eyes left his back to rove the room and fell on the thick green foliage in the corner.

Roger loved plants, and his inner office was a veritable jungle of greenery. She had threatened, more than once, to hire a professional to come in and take care of them, but he preferred that she do it herself, knowing her mother's flower garden was the most beautiful in town, and knowing, too, that she took care of it now that the older woman had passed on.

"I came in to take a look at your plants," she announced suddenly, her eyes lighting on the brown curling leaves near the base of one. "I noticed some leaves turning brown on the ends of the fichus the other day and decided to come in early and check to see if it was getting root-bound," she improvised quickly.

Slipping a white lab coat over his pale blue shirt, Roger straightened his tie and turned to take a look at the plant to which she referred. "It does look a bit peaked. Maybe I should prescribe something for it. Vitamins, do you think, or perhaps a strong tonic?" he murmured seriously, then shot her a teasing grin.

Blair smiled obligingly, feeling like a heel for lying to him. Why didn't she simply tell him the truth? Michael wouldn't have to know what she'd done. It would be so much simpler to ask him for the information than to sneak around behind his back.

Roger slipped his hand into the pocket of his faultlessly creased trousers and withdrew a wallet, two sets of keys and some change. He was meticulous about keeping all his personal belongings locked in his desk drawer during office hours.

Laying his things on the desk, he buttoned the lab coat neatly down the front and excused himself as he stepped through to his private bathroom.

"Maybe we should do as you suggested in the past and get a plant doctor in to take a look at them," he called through the door. "What do you think?"

Blair didn't answer immediately; she was busy trying to figure out how to get the key to the filing closet off its ring without him hearing. She took a step toward the desk, one hand reaching toward the key ring, and halted guiltily.

"I said, maybe we should get a professional in to look at them," he repeated as he came back into the room, having rinsed his mouth with mouthwash and recombed his hair.

She looked at him blankly. "What? Oh, yes, maybe we should. I'll see to it." It was too late; she'd blown it.

"Well," Roger looked down at the heavy gold watch adorning his left wrist, "the troops will start arriving any moment now. Can I treat you to a cup of coffee?"

She'd forgotten to make the coffee! "I'm sorry, I was so worried about the plants that..."

"That you didn't make any coffee," he finished for her. "It's all right." Placing his arm around her shoulders, he gave her a brief pat. "Don't look so upset. I won't fire you for forgetting to make coffee. As a matter of fact, I'll make it. You go get ready for our first patient, and I'll make you the best cup of coffee you ever tasted."

The morning sped by, leaving Blair without a moment to spare to think about keys and locked doors. She'd planned a visit to the nursing home where Tom Wallace was a patient, but an emergency kept her and the doctor working right through their lunch hour. And there was no opportunity to call John Saunders as Michael had wanted her to do, either.

At four-thirty the spate of patients died down, and by five the office was almost empty. The doctor was busy seeing his last patient when Blair took a moment to pour herself a cup of coffee and catch her breath.

Roger hadn't been bragging when he'd said it would be the best coffee she'd ever drunk—or at least, it had been that morning. Now it tasted bitter, like all the rest.

"Well, that's the last of the lot."

Blair glanced at the man standing in the doorway and gave a tired nod. "Want a cup?" She indicated the coffee-pot beside her.

Roger looked at the oily black liquid and declined. "No thanks. Caffeine at this time of the day is *not* what the doctor ordered." He sighed tiredly. "I need a drink."

Blair grinned.

Roger eyed her a moment in silence before asking, "The Baldwin auction is Saturday. Have you changed your mind about going?"

"No." She shook her head. "I have to go." She gave a little shrug.

The phone rang, and she made as though to move past him to answer it. "Finish your coffee," he told her. "I'll get it."

She heard the low murmur of his voice, and a moment later he reappeared in the doorway, shrugging hurriedly into his jacket.

"An emergency—sounds like a ruptured appendix. Get me Brian Harding's chart."

Blair put her cup down and hurried to do his bidding. She took the file into his office only to find he wasn't there, and then she heard him in the bathroom. She was in the process of leaving the room when a glimmer of light winked at her from beneath the file folder. She lifted the edge and took a peek.

Roger had removed his wallet and keys from the drawer, but he hadn't yet put them in his pocket. Blair glanced up at the closed bathroom door. With little more than a moment's hesitation she picked up the key ring and stared at it.

There were four keys on it; it took two tries to find the right one. Slipping the appropriate key from the ring, she placed it in her pocket.

Her fingers shook so badly she could hardly refasten the thin piece of metal. Eyes darting continually toward the bathroom door, she fumbled until it clicked into place. As though it burned her fingers, she dropped it back where she'd found it.

Immediately her conscience began to bother her. She was taking advantage of her position of trust to pry into things that didn't concern her. What if Roger noticed a key was missing? It could cost her her job!

The door to the bathroom opened, and Roger moved into the room, smoothing his jacket into place. "Good, you found the file." He picked it up, saw his wallet and keys and automatically swept them up into his hand.

Blair swallowed quickly, but she couldn't seem to take a breath until the man slid the wallet and keys out of sight into his pocket.

"I'm off. See you in the morning. Don't forget to lock up." And then he was gone.

She'd done it now! Blair slipped a hand into her pocket and gripped the cool metal key with icy fingers. What if Roger should discover it was gone? Would he remember he'd left the keys lying on his desk and that she'd been the only one in the office?

How would she get the key back onto the ring without his knowing?

Tomorrow was Friday; if she didn't get the key back by then, it would be Monday before she had a chance to put it back. Two whole days for him to discover it was missing. What had she been thinking when she'd taken it?

Fifteen minutes later the little kitchen behind her office was clean. Another fifteen minutes and all the files were restored to their proper places and her office and desk were in perfect order. That left the examining rooms...and the doctor's office.

Blair glanced down at her watch, feeling the key burning a hole in her pocket right through to her skin. She'd planned to visit Tom at the nursing home that evening, since she hadn't made it at lunchtime, but it looked as though that would have to wait until tomorrow.

It was a quarter till six and the examining rooms were spotless, ready for the next day's patients. She worked off some of her guilt and at the same time rationalized what she'd done by reminding herself that she was helping Michael.

She certainly wouldn't make a very good thief, she thought wryly, entering the doctor's office. If today was any example of her abilities, by the time she got around to actually stealing whatever it was she was after, she would probably be locked behind bars.

Once in the room with the door closed, however, Blair wasted no time in unlocking the file closet and reaching for the light switch. She stood looking around the small, windowless room, breathing the stale air, tasting the papery smell of its contents.

Floor to ceiling shelves covered three walls, and Blair felt her spirits sink as she gazed from one to the other. They were overflowing with file folders. This was going to take forever.

In one corner a small metal stepladder rested against the wall. Blair propped the door partially open and turned to confront the mass of folders. Where in this mess was the one she wanted?

It took her half an hour to figure out that the files were divided into two major categories. One constituted the patients who had died and were no longer under Roger's care, and the other were those who had gone on to other doctors. At first Blair thought Michael's father's file would be in those who had changed doctors, but after half an hour of sorting and resorting, she decided it wasn't there, after all.

She moved on to the files of those who had expired, and wasted more time determining that they were arranged according to the year and month in which the patient had died. It was a strange system for filing, but Roger had always maintained that no one understood his filing methods except him.

Most doctors only kept records for ten years, but Blair was discovering that Roger had records that went back twenty years. Obviously he was a bit of a pack rat, something she wouldn't have suspected of him.

Cheryl's husband would have his work cut out for him when he returned and tried putting his modern methods of filing into effect. Roger could be quite stubborn when he chose, and Blair decided right then and there that she would take her vacation while the battle raged between the two men.

After what seemed like hours of searching, Blair finally found Mark Baldwin's folder. It had been filed with the deceased patients. As she studied its contents, she discovered that the last entry was dated almost two months before his disappearance at sea.

Taking the folder with her, Blair moved out of the small airless room and sat at the desk. She removed a small notebook and pen from her pocket to make notes and began to read.

After a moment, with a puzzled frown, she paused and went back over what she'd read. What was this? According to the file, ten years ago Mark Baldwin had been a very healthy forty-seven-year-old man. The only notation on a medical problem appeared to be an ingrown toenail on the big toe of his right foot.

Blair leafed down through the chart, reading the doctor's notes. There was no mention of his being hypertensive. The last blood pressure reading had been taken and charted on his final visit, the date on the front of the folder, and it had been wholly within the normal range.

Blair looked closer. The date on the entry corresponded with the approximate time Michael had given for his father's poisoning.

Why had Mark Baldwin told his son he was seeing another doctor for a disease he didn't even have?

There was no mention of a referral to another doctor. There were also no notes concerning a poisoning of any kind.

Had the poisoning really taken place? If he'd gone to the local hospital through the emergency room, there would be a record of it. Blair decided to make a visit to the hospital and see if she could find out.

After making a few notes, she put everything back in the folder and returned it to the shelf where she'd found it. Glancing down at her watch, she realized it was a little after eight. Everyone would be gone from the building, and the night security guard would be coming on. It was time for her to leave.

Blair switched off the light and locked the door. She was rounding the doctor's desk when she heard a sound in the outer office and froze.

Who could it be? The security guard, wondering what someone was doing here so late?

And then she heard Roger Prescott's deep tones, followed by the low murmur of another voice. What was he doing here this late? Had he discovered the missing key?

Blair panicked. What explanation could she give for being here so late—and in his office?

"Blair?" Roger called. "Blair, are you here?"

Blair closed her mouth tightly, eyes darting around the darkened room in panic. Where could she go? The file closet she'd just left? No, what if that was why he'd returned, to look something up, or remove a file from its confines?

Her eyes moved toward the bathroom. Praying he wouldn't be in need of its facilities, she dashed across the carpet in the dark, managing, somehow, not to bump into anything, and hurried inside, closing the door with a soft snap.

"Where do you suppose she's gotten to?" a voice she recognized as that of Marvin Welborn asked curiously.

"I don't know. It isn't like her to leave the office unattended, and what is she doing here at this time of night? She's been acting a little strange the last few days—in fact, ever since she returned from a weekend trip down south," Roger commented.

"Maybe she's in love," Marvin snickered, surprising Blair. She'd never heard him use that particular tone of voice. Pressing her ear to the door, she listened as the two men moved about the room.

"Maybe she spent the weekend with a man," Marvin continued with relish. "She's a very attractive little package, or so I've always thought. She's shown very little interest in men over the years, maybe she woke up and realized she's headed toward becoming an old maid. I've always wondered what she'd be like in bed. You know what they say about the quiet ones." He laughed mockingly.

Blair's face flamed as she cringed in revulsion, shocked at this unexpected glimpse inside Marvin Welborn's vulgar mind. She'd never suspected him of such foul thoughts. To the world he was a quiet, soft-spoken man, friendly, but not overly so.

"Keep your loathsome thoughts to yourself," Roger said. "Where the hell are those papers?"

"What did you do with them?" Marvin asked, not at all offended by the other man's remark.

"If I knew that, I wouldn't be standing here looking for them, now would I?" Roger asked sarcastically.

"Do you suppose she's all right?" Marvin returned to the more interesting subject of Blair Mallory.

"Her car's still in the parking lot, and her purse is on her desk. She must be somewhere in the building."

"You know, it isn't safe—especially for a woman—to be all alone in a building like this at night. I watch that television program about missing people all the time." Welborn's voice took on a note of fascination as he continued, "Women get taken right out of their offices and are never seen again—" He broke off to suggest in ordinary tones, "Maybe you locked the papers in your secret hideaway."

Blair felt the perspiration freeze on her skin at his words. She clutched the key in her hand so tightly it cut into her palm. Oh, God, she prayed, don't let him try to unlock the door. She should have listened to Michael.

"I had them this morning, and I haven't been in my 'secret hideaway,' as you call it, all day long." Roger threw the other man an impatient look.

Blair inched her way to the other side of the dark bathroom. In her immediate anxiety she'd forgotten about the other door that opened onto the main hallway. It was there to allow the doctor to leave on an emergency call without being seen by a waiting room full of irritable patients.

She opened it cautiously and peered outside, up one end of the hall and down the other.

The building was shared by three other doctors, and occasionally they had a few late appointments. However, it was well past eight, and it looked as though she was the only one who had stayed late. Carl, the building security guard, was nowhere in sight.

She moved into the hall and leaned back against the cold marble wall, breathing a long sigh of relief. She wasn't certain what to do next. She could make a run for her car—no, she couldn't do that. Roger and Marvin had mentioned seeing her car on the way in, and besides, her car keys were in her purse lying on her desk in the office. Damn! She hated this!

If she could just manage to get to her office...

"Well, hello, what are you doing here this late at night?"

Blair whirled around and stared up at the young man with orange spiked hair.

"Carl! You frightened me." Swallowing tightly, her heart in her throat, she managed a grin. "I—had some last-minute filing to do and the next thing I knew..." She lifted her hands in a helpless gesture.

"I saw your car out front, so I knew you were here, but I peeked in your office a while ago and you weren't there. I was a little worried." Carl was very fair-skinned, and at the moment his cheeks were bright red. He was twenty-three years old and had a monumental crush on Blair. "I've been looking around the building trying to find you."

"Thanks for being concerned," Blair broke in. Out of the corner of her eye, she saw the door to the right of her begin to open, and Roger and Marvin moved into view.

"Well, I''d better be going." Blair raised her voice enough so the two men would be sure to catch what she said. "It's been nice talking to you, Carl."

Carl smiled and nodded and, with his cheeks flushed a bright red, moved slowly away. Blair watched him for a moment before turning toward the two men.

"I didn't expect to run into you here tonight, Blair," Roger said as she joined him outside her office door.

"I was just getting ready to leave when Carl came on, and we got to talking." She lifted her hands in a shrug. "One thing led to another and—look at the time!" She glanced down at her watch.

She hadn't looked directly at Marvin Welborn since joining the two men, except for a brief, all-encompassing first glance. Now she couldn't help but notice the speculative glance he threw her at the mention of the time she'd spent with Carl.

"What are you doing back here?" Blair asked. "Is Brian all right?"

"He's fine," Roger assured her. "They had him in surgery, waiting for me, when I got there, and the operation was fairly routine. I left him in good hands. Tracy Randall is specialing him tonight."

Blair knew the nurse and knew she was especially good with children. "I'm glad."

"I came back for these." Roger fluttered a sheaf of papers before her eyes. "Marvin and I have a dinner engagement with some prospective investors. We hope to interest them in a new business venture, and I need these."

"Really, what kind of business venture?"

Marvin gave Roger a slight smile and answered for him. "We're considering investing in something that will employ hundreds of people and benefit animal lovers all over the world."

Blair looked from one man to the other. "That would be wonderful. I wish you luck with it."

"Thank you, my dear. Now we'd better be running along, and so had you. It's getting late, and I'm sure you haven't had your dinner yet, either."

"You're right," Blair acknowledged. "Good luck and good night. I'll see you in the morning."

"Would you like to join us?" Marvin asked abruptly as she was turning away.

Blair hesitated. She didn't really want to spend any more time in Marvin's company, yet a part of her was interested in this business venture. It sounded as though it was going to be something on a very grand scale indeed. Could it have anything to do with the Baldwin land? "I—"

"I don't think that would be a good idea," Roger broke in quickly. "I'm sure Blair has things she needs to do at home, and this business dinner is just that. I'm certain she'd be bored to tears."

"I appreciate the invitation, but you're right." She was thankful to Roger for getting her off the hook. "I'm very tired."

"Another time, perhaps." Marvin gave her a smile and turned away.

Not on your life, Blair was thinking as she watched them leave the building. In her office, she gathered her things and locked up. On the drive home she thought back over the night's events and what she'd learned.

For some reason Michael's father had lied to him about his health. And Marvin Welborn presented one face to the public and another, totally different one, in private.

She didn't know which discovery disturbed her the most.

Michael was positive his father's killer was someone his father had known and done business with. Was Marvin Welborn capable of murder? It was a chilling thought.

Blair had intended to go straight home, but after checking her watch, she abruptly decided to make a detour.

It was nine o'clock when she arrived at the Golden Sands Nursing Home, and visiting hours were about to end. Carol Stanton, the night nurse on duty, was a friend of Blair's. They'd gone through their training together. Blair was confident the other woman would allow her a few minutes with Tom before she had to leave.

After making a momentary stop at the nurses' station to get permission, Blair made her way to the private room where the old man lived alone. His wife had been dead for seven years now, and it was only five years ago that he'd finally agreed to give up living in his home and move here. He'd admitted, finally, that he was forgetting things, like paying his bills and when to eat.

Blair had made many visits to the old man over the years, cementing their friendship with a deep affection. It wasn't unusual for him to look up and see her standing in his doorway.

"Tom?"

He was a mere shadow of his former robust self. Michael wouldn't recognize him. His clothes hung on his thin frame, but his blue eyes still lighted up at the sight of her. He looked up from the picture he was holding as she spoke his name, a confused expression on his face.

"Sadie?"

"No, Tom, it's me, Blair." She stepped into the room where the light could strike her face.

The old man continued to squint up at her, smiling all at once in recognition. "Girlie, how are you?"

"I'm fine, Tom. How are you?"

"Fair, fair." He placed the picture on the table beside him with shaking hands and began to rock. "What's that you got in yer hands?" he asked, knowing, but asking all the same.

"This is for you." She handed him the box of chocolates she'd taken the time to purchase on the way over.

She never visited the nursing home without a present, and candy was something all the residents loved to receive. It was better than money as far as they were concerned. Tom was no exception, and as long as it wasn't against his dietary orders, Blair kept him supplied with his favorite.

Tom opened the box and offered her the first piece. She obliged him by taking a small square of chocolate and popping it into her mouth. He immediately followed suit, a smile of delight on his wrinkled face.

Pulling up a chair, Blair sat down, and they sucked on their caramels for a time in companionable silence.

"S'nother storm blowing up," the old man commented all at once around the candy in his mouth.

"Really?"

"Yup. The sky was red this morning, and it's too calm this evening. I took a walk along the beach a while back, an' I could smell it brewin'."

"You love the ocean, don't you, Tom?"

"Yup. Never lived any place else in—" he paused to calculate in his head "—seventy-five years, next month. That's a whole lotta time to pass in one spot."

He rocked and chewed, then slowed, turning his faded blue eyes toward the photograph he'd been holding when Blair first arrived.

"You miss her, don't you?"

"I do." He nodded. "She was all I had. The Lord never seen fit to bless us with little ones. She wanted a big family..." His voice quivered and died.

"Is she the reason you retired from the police force so early?" Blair asked softly.

The old man nodded. "I'da done anything she asked of me, given her anything—died for her if I could—but I couldn't give her the one thing she wanted most in the whole world...."

Tears gathered in the creases at the corners of his eyes. "I couldn't give her babies—" His voice broke, and he bowed his head, shoulders shaking.

Blair left her chair and went down on her knees beside him, removed the box of candy and took both his hands in hers. She laid her cheek against them, unconsciously aware of the thinness of the skin, the blue, ropy veins, the brown liver spots dotting their backs.

"It's all right, Tom. She had you, and that's the most important thing you have to remember. Sadie loved you, loved you more than anything else in the whole world. I heard her say that more than once."

"You did?" he looked up to ask.

"I sure did. And she was proud of you."

"Yeah." He looked toward the picture. "She used to say she loved a man in uniform." He grinned weakly. "But the time came," he added soberly, "when she just couldn't take any more of the fear and worry about me being a cop."

"Didn't she mind you working as a security guard?"

"Naw, she didn't mind that." He pulled his hands free and rubbed at the moisture gathered on his cheeks.

"That was a happy time for you, wasn't it, Tom?" Blair asked gently. "The time you worked at the marina?"

"It was the best job I had after I retired from the force," he agreed. "I could spend the days at home with Sadie, and at night, I had the ocean.

"You know—" he wiped at his nose with a large white handkerchief he'd pulled from his pocket and straightened in his chair "—I used to want to go to sea. I wanted to be a fisherman or something—anything—on a boat when I was younger."

Blair got to her feet and brought her chair closer, resuming her seat. "Really? Why didn't you? Because of Sadie?"

"Naw." He grinned and looked up at her from the corners of his eyes. "I got seasick."

"Seasick?" she asked in surprise.

"Yeah, ain't that a kicker? I love that ocean so much I couldn't live if'n I didn't have it within sight every day, but I can't stand bein' out on it."

"That's too bad," Blair sympathized. "You know, there's medicine you can take—"

"Yeah, I know, but I don't like to take medicine." A faraway look crept into his eyes. "I ain't takin' nothin' that makes me sicker than I was before I took it. I don't care what anybody says. I may be old, but I ain't stupid." He leaned closer, a crafty expression on his face. "I know what goes on here. I may be forgetful, but I got eyes in my head, and I got nothin' but time to watch and listen. Ain't I seen 'em bein' carried out one after the other, 'cause they took the damned stuff?

"'Sides—" his wandering mind changed subjects abruptly "—I'm too old now to worry about goin' to sea. Pert near too old for anything, it seems, since they won't even let me live in my own house anymore."

His attitude became belligerent. "I don't care what that lawyer fella says—I ain't sellin'. My Sadie loved that house. She fixed it up just the way she wanted it, and I ain't gonna see it torn down just so another damned shopping center we don't need or another fast-food joint can be built. My Sadie loved that house...." His eyes became fixed on the photograph.

"Tom, do you remember Mark Baldwin and his son Michael?" she asked gently, puzzled by his words, but intent on learning what he might know about the night before the accident.

"Who?"

"The Baldwin family..."

"Oh, yeah, I remember. It's a shame, what happened. I always wondered..."

"What?" Blair asked intently. "What did you wonder?"

Tom looked at her consideringly, then glanced away. When he spoke again, Blair knew it wasn't what he'd been about to say.

"I saw the two of you that last night. The two of you was always like two peas in a pod all the time you were growin' up." He shook his white head in bewilderment. "I still can't figure out how you let him get away. Mark told me he thought you'd get married someday."

"Tom..." She spoke quickly, wanting to bring his attention back to that last night while he was still lucid. "Do you remember seeing Michael leave his father's boat?"

"Yeah, sure I do. I was makin' my rounds—just about four in the mornin', it musta been. We stopped to talk a minute. He wanted to know how it had been with me, when I fell in love with my Sadie. I told him it was like a bolt of lightnin' hittin' me right between the eyes. He just stood there grinnin' fer a minute, then he slapped me on the back and said, 'Yeah, that's what it was like for me, too.'"

Blair swallowed and cleared her throat. The past still had the ability to cause her great pain, even knowing Michael was alive and nearby. "Do you remember seeing any strangers around the marina that night?"

Tom stopped rocking and focused his rheumy eyes on her face. "There weren't no strangers messin' about that night. If there'da been, I'da known it and I'da told someone."

She didn't want to offend him. "Well, do you remember anyone you know, besides Michael and me, who might have been on the Baldwin boat or anywhere near it?"

"It was warm weather, as I recall. There was a lot of people at the marina that night gettin' their boats ready to go out in."

"You don't remember anyone in particular who could have been on Michael's boat after he left?"

"The only one I 'member 'sides you 'n' Michael is Mark. We spoke for a few minutes 'fore I went home."

"Did you talk about the fishing trip?" she asked, watching him closely.

A hooded look came over his eyes. "We didn't talk about anything you'd be interested in," he answered.

Blair frowned. "Tom, it's very important—"

"I told you," he interrupted. "I don't know nothin'."

Sighing, recognizing the stubborn glint in his eyes, she asked, "You're sure you didn't see anyone else around the boat?"

"Naw, you know how it is down there in the summer."

"That was a long time ago. Think, Tom. Are you sure?"

"I told you—I'd a said somethin' if there'd been anything funny goin' on. And my memory ain't as bad as certain people would like it to be."

He cast a swift glance toward the door and leaned closer to her, lowering his voice in a conspiratorial manner. "See, I've figured out what they're doin'—ain't got no proof, yet, though, and that's why they want to get rid of me. But I'm too smart for 'em, 'cause I ain't senile, just—" a note of weariness made his voice sound gruff "—gettin' old."

Blair sat with him a little while longer, until his eyelids began to droop. Then she roused him, helped him get ready for bed and tucked him in before she left.

On her way out she stopped at the nurses' station to have a word with her friend, Carol. She asked if Tom was taking any medication. The nurse told her he refused everything, that he had some crazy notion they were trying to poison him.

For a while Dr. Prescott had asked them to put his medicine in his food, but somehow Tom always seemed to know when they did and refused to eat or drink. They'd had to stop for fear of his becoming malnourished or dehydrated.

Blair left the nursing home feeling very confused. What had he meant when he'd said he knew what they were doing? Who was the *they* he was referring to? The nurses at the nursing home?

Sometimes the elderly became paranoid. Was Tom paranoid? Or was it something else? Was Roger Prescott one of "them"? Or was it just the rambling of an old man who'd lost everything he had ever cared about and was trying to hang on to life through fantasies?

Blair was becoming depressed just thinking about it. Tom and his wife Sadie had been a part of her childhood that she'd always treasured. They had been aunt and uncle to every kid growing up in Baywater for as long as she could remember. But Sadie was gone now, and Tom was beginning to fade into the past more and more each day.

Blair pulled into her driveway and sat there without moving. She'd hoped to surprise Michael with good news when he returned from Saint Augustine, but what she'd learned was puzzling at best.

Why had Michael's father lied to him? And if he'd lied about one thing, could he have lied about the rest? Why had Roger filed Michael's father among the dead months before he'd actually died? Was it only an error? And what was it that Tom Wallace thought he knew?

Chapter 7

By Friday afternoon Blair was a nervous wreck. She hadn't found an opportunity to slip the key she'd taken the evening before back on Roger's key ring. It seared her skin with guilt every time she reached into her pocket and touched it. And every time Roger stepped into her line of vision or came up behind her and spoke her name, she broke out in a cold sweat, expecting him to accuse her of stealing it.

If necessary, she decided, she would simply throw the key on the floor and pretend to find it. There was no reason for him to suspect she hadn't.

She found herself watching him, feeling uncomfortable in his presence, and not only because of her own sense of guilt. She was beginning to wonder if she knew him as well as she'd always thought she did. She'd certainly been wrong about Marvin.

Was there reason for Michael's conviction that one of his father's friends had murdered him? So far she hadn't found anything to point to that fact, but there *were* questions running through her mind.

When five-thirty rolled around and Blair had still had no opportunity to replace the key, nor the opportunity to drop it and pretend to find it, she left the office with a deep sense of anxiety. On Monday morning she simply must get the key returned!

After a lonely dinner that she only pretended to eat, wondering when Michael would get back into town, Blair decided to take this opportunity for one last walk through the house next door. After tomorrow she would no longer be free to roam its rooms and halls at her leisure. It would belong to someone else.

In the past week much had happened to bring about a drastic change in her life. In the length of time it had taken to read a one page letter, she'd become another person.

A week ago she would never have had the nerve to steal her employer's key and delve into his private papers. She'd always lacked the courage to fight for what she wanted, preferring to take the easier road of least resistance, using her parents' overprotective attitude and even Michael's friendship as a buffer against the unpleasantness in the world.

Thanks to Michael's having come back into her life, she was finding the courage to fight for what she wanted. But would it do her any good? Or had her courage come too late?

The Baldwin house was a two-story, L-shaped weatherboard frame house. It had five bay windows and was fronted by a full-facade two-tier porch that faced the ocean. Blair entered through the back door and stepped into the kitchen.

She'd been in and out of this house many times over the past few years, keeping an eye on things, making certain the house and its contents were kept clean and in good repair. It had truly been a labor of love.

She paused and looked around at the kitchen's emptiness, remembering what it had been like when Michael's mother had been alive. She'd been something of a gourmet cook, and dried spices had hung among the pots and pans suspended from the ceiling. The air had always seemed to be permeated with the smell of wonderful things to eat.

Passing through the kitchen to the hallway, she moved toward the front staircase. There was another at the back of the house, leading up to the servants' quarters, which had been in use until sometime in the late forties; the front staircase led up to the family's quarters. Upstairs, there was no access between the two separate sides of the house.

Michael's grandfather had added plumbing in the early fifties, but he'd kept the rest of the house as it had been. And for history's sake, Michael's father had done the same.

Blair stopped at the foot of the stairs to peek through the wide double doors into the large formal dining room. The furniture was covered with dust sheets, but the late-evening light coming through the tall windows made the crystal chandelier sparkle and shine.

Michael's mother had not only been a great cook but a great entertainer, as well. There had always been parties and gala dinners at the Baldwin mansion, and Blair and her parents had had a standing invitation to every one of them. Except one.

Tears clogged the back of her throat as she forced herself to step away from the door and move onto the first step of the steep staircase. She ran her hand lovingly over the dark oak banister, feeling its polished smoothness.

How many times had she run up these stairs laughing and shrieking, making a terrible racket as only children at play can, with Michael right behind her?

At the head of the stairs she hesitated. She'd had a destination in mind when she'd decided to say goodbye to the house... Michael's room. She'd spent a lot of time during her adolescent years in that room, playing games, listening to music, watching television, exchanging secrets with her best friend.

That had been before Cheryl had really entered their lives. Cheryl's childhood had been far different from theirs. She'd been away, traveling with her mother during much of her earlier years. She'd spent a great deal of that time in New England, where her mother's family lived.

Blair stood for a long moment outside Michael's door before reaching out to touch the handle. She opened it slowly—and stopped dead in her tracks.

Michael looked up from the worn catcher's mitt he was holding in both hands.

"I didn't know you were back." She felt unnerved by coming across him so unexpectedly, and couldn't seem to think of anything else to say.

"I got here a little while ago. I was coming to see you in a few minutes."

Blair nodded, her gaze lowering to the battle-scarred mitt in his hand. How could the sight of something so ordinary make her want to laugh and cry at the same time? "Do you remember the year we were twelve? The summer of the big playoff between your Little League team and the town champs?"

"I remember," Michael murmured reluctantly. He'd been in this room for over an hour looking around, touching this and that, remembering, and he'd seen a part of Blair in everything he touched and all that he remembered. "It was to be my finest hour. I was going to pitch a no-hitter for that game."

"But you came down with measles the day before," Blair reminded him.

"You gave them to me." He glanced up accusingly.

"And I pitched the game."

"Because they couldn't find anyone else on such short notice. Billy Gresham, my backup and another of your victims, was out with the measles, too. And you convinced the coach I'd taught you to pitch my famous fastball."

Blair moved into the room and took up the story. "You spent the morning before the game dodging your mother, because she was trying to keep you in bed. But you were determined to teach me how to pitch. And we won," she added with haughty pride.

"Only because their best batter fell off his bicycle the morning of the game and broke his arm." Michael shook his head derisively. "You were a lousy pitcher."

Blair pretended to be offended, but she couldn't hold back a grin, and after a moment Michael grinned back.

She caught her breath. It was the first time she'd seen him smile in over ten years.

"We share a lot of good memories," she whispered, feeling as though her heart was about to burst from the sight of that grin. Just for an instant it had looked exactly like his grin from the old days. "We had some good times when we were kids, didn't we? It's good to remember—"

"I just wish I could forget," Michael broke in harshly, the smile wiped from his face. He slammed the catcher's mitt down onto the shelf beside a scratched football helmet and stood looking at it with angry eyes.

"Why?" she asked, without letting him know exactly how much his words had hurt her. "Why do you want to forget?"

"Because memories are a trap, a trap binding you to places you can never return to and people who are gone, lost to you forever. I don't want to get caught up in that endless cycle of nothingness!"

"Is it the whole past or only the past *we* share that you want to forget?"

"If I could," he answered simply, honestly, "I'd forget I ever existed before ten years ago."

Blair felt a flash of wild grief storm through her. She was a major part of that other life he wanted to forget.

What was it he wanted so desperately to forget? She was no nearer to discovering what he was hiding than on the night he'd come to her house and caught her in the shower. There simply must be a point where they could communicate, a point of reconciliation for the two of them. But without Michael's help, she would never be able to find it.

Tears trembled on her thick dark lashes as she lifted her gaze from the sight of Michael's clenched fists to stare at the tormented expression on his restless face.

She should never have come here tonight. Michael had virtually told her that he wished she didn't exist—had never existed. Yet he'd come to her for help when he felt he could go to no one else. And he'd made love to her.

Suddenly she felt very fragile, too fragile to stay in the same room with the cause of her distress. Without warning she left him, whirled from the room and hurried down the hall.

Michael started to let her go, but something wouldn't let him. He caught up with her at the top of the stairs. "You don't understand—"

"Am I interrupting something?"

Neither Blair nor Michael had noticed the silent witness to their distress. Roger Prescott stood looking up at them, his glance going from Blair's white face to Michael's carefully blank one.

"Are you all right, Blair?" Roger asked, poised to go to her rescue should she appear to need him.

Blair felt the awful tension in the rigid fingers clutching her arm and tried to compose herself before speaking. Would Roger recognize the man beside her? This was the place in which Michael had grown up, it was his home—how could Roger not know that?

Blair forced a smile, withdrew her arm surreptitiously from Michael's grasp and answered, "I'm fine. Roger, I'd like you to meet a new friend of mine. This is Mich—"

"Mike Wilson," the man beside her replied in a gruff voice.

"This is Roger Prescott, Mike," Blair continued. "Dr. Roger Prescott, my friend and employer."

Speaking directly to Roger, she explained, "Mike and I met, or, should I say, renewed our earlier acquaintance, quite by accident a little while ago when I stopped at the grocery store on my way home. We got into a discussion about antiques, and I mentioned the sale here tomorrow. I brought him with me for a last look around, because I thought he might like a sneak preview of what would be going on the auction block."

"Really?" Roger murmured, giving Michael a measuring look. "Which interests you more, stately mansions or their contents?"

"Both."

"Is that so?" Roger asked with interest. "Do you live around here? There are a great many houses of note in the area."

"No," Michael replied somewhat shortly. "I'm interested in older houses purely for their aesthetic value." He turned abruptly to Blair. "And now, if you will forgive me, I have an appointment early in the morning, and I'm rather tired. Perhaps I'll see you at the auction," he couldn't help adding for Roger's benefit.

"I didn't see a car outside, can I give you a ride to wherever you're headed?" Roger offered with equanimity.

"Thank you, but no, I enjoy walking," Michael responded coolly, giving Blair a brief nod before descending the stairs and making his way around the other man.

"Isn't that the man from the restaurant?" Roger asked, watching Michael's rigid figure disappear out the door.

"Yes, we met quite by accident, but he seems a pleasant sort." She dismissed Michael with a careless flutter of one hand.

What she really wanted was to hurry after him and ask if he would come to see her later. She had things to tell him. They'd gotten caught up in the past, and she'd neglected to tell him what she'd learned since she'd last seen him.

"I found him rather... abrupt. What's wrong with his voice?"

Blair moved slowly down the stairs. "I didn't ask. That would have been rude. Perhaps he's a heavy smoker, or a victim of some throat disease."

Roger watched her with concern and said, "You know, my dear, it isn't safe to take up with strange men. Young women disappear all the time," he said, unconsciously echoing Marvin Welborn's words of the day before. "I'd make it a point not to be alone with him, if I were you."

"I'm not afraid of him. I'm a grown woman, not a child. I can take care of myself."

"Oh, dear," Roger murmured contritely, "now I've offended you, and that wasn't my intention at all. I'm sorry. I was only concerned for your welfare. You seem to be going through a rough period right now." She started to protest, and he raised a hand to silence her. "I simply mean that you seem a bit unlike your usual calm self. When Marvin and I spoke to you at the office last night, I thought you seemed agitated.

"After my dinner tonight, I felt compelled to come by and make certain you were all right. When I didn't find you at home, though your car was in the drive, I thought I might find you here. It's tomorrow, isn't it?" he asked gently. "You're upset about the auction."

"No," she protested quickly, then added, "Well, perhaps."

"You know, Blair, there isn't anything I wouldn't do for you. You've been Cheryl's friend since the two of you were little more than children, and I feel as though we're family. If I can help, you'll let me know?"

"That's nice of you, Roger." She didn't know what else to say. Now that she'd accepted Michael's idea that there was a killer in their midst, and in light of what she'd discovered in this man's file closet, she didn't know what to think. Roger Prescott had been as much a part of her life as Cheryl had.

"I think the auction is affecting me more than I expected it would," she offered lamely.

"I see, well, it's affecting all of us, you know. None of the older generation will ever forget what a good friend we lost in Mark Baldwin. And I know you feel the same about Michael." He paused, then added, "Tomorrow it will all be over, really over. Perhaps then we'll all be able to get on with our lives and put the tragedy behind us once and for all." Taking one of her hands between both of his, he murmured, "It's late. Come along, my dear, I'll see you home."

Blair knew it would only be polite to ask the man in for coffee, but she couldn't bring herself to issue the invitation. She didn't want to prolong his stay, because she was hoping that Michael would return.

After Roger left she waited until well past midnight, pacing the floor in anxiety, but Michael didn't put in an appearance. She hadn't thought to ask where he was staying, and he'd never offered the information. She supposed she could call every motel in town looking for him, but the idea didn't appeal to her. She would be seeing him in the morning; what she had to tell him would simply have to wait until then.

The sale of the Baldwins' household contents was almost over. John Saunders had just purchased the last item on the list, an antique desk that had been in Mark Baldwin's study for as long as Blair could remember.

She was sitting at the back of the room listening to the auctioneer's ringing voice when she became aware of a slight ruffling of the short hairs on the back of her neck. A moment later a hand fell briefly onto her shoulder, and she knew Michael had arrived.

He took a seat behind her as the house itself came on the auction block. As the bidding began, Blair was nervously conscious of the fact that the rightful owner was sitting directly behind her, watching as it passed out of his grasp forever.

A part of her wanted to jump to her feet and shout that fact to the people gathered there. But she didn't have the right to do that. It was Michael's decision, and he'd made it, so the business at hand continued without interruption.

There was little competition for the house, because it needed plenty of ready cash to maintain it. Most people weren't willing to put that kind of money into an older house, even if it was something of a landmark and had held up through over a hundred years of stormy weather.

Marvin Welborn was the exception, and he walked away with it for below market price. Blair didn't know whether to be glad or upset.

A moment later, very conscious of the man behind her, she felt a new tension in the air and glanced up to see Roger Prescott walk past. She was surprised to see him, because he'd told her he wasn't planning to attend.

As he passed by her without glancing to either side, the man behind her leaned slightly forward and muttered, "They're all here."

Blair straightened her short pleated skirt with stiff fingers and swallowed tightly. If Michael was correct in his assumption, in a short while one of the three men who had been Mark Baldwin's business associates and his closest friends would unwittingly reveal himself as a possible murder suspect.

At last everything had been disposed of except the various pieces of undeveloped land. Blair could feel tension radiating in waves from the man seated behind her as pictures of various properties owned by Mark Baldwin were shown and then bid on. It was late in the afternoon when the last piece of property, the piece Michael had focused his attention on, located at the north edge of town, came up for bid.

The bidding began low and never really got off the ground. Only two people made offers for it, and after a couple of bids one dropped out, leaving it in the hands of the other man.

Blair didn't know how she felt. Was it relief because the two bidders were complete strangers, or disappointment because now she and Michael appeared to be back to square one?

She wanted to turn to Michael and offer him a word of comfort. He'd hoped that the man who walked away with the property would be someone familiar who would give him a lead to a killer.

He'd been certain that anyone who was willing to kill for something, then wait ten years to take actual possession of it, would make damned certain, by whatever method necessary, that no one, except himself, got hold of it. Where had he gone wrong in his thinking?

The auction was over. Blair sat for a moment without moving, waiting for a word or a sign from Michael. Finally, when he didn't speak, she stood and turned around.

He was gone. She looked around the room for his tall, broad-shouldered figure, but she couldn't spot him. People were milling about, talking in small groups, but he wasn't among them.

Blair saw Marvin Welborn nod to Roger Prescott, and a moment later the two men were standing close together in deep conversation. She was reminded of the night she'd almost been caught in Roger's office, and a slight shiver rippled down her spine.

She didn't want to suspect either man of any wrongdoing, least of all murder, and under the circumstances there wasn't any concrete reason to do so, but all at once she wished she could hear what they were discussing. She'd told Michael she would be looking for evidence to prove his father's death had been an accident, but if she had to choose someone as a likely suspect, she wanted it to be Marvin Welborn.

Deciding that she needed to find Michael, Blair made her way out the front door and down the porch steps, searching for him. As she moved around to the side of the house, a figure stepped out in front of her, halting her in her tracks. She found herself staring into Michael's dark eyes.

"Do you know the identity of the man who bought the property?" Michael asked tautly.

Blair shook her head. "I've never seen him before."

"Go back inside and see what you can learn about him. They'll need his credentials for the bill of sale. I'll wait for you in the gazebo."

"But—"

"Just do it!" he muttered curtly.

Realizing how upset he must be, Blair made no further protest. She made her way back along the sidewalk to the front lawn and up the front steps to the house. John Saunders stood smoking a cigar outside the front door.

"Well, it's over." He took the cigar out of his mouth and flicked the ash into a can of sand standing beside him.

"Yes," Blair responded, wondering how to elicit the information she needed without arousing his suspicions.

"I've been wanting to tell you what a good job you've done in taking care of the place," John continued, adding, "I only wish you'd allow me to compensate you for your time and trouble—"

"No," Blair cut him off. "Thank you, though. But I didn't do it for money. I wanted to, for old times' sake.

"We had a good turnout," she said, changing the subject abruptly. "More people showed up than I expected."

"Yes," the lawyer agreed. "Auctions like this attract people from all over the state and sometimes all over the nation."

"The two men who bid on that last bit of property, I thought one—the man who purchased it—looked familiar. I must have seen him around town, but I can't for the life of me remember where." She frowned a moment in pretended concentration, then asked, "Do you know his name?"

"Name's Russell, Todd Russell. He works for Unico Corporation. They own a lot of land in the area."

"Unico," Blair echoed softly.

"Yes." He gave her a curious look. "Do you know the company?"

"Oh, no, I just heard someone mention it the other day, that's all."

"Oh. Well, I see someone has come looking for me." He put his cigar out and popped a mint into his mouth. "I suppose they need me for paperwork. Keep in touch, Blair, don't be such a stranger. I'll have June call you and have you over to dinner real soon. Rob, our youngest, will be in town in a couple of weeks, and I'm sure he'll want to see you."

Blair murmured a polite rejoinder and watched as he turned away. "John!"

"Yes?" He turned back.

"I—can I come by your office or the house sometime after the first of the week? There's something I need to discuss with you."

"Certainly. If my secretary can't fit you in, just drop by the house anytime next week in the evening. We'll be glad to see you."

"Right. Thanks."

"Is anything wrong?" he asked before turning away, sensing something more behind her request.

"N-no." She shook her head. "Nothing. I'll see you sometime next week."

A few minutes later she joined Michael in the gazebo behind her own house. "Well?" he asked impatiently. "Did you find out who he is?"

"Yes. His name is Todd Russell and—" she hesitated "—he works for Unico Corporation."

"Damn!" Michael slapped a hand against the wall of the building, dislodging leaves from the ivy climbing its way up the wall. Dropping onto the bench, he sat with clenched jaw, staring at the ocean in the distance.

"What does it mean, Michael?" Blair asked when he remained silent. "Do you think someone at Unico had your father killed?"

"I don't know." He shook his head. "It doesn't make any sense. Dad said—"

"Michael," she interrupted, "your father...lied to you."

"What?" He glared up at her. Getting to his feet, he towered over her, anger in every rigid line of his face and body.

"Michael, please..." She laid a light hand on his arm. He shrugged it off. "I'm sorry. I didn't mean to blurt it out that way. I know how much you loved your father—you know I loved him, too. But...I did some investigating at work the other day."

"You didn't tell Prescott about me!"

"No," she muttered, pushing the hair back from her forehead. "I took a key from Roger's key ring and went through the patient files he keeps in the locked closet behind his desk." She paused, knowing this was going to hurt. "According to your father's medical records, he was in perfect health when he died. He didn't mention another doctor's name to you because he wasn't seeing one. He wasn't ill."

Michael stared at her as though expecting her to say something more.

"Do you understand what I'm saying? He lied about going to a specialist in Saint Augustine, because he didn't need one. He didn't have hypertension."

"Why would he lie about that?" he asked harshly.

"I don't know." She moved away from him, turning to face the water. "There's something else. Nothing on his chart indicates he was treated for poisoning."

"Are you implying he lied about being poisoned?" Taking a quick step forward, he jerked her to face him with a cruel hand at her elbow.

"I didn't say that."

"But you're implying it! Why? What possible reason would he have to lie to me about either of those things?"

"I don't know. Maybe he thought you'd believe whatever else he had to say more readily if you thought he was in actual physical danger."

"There's no mention at all of the poisoning?"

"None, but..."

"But what?"

"Well, the last notes on the chart were made two months before your father...before the accident. There's something else, I don't know if this means anything or not, it could just be the way he files."

"Who?"

"Roger. He files the charts of patients he no longer sees under two headings. One is for patients who have moved on to other doctors. The other is for those who are deceased. Your father was listed among the deceased."

"So?"

"The chart was dated for two months *before* the accident. That must have been right about the time your father was poisoned."

"Son of a— So it's Prescott we're after."

"I didn't say that. Besides, it was Unico who bought the land you're so certain someone was after. What does that have to do with Roger Prescott?"

"You're right." Michael ran a hand through his hair. "It's a damned maze. I didn't find out a single useful thing in Saint Augustine. Naturally, since apparently Dad wasn't seeing a doctor there, I didn't find anyone who would admit to having him as a patient. And as for the Unico Corporation—it's a dummy company for something called Tritran. They didn't have a phone number, so I went to their address and discovered a small empty office with a mail slot in the door.

"The building manager said the lease was paid by check, sent through the mail each month. He's never seen anyone in the office. He said someone must come and pick up the mail, though, because he'd seen the mailman push things through the slot, and once, out of curiosity, he'd peeked through it and the mail was gone."

"There's something else," Blair said. "I went out to the nursing home and spoke with Tom Wallace."

"I told you—"

"I know, I know," she cut him off in mid protest, "but you were gone, and I wanted to find out if he could remember anything about that last night before you and your father left, something that he hadn't told the authorities."

"And?"

"Tom said he spoke with your father before the two of you left that morning. But he didn't say what they talked about. He acted kind of strange, almost secretive, when I asked, as though there was something he knew and wasn't saying."

Michael eyed her closely. "Do you think it has anything to do with Dad's death? The Tom I remember wouldn't hurt a fly."

"No, no." She shook her head. "You don't understand. I don't think Tom had anything to do with your father's death, but he might know something that would help us find the man who did."

"What makes you say that?"

"He was talking strangely. I know he's getting up there in years, and he's gotten forgetful, but . . ."

It was hard to explain. What Tom had said hadn't really made any sense, but it had stuck in her mind.

"I don't know." Michael shook his head. "I'm not certain about anything anymore. I thought I had things pretty well pinpointed, but now . . . I just don't know."

Michael shoved his hands in his pockets and moved down the steps toward the beach. He hadn't thought it would be easy, but he'd thought it would all make sense in the end. And now nothing made sense.

Why had his father lied to him? And which of the three men, Prescott, Welborn or Saunders, if any, had been involved in his death?

Blair watched him go, pain squeezing her heart. She was partly responsible for the dejection bowing his shoulders. Perhaps she should have learned what she could at the hospital before speaking to him. Maybe she should have had another talk with Tom.

"Michael!" She couldn't let him go this way. "Michael!" she called, hurrying after him. "Wait, please!"

She caught up with him in her mother's garden near a row of crepe myrtle. "We'll find the killer—"

"I thought you didn't put much stock in his existence?" he came back at her angrily. "You've resisted the idea all along."

His glance shifted from her pale face. "Maybe you're right. Maybe it was an accident, maybe I made up the whole incident in my head. Maybe it was all a nightmare I had

while I was unconscious. Maybe I've lived a lie for the past
ten years.''

''Michael, don't . . .'' Tears blurred her vision. She didn't
know when she'd begun believing in his story, perhaps
sometime between talking to Tom and the auction, or maybe
just now. But he believed it so strongly that she had to believe it, too.

A sudden breeze blew a large, deep red blossom off the
tree behind them, and it landed in Blair's dark hair. Michael reached up to remove it. He held it on the palm of his
hand for a long moment, staring down at it.

Blair watched his face. It wasn't the face of the man she
remembered, but she was hardly conscious of that fact any
longer.

He was different inside, too, but the gentleness she remembered as being an inherent part of his makeup was still
there. Every now and then it made itself known in a glance
or a gesture, as now, when he smoothed the hair back from
her cheek and tucked the large, bloodred blossom behind
her ear.

His hand lingered in the air near her, and it was all she
could do to keep from leaning toward it, wanting so badly
to feel its warmth against her cheek.

Something of what she was feeling must have registered
in her eyes, because Michael couldn't seem to draw away
from her. A change began to come over his face, and Blair
knew he was going to kiss her. Her eyes drifted shut as she
swayed toward him, completely under his spell.

Michael's insides were churning. He wanted to kiss her,
wanted it so badly he knew he couldn't.

Clenching and then dropping the hand near her face, he
whispered, ''I need time to think, time to get my thoughts
together and make some sense of all this. We're missing
something, somewhere. I need to get away from Baywater
for a little while.''

Blair's eyes snapped open, a feeling of panic sending her
heart plummeting. He was leaving?

''Will you come?''

Blair froze. ''You want *me* to go with you?'' she asked,
trying to hide the joy flooding her heart.

"Yes, if you want to." He hesitated before adding, "I'd like for you to come."

It scared her a little the way her spirits suddenly lifted and her heart began to sing. It scared her to know he had that much control over her emotions. What would she do if she couldn't find a way to make him stay and admit he still loved her?

Chapter 8

"So, you like convertibles. I didn't know that."

He saw her smooth back a strand of hair blowing into her eyes and asked, "Would you prefer the top up?"

"No, I like it down."

They rode in silence until the strain finally began to get on Blair's nerves. She wondered if he was regretting his impulsive invitation. She'd hoped the invitation might signify some progress in their relationship, but here he was backing off again, and it made her a little angry.

"Are you worried about us being seen together?" she asked testily. "You should have thought about that when you asked for my help."

He threw her an impatient look. "I don't want to shove it under their noses, that's all. I don't expect to be recognized, but I don't want Prescott and the others asking too many questions, either." After a minuscule pause, he added, "And there are a great many things you don't know about me."

"I suppose that's true," she agreed after a moment. "Ten years is a long time. But there are a great many things I *do* know, too." And she proceeded to list them first on the fingers of one hand and then the other.

When she'd run out of fingers and was beginning to go back for a second round, naming things like frogs and chocolate ice cream in the same breath, against his will he laughed and said, "Okay, okay, I admit you know a lot about...my childhood."

Surprised to hear real laughter coming from him, she glanced over at him, but his expression was sober. "Michael, do you remember the summer we were both fifteen?" she asked abruptly.

"I remember."

"Do you recall the week I spent at your house because Mom and Dad were going to Chicago for some tests Dad needed?"

"I remember," he repeated gruffly, and she didn't know how much of the gruffness was caused by his throat injury and how much by emotion.

She twisted her hands together on her lap. "I heard you and Billy Gresham upstairs in your room...talking...the night of your birthday party."

"Yeah? So?"

"You were talking about a girl...and the way you described her, you sounded as though you were...in love with her...." She knew he was looking at her, but she couldn't meet his eyes. "I couldn't figure out who it was, then later, at the dance, I knew...it was Cheryl."

"What exactly did I say?" he asked in a guarded tone.

"You said you hadn't realized how beautiful the girl was...and then, one day—"

"I looked up and found I couldn't speak because of her beauty," Michael finished for her, recalling the conversation.

"Yes, and I was so...jealous." Blair bit her lip and stared at the passing scenery.

She'd seen Michael dancing with Cheryl, holding her close, and realized suddenly that they were both growing up and he would no longer be her exclusive property. Puberty had struck; Michael had discovered girls.

"It was you." His husky voice was barely above a whisper. "The girl I was describing was you."

Blair's head whipped toward him. "M-me? I don't believe you!" She stared at his profile, looking for a sign that he was joking, and it was a cruel joke, at that.

Michael's eyes left the road long enough to meet hers. "Believe me. And if you're surprised, just think how I felt. One morning I went to get my buddy for a day's fishing and instead I found this incredibly beautiful creature with long dark hair streaming down her back, wearing a white bikini, revealing curves I didn't even know she had, waiting for me on her porch."

"Then why—"

"Why did I start dating Cheryl right after the party?"

Blair nodded.

"You ignored me. At the party all evening, every time I came near you, you looked at me as though I'd crawled out from under a rock. I didn't know what I'd done, but I figured it must have been pretty awful. So I stayed away from you, to give you time to get over whatever was bugging you.

"Later, after the party, when I tried to talk to you, you wouldn't talk to me. I went to your door and knocked. I wanted you to come with me for a walk along the beach, so we could get things straightened out between us. I was pretty confused and you always said the ocean helped you think more clearly.

"But you locked your door and pretended to be asleep. I sat on the floor outside your door and waited. I figured I'd wait until you woke up." He shrugged. "Then I heard you moving around inside, and I knew you'd only pretended to be asleep because you didn't want to talk to me.

"At fifteen I was very sensitive about my manhood." He grinned wryly, sobered, and tried to explain. "I was dumbfounded to find myself looking at you, someone I'd always considered a sister, and thinking about you like…that. You can't imagine how confused I felt.

"While I was sitting outside your door that night, I tried to figure out what I'd done to make you mad. And then it came to me." He threw her a sideways glance. "I thought you *knew* about the feelings I was struggling so hard to hide and that was what was wrong. By ignoring me at the party and refusing to speak to me afterward, I figured you were telling me to back off.''

Blair wanted to protest, but she held her tongue. She remembered quite well how she'd acted that night, and she could easily see how he'd reached that conclusion.

It seemed they'd both been at cross-purposes that night. Blair had come to the realization that Michael was an attractive young man, ready to test his manhood, and he had discovered that she was becoming a woman, and neither had known how to handle the changing situation between them.

"What about Cheryl?" she murmured softly.

Michael frowned. "You bruised my ego. Cheryl soothed it. Everyone, including you, seemed to like the idea of us seeing each other. After a while—'' he shrugged ''—I convinced myself I was in love with her, and I never questioned my own feelings again—until that night on the beach...."

Blair felt the need to explain her acceptance of Cheryl into his life. "I guess, after getting over the shock of discovering you were actually interested in a girl other than me, I realized your relationship with Cheryl had nothing to do with our friendship. If you'd cut me out of your life altogether, or picked someone who wasn't my friend, I would have been resentful and stayed angry at you. But the very next day you invited me to go sailing with you, and you didn't invite Cheryl.''

Michael kept his eyes on the road. "We took a long time to grow up.''

Forty-five minutes later, in a small inland town southwest of Baywater, Michael pulled up before a bungalow and switched off the car's engine. It was a large, sprawling house with oleander and acacia trees growing in the yard.

"Where are we?" Blair looked from Michael to the house as he assisted her from the car.

But his answer never came, because at that precise moment a young voice chirped, "Daddy! Daddy!" and a small body came flying out the front door and launched himself at Michael, wrapping chubby arms tightly around his knees.

Daddy?

Blair looked from the little boy, who appeared to be about four years of age, to the man lifting him high in his arms.

The child, she noted in amazement, was the spitting image of the man at that age, except for a shock of wheat-blond hair falling across his forehead into huge dark eyes splotched with gold.

"Who's she?" the child asked, pointing a finger at her, once he'd greeted his father.

"She's a friend," Michael responded, turning toward her. "Blair, I'd like you to meet my son Mark."

The child was so perfect, so sweet and loving. He insisted on giving her a kiss, too, once he'd realized she was his father's friend. Blair stiffened for a moment as his chubby arms closed around her neck, thinking that this child, a small edition of the man she loved so much, could have been hers—*should have been hers!*

Closing her eyes, she slowly wrapped her arms around him and pressed her face against his soft, baby-fine hair as she felt his moist lips touch her cheek. He smelled like baby oil, sunshine and worn sneakers. And she wished with all her heart that he was hers.

A moment later Blair was introduced to Michael's sister-in-law and her husband. They welcomed her warmly, explaining how much they loved having Mark with them while Michael took care of business. No one mentioned what that business might be, and Blair wasn't certain if that was because the couple knew all about it and understood, or because they knew nothing and preferred it that way.

Coffee was served soon after they entered the house, with milk and cookies for Mark. Blair watched, her heart twisting painfully inside her breast, as Mark fed Michael part of his cookie and insisted he have a drink of the milk.

Obviously the boy and the man shared a very close, loving relationship. *She should have been a part of that family group!* A moment later Mark was on her lap, holding the remainder of his last cookie beneath her nose, demanding, "Bite."

When it was time to leave, Blair got to her feet with a very real reluctance. There were cookie crumbs down the bodice of her sundress, grating between her breasts, a milk stain on her skirt and a smear of chocolate on one cheek where Mark had kissed her—and she'd never felt so alive in her life.

After a tearful goodbye, Michael gave his son one last hug and ushered Blair out to the car, assisting her inside. She sat without speaking as Michael pulled away from the curb and turned the car toward home, a picture filling her mind's eye of large dark eyes swimming in tears as Mark had told her goodbye.

"Is he the real reason you came back to Baywater?"

Michael made no pretense of misunderstanding her meaning. "Yes. Once it's safe and the killer is no longer free to hurt anyone else, I want him to know all about the history of our family and the part they played in settling Baywater. And I want him to know all about his grandfather and what a good man he was." His hands gripped the steering wheel tightly. "I want him to know all about his heritage."

"Then why didn't you simply make your identity known and claim the house that's been in your family for generations?" She turned toward him on the seat. "That should be his, too."

"I told you before," he answered stiffly. "I didn't come back for the property or the money."

And you didn't come back for me, either, Blair was thinking as she stared straight ahead. Damn you for showing me what heaven could be like! Damn you for making love to me and introducing me to your child! Damn you for planning to leave me again so soon....

"He looks very much like you when you were a boy," she murmured, "except for the hair." She wanted to be angry with him. He'd taken her to see the child because he'd hoped to scare her off. How could he have thought that wonderfully small edition of himself would make her love him any less?

"Mary was very fair. She was also one of the kindest people I've ever known, a good nurse, a loving wife and a wonderful mother."

She sounded like a paragon of womanhood. How did you fight a paragon—or the memory of one?

"How did she get pneumonia?" Blair ventured softly.

He didn't respond immediately, and for a time she thought he wasn't going to. Finally he cleared his throat and said, "I told you how short-staffed the hospital was while Mary was in training. Well, it wasn't any better when she qualified and became part of the staff. After a year or so, when I was finally able to do things for myself, we got married, but she was still working those long hours. I wasn't fit for work, wouldn't be for a long time to come, or so I was told by the doctors."

Blair could hear how painful the memories were for him. She sympathized with his pain, but at the same time she wanted to know about the woman who'd given him a child.

"Mary worked all kinds of crazy hours, and I hated it." His hands tightened on the steering wheel. "Hated waiting at home while she earned our living. At the time I still wasn't clear on everything that had taken place on the boat before the explosion. My memory was still pretty foggy. I recalled the explosion, but it wasn't until I finally had the courage to go through the box of things the hospital had given me when I left—the things I'd had on me when I was found—that I came across the safe-deposit-box key. Then the rest of it came to me in a series of quick moving pictures, like a speeded-up movie reel. The money, the memory of Dad telling me about it, and the new identity he'd said he'd had made for me, played through my head. By that time, though I hadn't found a steady job, I was doing some crewing on fishing boats. The money I made wasn't a lot, but it added something to the household."

Blair realized Michael's pride wouldn't have allowed him to live for very long solely on his wife's income.

"Anyway," he continued, "I found the key and made a trip to the city where the bank was located. I'll never forget that day. I unlocked the box... and just sat there, staring. There was a small fortune in cash inside, along with the fake identity. I didn't know what to do. So I panicked."

"Panicked?" Blair frowned. "Why?"

It was hard for him to admit, even now. "I wondered where all that money had come from. I knew Dad had been comfortable, but I just never really thought about how much money there was or where it all came from...."

And suddenly she realized what he was getting at. "You thought your father had done something illegal!"

"I—I don't know. I just knew I couldn't touch it. I locked the box and just left it there. I was...mixed up, still not clear on everything about the accident. I went home and put the key back where I'd found it without saying anything to...anybody.

"I should have told her—I wanted to, damn it, I wanted to—but...I hadn't even told her about what really happened on the boat." He seemed to be talking more to himself than to her.

"You mean you never told Mary about your father?"

"She knew I'd been in an accident, I just didn't tell her what took place before it. Or who I was...or anything about my father being on the boat." Michael shook his head. "I really couldn't remember everything at first, and it didn't seem to matter to her. And then, later...I just couldn't tell her. I was afraid," he admitted. "I mean, someone had killed my father and almost succeeded in killing me.

"I was confused. I didn't know what to think about Dad's death." Michael hit the steering wheel with the palm of his hand. "I didn't know whether he'd been involved in something he shouldn't have been. I wasn't thinking clearly, the conversation we'd had was still choppy in my memory...and I was afraid for Mary."

For the first time since he'd returned, Blair saw a vulnerable look enter the dark eyes. "She'd done so much for me," he tried to explain. "I couldn't take the chance of bringing something like that down on her head. You understand that...don't you?"

What he wanted was reassurance that he'd done the right thing, but the only one who could truly give him that was gone.

"I knew that if I told her about the money," he continued, when Blair remained silent, "she'd want to know where I'd gotten it. And...I couldn't tell her..." His voice trailed off.

"Oh, Michael." Blair wished she could tell him that he'd done the right thing, but she knew he should have told Mary. If it had been her, she would have wanted to know everything about him, and she would have sensed it if he'd tried hiding something so important from her.

"I know, I know." A note of anguish entered his hoarse voice. "I shouldn't have doubted my father—and I should have told Mary.

"A few weeks after I found the money, I got a good job at one of the local banks. I told myself it was better that she didn't know about my past. And by then, you see, I had another, better, reason for keeping it from her. I couldn't endanger her life—or that of our unborn child.

"We had a healthy son, and we were talking about buying a house. Then I had a relapse. Mary went back to work, and between taking care of me and the baby . . . it was too much for her. She got sick. It all happened so fast, there wasn't time to think about the money, or the lies. . . ."

"Michael, I'm so sorry." She wanted to touch him, but she didn't.

"It took awhile for me to get things together again after her death. I left Mark with Elaine, Mary's sister, and quit my job at the bank. I never liked it much anyway. I hired out on some sailing vessels and stayed on the ocean as much as possible. When I got back on dry land and saw Mark again, saw that he was beginning to grow up, I knew I couldn't put it off any longer. Mary was gone, she could no longer be hurt by what I'd kept hidden. But Mark deserved to know the truth about his heritage.

"If anything happened to me, I knew the money in the safe-deposit box would put him through college and take care of him for the rest of his life. Elaine and her husband can't have any children of their own. They love Mark as much as I do. I knew he'd be safe with them. Because I knew I had to come back to Baywater and find my father's killer. Nothing would make any sense until I put that demon to rest."

"So you wrote me that letter," Blair said.

"Yes."

"Why didn't you tell me you had a son?"

"I didn't deliberately keep it from you."

"Didn't you?"

"All right," he admitted, reluctantly, "I didn't want to hurt you."

He'd known it would hurt her. That meant he knew all the rest would hurt, too, but still he'd contacted her, because he couldn't accomplish what he had set out to do without help. And he'd known all along that of the two women, herself and Cheryl, *she* was the one who had cared enough, the one it would be easier to convince, to do what he wanted.

Had he made love to her with that thought in mind? Again that ugly question surfaced in her mind. She couldn't bring herself to ask him point-blank, but it hovered, unspoken, in the air around their heads.

Michael glanced over at her, wishing she would say something. She looked so small, so defenseless, huddled against the door, eyes staring straight ahead. He knew what she was thinking, and he wanted to tell her it was a lie. But he didn't.

He couldn't offer her hope of a future between them, and he knew that was what she wanted. He didn't deserve happiness; Mary had offered him that, and look what he'd done to her.

Once he was gone from her life, for good this time, Blair might be able to look back on their brief time together without bitterness. Until then, her anger at him would sustain her through what lay ahead, just as his own lust for revenge would sustain him.

But that rationalization didn't stop his insides from feeling as though they were being ripped to shreds in the struggle to keep his distance from her. Nor did it help in the fight against the compelling need to have her that raged inside him, becoming fiercer with every passing day.

He knew he had to finish the job he'd come to do and get out of Baywater before he changed his mind and stayed, causing them both irrevocable pain.

As they passed through Baywater and drew near her house, Michael mentioned that he was going to Tallahassee sometime on Monday, to the office of the secretary of state, to get whatever information about Tri-tran he could find. He'd come to a dead end in his search, and he hoped that the visit would put him back on track again.

"Will I see you tomorrow?" he asked diffidently, knowing he should let her go, yet not quite able to.

"I've made plans."

He wanted to ask what those plans were, remembering Roger Prescott's show of concern the evening before, but managed to hold his tongue.

"Before you go, may I have the name and phone number of the motel where you're staying, in case I need to contact you?" Blair asked.

He gave her the information and was preparing to leave when Blair stopped him dead in his tracks by murmuring in a soft voice, "It didn't work, you know."

He gave her a questioning look.

"The fact that you have a child," she explained, "hasn't scared me off. I love children."

The next morning Blair phoned a friend from her hospital days who worked in medical records and asked the woman for a favor. A couple of hours later, she was reading the computer report on Mark Baldwin's trip through the emergency room, two months before his disappearance at sea.

It seemed Mark had been brought into the emergency room suffering from severe stomach pains and vomiting. He'd been having dinner at the country club with friends when he'd been taken ill. The diagnosis, after an examination by the emergency-room doctor and several tests, showed that somehow he'd ingested a small quantity of a rather toxic weed killer.

Notes made by the attending physician indicated that material from the patient's stomach had been analyzed, and it appeared that the salad Mark had eaten had been the cause of the poisoning. It was theorized that perhaps the vegetables hadn't been thoroughly washed.

The club had been notified quietly, Blair read, but no one else had come up ill, and the whole incident was thought to be an isolated case. Blair read a little further and discovered that Roger Prescott had been the one who'd brought Mark to the hospital, though the emergency-room doctor had treated him.

Why? Roger had been right there, his own doctor; why hadn't he taken care of Mark? And why did Mark stop using Roger as his personal physician about that time?

Nothing of what she'd read was conclusive. She needed more than these meager facts to be satisfied that Roger was guilty of anything other than keeping incomplete records and a bit of misfiling.

From the first she'd resisted the idea that Roger Prescott had anything to do with the fantastic story Michael had told her. Little by little, though, she had to admit, things were beginning to look bad for him. But there was still one thing missing—motive.

Was the desire for a piece of property enough to make a man like Roger Prescott kill his daughter's fiancé and a man he'd been friends with since childhood?

"Tell me, Jan, does this—" she looked at the screen "—Simon Farrell still practice medicine around here?"

The other woman shook her graying head. "No, he went to the West Coast, I believe."

"How long ago?" Blair asked.

"Oh, gosh…" Jan narrowed her dark eyes in thought. "I'd say nine, maybe ten, years ago." Giving Blair a curious look, she said, "Now let me ask you something. Why are you interested in something that happened so many years ago?"

Blair switched off the computer screen before answering. "I'm doing some reorganization in the office, trying to get the files in order before Roger's new partner gets back from his honeymoon. It's something I've needed to do for a long time, but with the way things are…" She shook her head. "There are never enough hours in the day."

"Don't I know it," Jan agreed. "When is the happy couple due back?"

"Not for a while yet, thank heavens. Listen, I'm sorry to have called you out on a Sunday for this."

"No problem," the other woman replied. "It's good that you came today. I'm not sure I should be letting you see these."

Blair shot the older woman a quick glance and caught her smile. "I'm only kidding. I'm sure there must be a copy of this file somewhere in Dr. Prescott's office."

"You're probably right about that." Blair returned her smile. "And I might even find it one of these days." Getting to her feet, she asked, "You wouldn't happen to have an address for this Simon Farrell, would you?"

"I don't, but the business office might. You'll have to wait until tomorrow to find out, though."

Blair thanked her again for coming out on a Sunday morning and made her way down the lonely hospital corridor toward the front door. She thought about going by Michael's motel to tell him what she'd learned but decided against it.

After stopping for a brief lunch, Blair headed home. She was unpleasantly surprised to find Marvin Welborn waiting for her on her doorstep.

"Good afternoon," he greeted her politely, flashing her a charming smile.

Blair returned his greeting with little warmth. She couldn't forget the vulgar inferences he'd made about her when she'd been hiding in Roger's bathroom on Thursday evening.

"I came to pick up the key to the house next door. I was going to mention it to you yesterday, but you disappeared from the auction before I found the opportunity." His gray eyes watched her closely. "I'm sorry to bother you on a Sunday. Hope I'm not interfering with any plans you might have made."

"Not at all," she answered without expression, unlocking the door and preceding him inside. "If you'll wait here a moment, I'll get the key." She left him in the front hallway and went to her room at the back of the house.

A few moments later, returning with the key in hand, she surprised him bending over her desk in the living room.

"Is there something I can help you find?" she asked coolly from the doorway, barely keeping her temper in check.

With great aplomb the man straightened slowly and turned. "There you are. I hope you don't mind that I came in here. You have a beautiful view of your mother's flower garden from these French doors."

But she knew it wasn't her mother's flower garden he'd been inspecting. She held the key out to him. When he moved to her side and took it, Blair made certain their fingers didn't touch.

A moment later, with a sense of relief, she ushered him from the house. Being in his company made her skin crawl. If she had to choose between the three men Michael suspected of his father's death, she would choose Marvin Welborn without a second's thought. After hearing what she'd heard from his own mouth and finding him snooping through her things, she wouldn't put anything past him.

Locking the door securely, Blair hurried to her desk to see what had interested him so much that he'd failed to notice her return until she'd spoken. Her appointment calendar lay open, with the page turned to Michael's address at the motel where he was presently staying.

Blair was positive the calendar had been in the top drawer of the desk. On the same page, below the appropriate date, was the address of the motel where they'd met the first time in New Smyrna Beach and the time of their meeting.

Why would Marvin be interested in Michael and where he was staying—unless he'd tumbled to Michael's true identity?

Blair decided she'd better tell Michael about Welborn, as well as what she'd learned at the hospital. The desk clerk rang through to his room, but there was no answer. Blair left a message for him to call her and hung up. For a while she paced the room, worried about his safety, but eventually she began to wonder if she was creating a tempest in a teacup.

In a little while, when Michael didn't call her back, she made certain her doors and all the windows, including the one in the laundry room, were securely locked. Then she retired for the night, vowing that in the morning she simply would get hold of Michael.

Chapter 9

The next morning Blair arrived at work a few minutes early, to be sure she got there ahead of Roger. She wanted to get the key back on his key ring at the first opportunity, and she was prepared to drop it, if she had to, and leave it for him to find.

Fortunately that proved to be unnecessary. Shortly after his arrival he discovered he'd left some things he needed in the trunk of his car and asked Blair to get them for him. Delving into his pocket, he came up with both sets of keys just as the phone rang with a call on his private line.

Handing her the keys, Roger had hurried to take the call in his office. Blair couldn't believe her luck. In a few moments the key was back where it belonged, with Roger none the wiser.

A little while later the phone rang again, and Blair answered it.

"Blair?" Michael's harsh voice rang in her ear.

"Y-yes," she answered, glancing at the open door across the hallway. Roger was sitting at his desk, poring over some papers.

"I want to talk to you. Can you meet me for lunch?"

"Yes," she answered softly. "I have something to tell you."

"Good, where do you want to meet?"

"The park," she answered, after only a moment's thought. "It's about a mile from my office on Inlet Avenue. I'll be there just after eleven-thirty."

"Right, see you then," he replied, ringing off.

"A problem?" Roger asked from the doorway.

Blair looked up as she put the receiver down and shook her head. "No, just meeting a friend for lunch."

"Really? Anyone I know?" he asked, coming into the room to lean casually against a filing cabinet, arms folded.

"Well...no," she hedged, not wanting to tell him the friend's identity.

"I see." He lifted a blond brow. "You don't want to discuss it, so that must mean it isn't a woman friend?" He turned the statement into a question.

"No." She kept her eyes on the file in front of her, giving nothing away.

"Not that Wilson fellow again?" Roger remarked disparagingly. "You left with him after the auction on Saturday. Is it getting serious between the two of you?"

Blair glanced up directly into his eyes. "I didn't know you saw me at the auction. I thought you said you weren't going to be there."

"I wasn't," he answered, sidetracked for the moment. "But John thought I should attend out of respect for Mark's memory, so I went."

"I think John was right." Blair began to stack the charts in order on her desk.

"Is Wilson your luncheon date?"

It was really none of his business who she met for lunch or otherwise.

"I know it's none of my business." He moved closer as Blair stood and opened the gray metal filing cabinet beside her desk. "I just don't want to see you get hurt."

Why this sudden concern for who she dated?

"I'm not going to get hurt. I'm only going to share a sandwich with him." She pushed the file drawer shut with a clang and went back to her desk.

"I'm sure you know what you're doing, just be careful, that's all I ask. I would tell my own daughter the same thing."

At the door to his office, he paused and glanced back. "I'm going to a small dinner party at the club tonight. Marvin will be there, and so will John and his wife. It's been a long time since we all got together. Not since your parents have been gone, in fact. Would you like to come? I know everyone would be pleased to see you. And I'll know you aren't angry with me for playing the heavy-handed father if you agree," he added with an engaging smile.

Blair started to refuse, then realized this would give her the opportunity to see all three men together. It might even give her a moment alone with John to ask him about the will.

"Yes, all right, I'll come," she answered. "Thank you for inviting me."

"My pleasure." He gave her a slight bow. "I'll pick you up about... seven-thirty?"

Blair nodded, and he left her. The morning flew by after that, and at eleven-thirty she made certain she was out of the office on time to keep her appointment with Michael.

He was waiting for her on a bench near the entrance to the park, with sandwiches and cold drinks. Blair felt her heart lurch at the welcoming glance he gave her and warned herself to play it cool.

"I wondered if you'd make it," he greeted her, handing her a sandwich and a soft drink.

She wished his concern had a more personal note to it. Biting into the thick, juicy sandwich she lowered her eyes to hide her thoughts from him.

"I thought you were going to Tallahassee today."

"I was, but I spent all day yesterday with Mark, and when I left he wasn't feeling well. I wanted to stay close, just in case."

Blair realized what he meant. His wife had died suddenly, and he wasn't taking any chances where his son's health was concerned.

"I've been hanging around town all morning, trying to get some answers to a few questions." He contemplated his own sandwich while he spoke. "I know you already spoke with him, but I went out to the nursing home to talk to Tom Wallace."

"Did you tell him who you were?"

"I didn't get the opportunity. He was having some kind of a bad turn, and they weren't letting him have any visitors."

"Oh, no," she said with quick concern. "I hope he's going to be all right. Did they say what was wrong?"

Michael shook his head. "I was just told he couldn't have visitors for a few days—doctor's orders. So I left and began making my rounds. There've been so many changes in the town, it wasn't easy. I looked for some of the people I remember Dad helping get loans at the bank and began to ask questions." He gave her a penetrating look. "Either I've been asking the wrong questions all morning, or no one knows a thing about Unico or much of anything else in this town."

Blair chewed quickly and swallowed. "I know something." Putting her sandwich down carefully on the wax paper, she scooted closer to him along the bench. "I went to the hospital yesterday and looked up the medical records on your father's visit there the night he was poisoned. Roger is the one who took him there that night—" she lowered her voice "—but another doctor took care of him after he arrived. According to Roger's records, he never treated your father after that night."

"So?"

"So, don't you get it?"

He shook his head, his eyes on her face.

"Why would one doctor let another doctor take care of his patient when he was in attendance? Unless the other doctor is a specialist, brought in on the case by the attending physician, it just doesn't happen."

"I still don't see what you're getting at."

"I think your father *refused* to let Roger attend him. And I think that must have been because, rightly or wrongly, he suspected Roger of poisoning him."

"I'll be damned!" He half rose from the bench.

"Wait, I'm not finished." Blair put a hand on his arm and pressed him back down. "I don't think Roger, if he's the guilty party, wanted to kill your father with the poison. If so, he would have done it. What if he only wanted to scare him by showing him how easy it would be to kill him—and in a public place like the country club, too? No one else who ate there became ill that night.

"Remember the will. If the will is as important as you think, so important that it had to turn up missing, whoever poisoned your father didn't want him dead—at least, not right then. They only wanted to make a point and perhaps force him into giving them what they wanted."

"Like a certain piece of property," Michael cut in quickly. A second later the light died out of his eyes and he shook his head. "But that idea doesn't hold water. Unico bought the property, not Roger."

"I know. I'm not sure about that part. I'm not even certain it's Roger we're talking about here. In fact, I'd prefer to believe it's someone else. But let's say, whoever it is, their meeting went something like this. Your father has learned something, something about a friend that he doesn't want to believe. I don't know what," she said, gesturing dismissively, "so don't ask.

"Anyway, he confronts the man with it, and he doesn't deny it, but perhaps he makes a veiled threat against your father. Your father becomes angry, and they have words. Another threat is made, but this time the threat isn't quite so obscure, and your father stalks out of the room. He's angry, but he still doesn't believe he's in danger from this man, because of their past association.

"Later, the friend responds by *showing* your father just how vulnerable he really is by slipping him the poison—in public. Naturally, after that your father is going to take him seriously. The man has made his point, and your father is scared, really scared, for himself, but mostly for you. Your father doesn't want to tell you who is trying to kill him, because he doesn't want you involved. That would put your life in real danger. So—"

"So he takes me on a fishing trip and tells me an edited version of what's going on," Michael took up the theory.

"Exactly." She stared at him, watching the various emotions chase themselves across his face.

"That puts us right back at square one. Three men, three possible killers, and no tangible motive."

Blair had one more thing to tell him. "Marvin was waiting for me when I got home last night. He came to collect the key to your house, or so he said. But I caught him snooping through the things on my desk. He didn't even bother to try and hide it. When he left, I looked and—" The more she thought about it, the more worried she became. "He was looking at my calendar with the address of your motel on it—and down below was the address of the motel near New Smyrna Beach."

"So that explains it!"

"Explains what?"

"When I got back last night, it was evident that someone had gone through my things."

"Oh, no! Michael, I'm sorry. It's all my fault."

"No, it isn't." He patted her hand. "It's all right. They didn't find anything."

"But that means they're suspicious of you. You don't think they know it's really *you?*"

"How could they?"

"I don't know, but—"

"Don't worry about me. I can take care of myself." Michael wrapped the sandwich he'd hardly touched and pitched it into the trash can. "I'm certainly not worried about me." He shifted his attention to her face. "But I *am* concerned about you. I don't want you doing any more snooping on my behalf."

Blair opened her mouth to protest, and he silenced her with a quick shake of the head and an impenetrable glance. "I mean it. If the theory you've come up with should be correct, even partly, and the killer learns you've been asking questions about events that took place ten years ago— well, it just isn't safe."

"No one suspects anything."

Michael looked up from crushing his empty soda can in one hand. "You can't be certain about that."

A soft breeze blew through the leaves of the trees overhead as Blair gathered her own trash and stood to place it in the bin.

"Blair, I don't want you getting involved in this any deeper. From now on I'll handle everything." Michael followed her as she moved along the path between the benches. "I should never have written that damned letter," he muttered.

"I'm not a child, Michael! I know what I'm doing."

He stopped in front of her, bringing her to a halt. Standing close, so no one around them could overhear, he urged, "Do as I say and stay out of this from now on."

"You're too late. I'm having dinner with Roger at the club tonight. Michael!" She pulled at her arm. "You're hurting me."

Michael immediately loosened his fingers and smoothed them over the red marks on her pale skin in contrition. "I'm sorry. I didn't mean to." His eyes touched hers and lingered. "Your skin is so soft...."

"I have to go." Blair managed to get the words past suddenly stiff lips, drowning in his eyes, wishing she could stay. "Let me go," she murmured breathlessly. "I'm going to be late."

He dropped his hand and stepped back, clearing the way for her to leave, and Blair strode quickly down the path to her car.

"Blair!"

She stopped to glance back over her shoulder. Michael was hurrying to catch up with her. "Remember what I said about Roger. Keep your distance. He could be dangerous."

"I'll talk to you later," she murmured ambiguously.

Michael stared after her retreating back. What was the real motive for his repeated warnings against Roger? Blair's safety? Or jealousy at the thought of her being out with another man?

Blair preceded Roger into the dining room of the Baywater Country Club and stood looking around, trying to spot the others.

"There." Roger touched her arm and nodded toward a table near the wide doors, standing open to reveal a portion of the terrace. At that instant Marvin caught sight of them and said something to John. Both men smiled and beckoned, while June Saunders lifted a hand in greeting.

"Don't you look lovely," the older woman murmured with a smile as Blair and Roger joined them. "Here, dear, sit beside me. It's been ages since we've gotten together like this."

"It's nice to see you." Blair smiled at the friendly woman and took the seat she indicated. Holding the full skirt of her yellow evening dress out of the way, she allowed Roger to seat her.

A few moments later a waiter came to inquire if they were ready for their meal. Blair asked for a glass of white wine and ordered a salad and shrimp scampi.

"You know," she said to no one in particular when the young man had left, "I read something the other day that alarmed me. It seems there were several poisonings somewhere in the state because people weren't washing pesticides off their fruits and vegetables before eating them."

Roger had been speaking in a low tone to John, but at the sound of her voice he stopped and gave her a brief glance. Blair looked from him to John, who was staring intently at something behind her.

She was on the point of turning to satisfy her curiosity when she heard, "Good evening, isn't it a coincidence, meeting again so soon like this?"

Blair stiffened. "Yes," she muttered, turning and giving Michael a dangerous look from flashing blue eyes. "Isn't it?"

Michael gave Roger a brusque nod and turned to the blonde beside him. "This is Jane Harris." He introduced the woman around the table, waiting for each of them in turn to supply their own names.

Somehow, a short time later, Blair found herself on the dance floor in Michael's arms, Jane Harris, the *Janey* from the tax office, having taken her place at the table.

"Shouldn't you have danced with your date first?" she asked.

"I'm sure she won't mind. She only came out with me because she's bored. Her fiancé is out of town at the moment, and she doesn't get out much."

"Oh."

They danced for a while in silence, with Michael fighting the urge to pull her closer. Finally he exerted a gentle pressure against the back of her head, and Blair laid her cheek against his chest.

It was a bad mistake, because in a moment his nostrils were filled with her unforgettable perfume and all he could think about was how easy it would be to get used to having her in his arms. He had to say something to break the spell, or in another moment he would be kissing her right there in front of everyone on the dance floor.

"That wasn't very smart, you know," Michael murmured against her curls.

"W-what?" Blair could hardly speak. She'd been in another world, peopled by only the two of them.

"Mentioning poison to those three," he answered, pulling back to look down into her face. "Are you asking the killer to come after you?"

"He doesn't know I know anything."

Michael gave her an exasperated look and warned, "You're playing with fire."

"I'm not! Besides, maybe that wouldn't be such a bad idea. At least then he'd be out in the open and we could find out who it is."

"Don't be a fool!"

"Hush!" Blair glanced at the man and woman dancing beside them and smiled. "Do you want someone to hear you?" she asked beneath her breath.

Michael jerked her up against him, whirled her across the floor and out through the open French doors. On the terrace they finished the dance in silence. When the strains of the music had come to an end, he took her hand and moved past the other couples engaged in taking advantage of the warm summer night for a romantic interlude and led her off the walk into the maze of flowers and trees opening out behind the terrace.

Blair offered no resistance, but asked, "Where are we going?"

"Someplace where I can talk some sense into your stubborn head without everyone hearing me," he answered half-angrily.

"Me!" She jerked her hand from his grasp. "What about you? Do you *want* those men—" she pointed back toward the building "—to figure out who you are?"

"I'm tired of pussyfooting around," Michael replied tautly. "I should have introduced myself as Michael Baldwin just now and not Mike Wilson. Wouldn't that have put the cat among the pigeons?" He laughed without humor.

"You're crazy!"

"Am I?" He grabbed her around the waist and hauled her up against him. "What about you?"

"Michael..." She glanced around them. "Don't. What if someone should see us?"

"What if they do?" he asked belligerently. On a softer note, he added, "Have you any idea how beautiful you look in that shade of yellow?" His eyes glowed down into hers, making it impossible for her to think clearly.

"But—"

Crushing her to him, he dipped his head, smothering her lips with hungry passion. After a long moment he drew away.

Blair wanted to protest his withdrawal, but he was only pausing for breath. His head descended again almost immediately, and with a series of slow, shivery kisses, he soon had her melting against him, her arms wrapped around his neck, her lips open beneath his, all thought of resistance a thing of the past.

"I missed you," he mouthed against her lips, kissing first the upper and then the lower.

"You don't know what you're saying," she whispered without conviction. She felt the tip of his tongue graze her cheek, and then his mouth settled along the sensitive skin below her ear.

"I just saw you at lunch—oh! Michael..." She quivered when his teeth nipped her earlobe, then pressed herself closer. "Someone will see us."

"I don't care," Michael panted, past worrying about discovery or the future. She was in his arms, and he wanted her.

Blair placed a determined hand against his chest and pushed him away. "Have you been drinking?"

Michael fell back a step. "No, I have *not* been drinking."

"We shouldn't be here alone." What was he doing to her? How could he make love to her in this way, knowing he planned to leave her? She wasn't adept at playing such games; she'd never learned the rules.

"Maybe you're right," he agreed shortly, turning away and catching sight of a small red glow in the distance, alerting him that they were no longer alone. "Let's go back to the others."

Blair followed him in mounting confusion. It was impossible to keep up with him and his quick changes of mood.

"We have company," he whispered against her ear under the pretense of giving her another kiss.

As they drew closer to the paved walk leading to the terrace, the odor of cigar smoke wafted to them on the evening air. A second later a dark shadow stepped in front of them and Marvin Welborn murmured, "Lovely night for a stroll, isn't it?"

"Lovely," Michael agreed, the hand against Blair's back stiffening in warning. "You go on ahead," he told her. "I want to speak to Mr. Welborn about some property."

Blair wanted to object, knowing Michael was baiting the man just to see how far he could go with this foolish masquerade. She wanted to ask him if he'd considered what would happen to his son if he ended up like his father, but she only turned away and hurried toward the French doors.

Inside, Blair found Roger and Jane sitting alone at the table. Jane was staring at the dance floor, a taut expression on her pinched face. Roger was glaring down into his drink. John and June were dancing.

By the time the music ended, Michael had returned to collect his date. With a brief nod in Blair's direction, he left without a word.

The rest of the evening passed without incident, but now Blair was uncomfortable with the three men. Several times during the meal a pall of silence fell over the table, and no one seemed inclined to break it. Even June seemed more interested in her glass of wine than in conversation.

Blair didn't know what to expect when Roger took her home a little while later. For all her brave talk about setting herself up as a target for the killer, she didn't look forward to being alone with him.

But she needn't have worried. Roger simply left her at her door with a few murmured words about seeing her at the office the next morning and drove away.

As she was getting ready for bed, Blair realized that she'd never gotten an opportunity to speak with John Saunders about Mark Baldwin's missing will.

Chapter 10

Roger was waiting for Blair the next morning when she arrived for work. He met her at the door with a murmured greeting and followed her into the small area at the back of the waiting room, where she kept her personal things during office hours.

As she sat to remove her outdoor shoes and replace them with her thick-soled nurse's shoes, he hovered in the doorway watching her. Blair looked up, waiting for him to say whatever it was he had to say. She noted the circles beneath his normally serene blue eyes, indicating a lack of sleep, and felt a moment's sympathy for Cheryl's father, until she thought about what might have caused his restlessness.

"I'm closing the office for a couple of weeks," he announced without preamble. "I hope you don't mind taking your vacation early."

Blair eyed him in surprise. "Is something wrong? Cheryl—"

"Cheryl is fine, nothing like that. I . . . haven't been feeling up to par lately, that's all. I've asked Charles Samuels to take my patients for a couple of weeks, and he's agreed. So, if you'll just call everyone today and cancel their appointments, let them know they're to see him, after that you're free to go.''

Without waiting for her to make a protest or ask any questions, Roger turned on his heel and strode toward his office. But Blair was too curious to let him get away with that.

''Are you planning to go on a trip?'' she asked as casually as she could manage, following him.

Roger paused with a hand on the door beside him and turned to face her. He appeared on the brink of saying something, then abruptly changed his mind. ''I really don't know what my plans are, except to take it easy for the next few days. What will you do with the time?''

Blair lifted her hands in a shrug. ''I haven't any idea. I wasn't expecting to take my vacation for another couple of months. Maybe I'll do some gardening. I wasn't planning a trip this year.''

Roger nodded, crossed the narrow hallway to his office and closed the door with a snap.

Blair stood staring at the closed door. What had happened since last night to upset him? Had she and Michael given themselves away?

True, she'd been foolish enough to mention the poisoning, and Michael had shown up out of the blue, flaunting himself before the three men. But they didn't know who he really was. Did they?

The first call she made that morning was to Michael. She caught him as he was heading out.

''Something's up.'' She spoke softly into the mouthpiece, keeping an eye on the door to Roger's office.

''What do you mean?''

''I'm being given a two-week vacation—two months early. And Roger isn't getting someone in to cover for me. The office is going to be closed.''

''Damn! That doesn't sound good. Did he in any way indicate that he was suspicious of you?''

''No, he simply asked what I was going to do with the time off. He said he was closing the office because he hadn't been feeling well lately. He doesn't look good, Michael. Maybe he really is ill.''

If Roger was guilty and suspected someone knew it, no wonder he looked sick.

Michael knew he'd been asking questions around town about things Roger—if he was guilty—wouldn't particularly want dredged up from the past. Could that fact have gotten back to his ears?

Neither he nor Blair had been the soul of discretion at the club the night before. She'd been foolish enough to mention poisoning, and he'd whisked her off to the dance floor and outside, right under their very noses. Roger might be a lot of things, but a fool wasn't one of them.

"You're going to Tallahassee with me," Michael decided on the spur of the moment. It was the only way he could ensure her safety while he was gone.

"Oh, don't be silly. I'm not in any danger."

"Then let's just say I'll feel safer knowing you're beside me, where I can keep an eye on you."

"But—"

"No buts. When can you be ready to leave?"

Blair glanced down at the list of patients scheduled to make an appearance that day. It was too late to call those who were coming in early that morning; she would have to tell them when they arrived.

No matter how she handled it, it was going to take at least half a day. "I should be through by noon," she answered slowly. "But I still don't think it's necessary—"

"I'll pick you up at your house at twelve-thirty."

The line went dead. He'd rung off without giving her the chance to change his mind. Blair dropped the phone into its cradle, casting a quick glance at Roger's closed door. Maybe Michael was right. Something in Roger's manner *had* put her on edge.

As she worked, part of her mind began to look for a reasonable explanation for his sudden decision to close the office. Except for half a day, he hadn't done that even for his daughter's wedding.

Had he discovered she'd been in his filing closet? She couldn't remember whether or not she'd put Mark Baldwin's file back exactly where she'd found it. She thought she had....

Or had he learned that she'd been making inquiries at the hospital? Would Jan have mentioned it to him in casual conversation? She should have made up some excuse to make certain the other woman wouldn't.

Blair shivered. On reflection, it might be a good idea to get out of town for a day or so. The one thing that worried her was that in the interim, whoever was responsible for what happened to Michael's father might find a way to block them from learning what really happened—and why.

Despite Michael's earlier suspicion of John Saunders because of his father's missing will, Blair wasn't convinced the man had anything to do with all this. Perhaps while they were gone she could convince Michael to talk to the man, maybe even take him into his confidence and tell him about what had taken place on the *Lazy Daze*.

With that thought in mind, Blair made her calls as brief as possible. When she'd finished, she tried to get the address of the emergency room doctor who had treated Michael's father after the poisoning, but the hospital refused to release the information. By the time eleven-thirty rolled around, she had one call left she felt compelled to make.

"Christy? This is Blair Mallory."

"Blair, how are you? Long time no see," her friend said, laughing.

"Actually, I've been out to the home recently, but it was at night, when you were off," she explained. "That's why I called—I want to know how Tom Wallace is doing. I understand he's been under the weather the last few days."

"He has been."

There was something in the other woman's voice that made Blair ask, "What was it—his heart?"

"No-o-o..." Christy hesitated. "He somehow got hold of another patient's medicine and took it."

"But why would he do that? He isn't on medication, is he?"

"No, it's kind of weird, isn't it, after the fuss he made about not taking any? But—" Christy tried to be objective about it, wishing she truly felt that way "—he'd been regressing to the past more each day. Everyone thought he'd given up, that he did it to join Sadie."

"Are you saying you think he took it *deliberately?* That he tried to kill himself?" Blair asked incredulously.

There was a long moment of dead silence. "I . . . can't really say one way or the other." Christy's voice had dropped to little more than a whisper. She continued in a confiding tone, "There was a new nurse on evenings at the time it happened, and not even she can be certain what actually took place. She remembers leaving her medicine tray on the cart while she helped a patient into the bathroom. That's a no-no, but she's young—newly graduated. She's pretty torn up about the whole thing. If Tom dies—well, it won't be good for her career."

"Is it that serious?" Blair asked anxiously. "What did he take?"

"We aren't certain. The medicines on the tray were all mixed up, and the drawer on the cart was open. He could have taken anything." She hesitated, as though she wanted to say more but couldn't, or didn't quite dare. "Lately he's been acting really paranoid. Did you notice that, when you visited?"

"Paranoid?"

"Yes, he had some crazy notion that someone was after his house."

"Can I see him?"

"Sorry," Christy responded with real regret, "I'm afraid not. We transported him to the hospital a little while ago."

"Hospital!"

"Yes, doctor's orders." All at once her voice became louder and more businesslike. "He wasn't responding well to treatment. The doctor wanted him where someone could keep a close eye on him around the clock. He isn't being allowed visitors just yet. Check with the hospital in a day or so."

"R-right, I understand." Obviously someone whom Christy didn't want to overhear her conversation with Blair had entered the nurses' station. "Thanks, Christy. Talk to you later."

Blair rang off and sat staring at nothing, her thoughts in a whirl. Why hadn't Roger mentioned anything to her about what Tom had done? He knew she cared about the old man and visited him on a regular basis.

She straightened her desk, put all the files back into the filing cabinet and prepared to leave. But as she picked up her purse, she knew she couldn't leave without doing one last thing.

Making her way across the silver-gray carpet to Roger's door, she knocked lightly.

"Yes?" He sounded irritable.

Blair opened the door and peeked in. "I'm just leaving. Everyone has been notified that the office will be closed for the next two weeks."

Roger had taken his jacket off and loosened his tie. His always-immaculate hair looked as though he'd been running impatient fingers through it all morning long.

"Fine, fine. Have a good vacation." He waved a hand in her direction. "I'll see you in two weeks."

He returned his attention to the papers on his desk, but, sensing she hadn't withdrawn, he looked up, a slight frown furrowing his brows. "Is there something else?"

"I just spoke to someone at the Golden Sands Nursing Home. I was told Tom is in the hospital."

He looked blank for a moment. "Tom?" His brow cleared. "Oh, Tom Wallace. An unfortunate incident. But I'm confident he'll pull through."

"I wish you'd told me when it happened. I should have been with him when he needed someone."

"I'm sorry. I know you visit him at the home, but I didn't realize you were that close to him."

"I want to visit him in the hospital."

Roger straightened, a sympathetic light entering his crisp blue eyes. "He's in a coma. He wouldn't know you were there."

"Coma! Christy didn't mention that!"

"Don't be too alarmed. It's caused by some medication he apparently ingested."

"When can I see him?" she demanded.

"In a day or two. By then we should have flushed the drug from his system."

Blair stood her ground a moment longer, determined to make him understand how important Tom was to her. "This is Tuesday, so by Thursday I expect it should be all right for me to see him."

Roger met her stare. "Yes, by Thursday he should be able to have visitors."

Blair was ready and waiting for Michael when he arrived shortly after twelve-thirty.

"I didn't know whether to pack an overnight bag or not, so I threw a change of clothing into my purse." She indicated the colorful cloth bag, looking more like a beach bag than a purse, standing beside the door.

"A change of clothes isn't a bad idea. I brought one myself." He indicated the strong wind bending the branches of the magnolia outside her front door, scattering white petals across the yard, and added, "It looks like we're in for a blow."

Blair glanced outside and murmured sadly, "Tom said he smelled a change coming."

Once they were seated in the convertible, with the top up this time, Blair recounted what she'd learned about Tom that morning.

"That's rough," he murmured sympathetically. "I hope he's going to be all right. He was a tough old bird ten years ago, so maybe he'll pull through."

"Michael, do you think Tom could have been ... poisoned?"

"Poisoned?" He threw her a questioning glance. "What makes you ask that?"

"Tom wasn't taking any medication. He told me that the day I visited him. He said something about it making him sicker."

"So?" He eyed her sharply.

"So if he was refusing to take his own medicine, why would he take someone else's? It doesn't make sense." She hesitated, then asked, "Do you think Roger could have given him the medicine ... to keep him quiet?"

"About what?"

"I don't know. Tom said something else that stuck in my mind. He said he talked with your father early that morning, before the two of you left."

"So?"

"I wonder what they talked about."

"Hell..." Michael shook his head. "Tom and Dad were fishing buddies. They could have discussed their next fishing trip—"

"Or something someone is afraid you'll learn from Tom," Blair put in quickly.

"I thought you believed in Roger's innocence?"

She wasn't certain what she believed at the moment. She didn't want to believe Roger could be capable of murder; she didn't want to believe *anyone* she knew was capable of such a horrible crime.

"In any case," Michael continued, "why wouldn't Roger have gotten rid of Tom ten years ago if he thought Tom knew something damning? Why wait until now to do it?"

"I don't know."

"Exactly."

"But I can't believe Tom willingly tried to put an end to his own life. That just isn't like him."

Michael could see that she was really upset about the old man's condition. He covered the hand lying on the seat between them.

"I want nothing more than to see Dad's killer caught. I want it so badly—" his gruff voice roughened, the muscles in his neck and jaw working strongly "—that I eat, sleep and dream it, day after day. We're getting close, Blair." He cast her a quick look, a glimmer of excitement in his dark eyes. "I know it!

"This trip is going to tell us who's behind Unico—or Tritran, or whatever they want to call themselves. I can feel it." He gave the hand he was holding a squeeze. "Maybe that's the key we've been looking for without even knowing it. And then this will all be over, and no one else will be hurt by this man ever again. I'll see to that."

"I hope you're right," Blair murmured feelingly.

Michael loosened his hand and returned it to the steering wheel. "Maybe Tom's problem doesn't have anything to do with this. Didn't you tell me he's in the home because he'd become forgetful? Could he have forgotten he was refusing to take medicine and gotten hold of some belonging to someone else, thinking it was his?''

''I suppose it could have happened that way,'' Blair conceded reluctantly. Before Tom had been placed in the home, he'd been found several times at night wandering the streets, lost and unable to remember where he lived.

It was possible she could be reading something more into Tom's verbal meanderings than really existed.

But what if she wasn't?

Tom could be in grave danger.

As the miles sped by, taking her farther away from the old man, Blair found it hard to relax. Doubt concerning his safety kept her on tenterhooks. Had she left Tom in the hands of a killer, someone who'd killed at least once already and gotten away with it?

There was nothing she could do about it at the moment, and at least Tom was in the hospital. That fact alone should give him a measure of protection.

The drive to Tallahassee took five hours under the best of conditions, but with the weather deteriorating more with each passing mile, it took longer. Nature's violence only served to add to Blair's feeling of disquiet.

It was late in the evening when they entered Tallahassee's city limits. Too late to consider anything more than getting a place to stay for the night.

''Tired?'' Michael asked as they sat at a traffic light waiting for it to change.

''I'm beat. What about you?''

''Same here. I'm glad you had the foresight to bring along a change of clothing. I guess I wasn't thinking very clearly when I talked to you this morning or I would have suggested it, myself.''

The weather had done a lot to drain Blair's agitation. Her head was resting against the back of the seat, but she turned to give him a languid smile. ''I feel like a fish in a plastic bag. If the humidity was any higher, it would be raining inside as well as outside.''

Tiny ringlets of damp hair curled around her forehead and ears, making her look younger than the night Michael had kissed her for the first time. Just for a moment he allowed his thoughts to return to that night, and without realizing it, his eyes filled with a deep tenderness.

An impatient horn honking behind them dragged Michael's thoughts from the past, forcing him to concentrate on the task at hand. But though his attention was given over to getting through the heavy traffic, his body was fully aware of the woman sitting only an arm's length away.

"I guess the best thing for us to do would be to get a room for the night." His words hung suspended in the air between them, rife with innuendo.

Blair's stomach tightened. She felt as though she were waiting for something—some unnamed thing—and her heart beat faster and the palms of both hands turned cold, while the rest of her body remained bathed in perspiration.

Straightening from her pseudo-relaxed position against the seat, she folded her hands on her lap and focused all her concentration on the view through the window at her side. It was impossible not to recall the last time they'd stayed at a motel together.

Michael shot her a series of short, awkward glances and kept right on driving, past several motels with vacancy signs. He couldn't see her face, but all the same he knew what she was thinking—because he was thinking it himself.

His glance fell to her fingers, gripping each other tightly on her lap. His insides felt like that, all twisted together in a tight, hard knot.

The car began to grow smaller, the space between them shrinking, and every breath he took seemed to be filled with a different fragrance, each one sweeter than the last—and each one reminding him of the woman at his side.

Why not? a voice inside his head was asking. *Why not do what you both want? What's the harm? You're both adults. If the past won't allow you to have her for the rest of your life, what's wrong with grabbing what you can right now, tonight? Grab it with both hands, before it's gone forever.*

But would that be fair to Blair? He suspected she still cared for him. Could he take her love so callously and then walk away?

By the time he found a motel, a row of cottages set a few yards apart from each other, he'd made his decision.

Without a word or a glance passing between them, Michael pulled beneath the covered portico outside the motel office and stepped from the car. Rain and wind slapped at him, shoving him toward the double glass doors.

A few minutes later he returned and pulled around to the end cottage. Stopping the car, making no immediate effort to get out, he held up a single key, dangling it in the space between them, waiting for Blair to glance in his direction.

She felt him waiting, and at last her head turned in his direction. Their eyes met over the top of the key attached to the red plastic tag with the number sixteen printed on it in black numerals. Not a word passed between them as they left the car, becoming instantly soaked in the driving rain.

Michael's fingers shook as he unlocked the door; then, standing back, he allowed Blair to precede him inside. He knew that what they were about to do was wrong—for the both of them—but he wanted it.... With every fiber of his being, he wanted *her*.

Blair stood in the center of the room with her back to the door, shivering in her damp clothes. The frigid air from the air conditioner caused gooseflesh to pop up all over her body. Rivulets of water dripped off the ends of her hair and ran down her face and neck.

Dropping her bag to the floor, she waited.

"Here," Michael said from beside her.

She hadn't heard him leave the door. Turning slightly, she looked up at him, her eyes on his face, but his eyes were on her, on her breasts. And suddenly she realized that the dress she was wearing had become soaked clear through, making it evident that she wasn't wearing a bra.

Michael was holding a towel in his hands, but as she reached for it, he began to gently dab at the moisture on her forehead, cheeks and chin. Blair swallowed tightly and closed her eyes.

The towel moved lower, down her neck to her shoulders. Suddenly it stopped, but she didn't dare open her eyes—not yet. Not while she was feeling so...exposed.

"I'm leaving Baywater once the killer has been dealt with."

Blair's eyes fluttered open. "Why?" One word was all she could manage, because she was drowning in his nearness.

"Nothing has changed."

Blair's breath caught in the back of her throat in sudden pain. He was telling her that he didn't love her.

"What about Mark? I thought it was for him that you came back?"

"He'll be all right. He's happy with Elaine and her husband."

"I don't understand. Are you saying you're going to leave him with them permanently?"

Michael turned away. "It's better that way, better for him. He'll have a real family—a father and a mother."

"You're his father! He loves you, you love him! How can you walk away from him just like that?"

"I'm not walking away 'just like that'!" he mimicked, whirling to face her. "Do you think I want to leave my son to grow up without me? I'm doing it for him! Can't you understand that? I'm doing all this—" he swept his arm around the room "—for him."

"Michael, please, you can't—"

Reaching for her, he hauled her up against him. "Shut up," he mouthed against her lips. "At least we have tonight."

For a moment she stiffened in protest, but his mouth opened hungrily over hers as he fused his body with hers, and all thoughts but one flew straight out of her head. He was offering her one night, one night out of the thousands she would have to live without him.

"I'll take it," she murmured, returning his kiss with ardor. "Make love to me, Michael. Make love to me now."

In answer to her words, he tightened one arm around her, renewing his assault on her lips. The other hand glided down over her neck, across her shoulder, and slid smoothly beneath the bodice of her dress, until he was cupping one small, firm breast in his warm palm.

Blair moaned as Michael's lips moved against the skin on her neck, leaving a trail of hot, moist kisses before returning to her mouth. His tongue laved her upper and lower lips, while his thumb and finger kneaded the taut nipple on the breast he held, causing shivers to run down her whole body.

Spreading one hand flat against his trousers, she smoothed her way upward, over rigid muscle to the inside of his thigh. He quivered, and the hand at her waist tightened, drawing her closer.

Both his hands moved around her waist to her spine, then slipped up her back to her shoulders. There his fingers slid beneath the thin straps of her dress, pressing them slowly down her shoulders.

The chill air in the room grew hotter, and the dampness on her skin turned to steam. Michael skimmed the dress from her upper body and down to her waist. There he paused, wrenching his lips from hers to draw back and look at her, devouring her with his eyes.

"You're so beautiful." He caressed her shoulders, his palms making swirling patterns against her smooth flesh. "Whatever else happened in the past, I never forgot you, not for a moment." A bleak look passed over his face.

"Michael?"

He pulled her close, lowering his mouth to hers in desperation. He couldn't seem to get enough of kissing her, touching her. His lips and hands were everywhere at the same time.

Blair thought she might pass out from the thrill of it. He took her like a starving man, storing up food for a bitter winter.

So much had transpired in both their lives to change them. Was he right? Were there too many memories between them, barring them from a future together? The thought terrified her.

And though she knew he would be making love to her out of nothing more than desire, she wanted him. Taking his face in her hands, meeting his eyes, putting into her voice all the love she'd carried around inside her for so long, she whispered, "Make love to me, Michael. Make it good. Make it very, very good." Standing on her toes, she pressed her lips to his.

Michael's hands slid down her slender waist to her hips, drawing her tight against him, intensifying the kiss.

In moments they were both undressed, her arms twined closely around his neck, their mouths fused together in the first of a series of hot, hungry kisses that burned hotter as their passion for each other grew. Michael walked her backward toward the bed, the dizzying power of his kisses and hands making her cling to him for support.

As he lowered her onto the cool sheets, his body covered hers. Blair accepted his weight as though it were a benediction, drawing him even closer, feeling the hair-roughened skin of his chest against her damp breasts.

The hair on his legs created a tickling sensation as they moved against hers. Her hands traveled down his back, exploring every sinew and tendon with eager fingers, smoothing their way toward the solid muscle of his flanks.

Her lips journeyed over his face, kissing every inch of it, feeling the rough prickle of a beard on his cheeks and lower chin, traveling over the scars on his larynx. There they lingered as she pressed a fervent kiss against the damaged flesh, as though the very depth of her kiss might somehow remove remembered pain.

Michael closed his eyes at the touch of her warm lips against the scars, remembering how even his gentle Mary had avoided them while making love. And just for a moment he wondered if this woman beneath him could make him whole again.

But on the heels of that thought came the fear.

What if he lost her, too?

Pushing everything except the moment at hand from his mind, he renewed his loving assault on her body with a fierceness that rendered Blair incapable of thought. She could only feel.... Michael's hands...Michael's lips... Michael's body, filling her with shivers of delight.

She quivered as his hard hands explored the soft lines of her waist, the contours of her hips, the firmness of her thighs, with a tenderness she'd imagined in lovemaking but never truly known. Michael's lips skimmed kisses from her shoulders across her breasts to the gentle hollow of her stomach.

She vibrated beneath his fingers as he drew circles on her flesh, small ones around her navel that grew until she felt all ice one moment and like liquid fire the next.

Eventually she found she couldn't lie still a second longer. Raising herself on her elbows, she gave him a gentle push, rolling him over onto his back. In a moment she'd slid against his side and over onto his chest.

Burying her face in the dark crisp hair, she breathed in the male scent of him, feeling intoxicated by it. She rubbed her cheek against him like a kitten, the short wiry hairs cushioning her skin. And then she relaxed against him, allowing herself the enjoyment of feeling his hands gliding up and down her hips, caressing her thighs, bringing her thrill after thrill from points of pleasure she hadn't known existed.

All at once she became aware of something small and pebble-hard pressing against one cheek. Turning her head, she took his small, tight nipple between her teeth and gave it a gentle nip.

Michael jerked slightly beneath her in surprise, hardly getting his breath back before she began to plant small kisses across his chest, giving him a gentle love nip now and then. She kissed a pathway down the rigid muscles of his chest to the quivering muscles of his stomach.

All at once he grasped her head in both hands and pressed her against him, letting the pure healing power of her love fill him body and soul. And then he was flipping her quickly over onto her back, positioning himself between her legs. With his body covering hers, he bent his head and took her mouth, his tongue darting between her lips at the same instant his body filled hers.

Blair gasped and rose to meet him, her body sheathing him in liquid heat. He moved, and the turbulence of his passion swirled through her, bending her to his will. She gave and he took, and it seemed that in moments it was over. Michael jerked against her and was still.

Blair held him while his heart pounded against her, his hoarse breathing filling her ears. Caught up in a passion that made the world appear slightly out of focus, she told herself it didn't matter that she hadn't made it over the edge, so long as he had. He had already given her more than she'd ever hoped to experience in lovemaking.

Her hands moved over his back soothingly, gliding over the sweat-slickened skin, feeling the hard muscles quiver against solid bone beneath. After a while his breathing became steady and his body relaxed against her.

She thought he'd fallen asleep, but all at once he stirred. His face moved against her, his lips seeking the soft mound of one breast. Her breath caught and held with the return of ecstasy.

This time he moved slowly, carefully, taking her to heights that dreams were made of. This time, it was all for her.

When she tried to return his touch, he gave a slight shake of his head, raised her hands and held them above her head with one of his own.

All at once Blair's head reared back, the muscles of her throat standing out, as the passion he extorted from her took her to the brink of paradise. "Oh—oh—Michael," she moaned. "What are you doing to me?"

His lips moved down the underside of her chin to her neck, his lips sucking gently, his tongue laving a trail of fire to her breasts.

"Is it good?" he asked hoarsely, thrusting firmly against her. "I want it to be good—better than good."

With each word he thrust more deeply into her, until she tore her hands free and clutched at his back, her nails biting into his flesh, needing to hold on to something real, something that would anchor her, because it felt as though she just might rise so high that she would pass right through the ceiling and disappear into the night sky overhead.

Wave after wave of sensation washed through her, spiraling her into a crystal void where she felt everything—color—sound—expression—and then came an explosion of feeling such as she'd never known. The pleasure lasted all too briefly, but the memory of it would last a lifetime.

Gradually she began to return to her surroundings, like a leaf floating gently toward the ground. When it was over, they lay in each other's arms, the cool air in the room floating over their naked bodies.

Michael was too exhausted to think, and fell immediately to sleep. But Blair lay with her eyes open, staring at his sleeping profile, wondering how this man could make love to her with such intensity of feeling only seconds after telling her he planned to walk away from her and never look back.

How could she change his mind?

Chapter 11

Blair glanced up from the television program she'd been half watching as Michael walked through the motel room door.

"Well?" she asked eagerly.

He shook his head and sat on a corner of the bed, dropping his hands between his knees and staring down at them.

"I went to the office of the secretary of state and spoke with his secretary. We looked up the articles of incorporation for Tri-tran." He looked up. "Guess what I discovered?"

"Roger Prescott's name—"

"Along with Marvin Welborn's and John Saunders's."

"John, too?" she asked in disappointment. Marvin's involvement didn't surprise her, and she'd conditioned herself to accept Roger's, but she'd thought surely John Saunders was above reproach.

"All three of my father's good friends—they're all in it together."

Blair wanted to take him in her arms, hold him as she would have held his son if he'd fallen down and hurt himself, but she knew without a doubt that Michael wouldn't have welcomed her compassion.

He'd been up very early that morning, had showered and dressed before she was even awake. And when she had awakened, only moments before he'd left in search of a morning cup of coffee, she'd known instantly, from his aloof manner, that their night together had changed nothing.

On his return he'd kept an invisible barrier raised between them. And later, when he'd invited her to accompany him to the statehouse, the invitation had lacked sincerity.

Knowing all this, she still loved him. Somehow, once they'd proved his father's death hadn't been an accident, and the murderer—or murderers—were brought to justice, she would find a way to change his mind. He needed her in his life, whether he knew it or not, and needed his young son, too.

Blair rose to her feet slowly. First things first. "So let me see if I have this right. Unico is a front for Tri-tran, which is owned and operated by Roger, Marvin and John."

Michael nodded.

"And Unico wanted the land your father owned on the north edge of town." Again Michael nodded. "But for some reason," she continued, "your father appears to have been determined to keep them from getting their hands on it. Why?"

"I don't know." Michael got slowly to his feet and began moving restlessly about the room. "I wish I did. Maybe then some of this would make sense." Stopping by the television, he asked irritably, "Are you watching this?"

"No, go ahead and turn it off." She gave the screen an indifferent glance and looked away, only to find her eyes darting quickly back. "No! Wait! Michael, wait! Turn up the sound."

"My God," Michael murmured an instant later, recognizing the area behind the newswoman on the screen.

"The bulldozers have already begun their work here at Baywater, Florida, a small community located a little less than an hour's drive south of the beautiful city of Saint Augustine.

"We've been talking to one of the men working here to-day, and it appears that the rumors this station has been hearing are true. A new multimillion-dollar quarter-horse race park is on its way to being built on this very spot.

"Though we've been unable to gather much information about the projected date of completion, or those who are behind its construction, it seems that before long, points farther south, like Hialeah and Tampa Bay Downs, may be getting a run for their money." She smiled brightly into the camera. "That's all for today. This is Terry Greene, for Channel Ten in Tallahassee, Florida."

Michael backed away from the set as though it were threatening him, backed until both legs struck something solid. Without bothering to look, he dropped onto the straight-backed chair and sat there without moving, staring at the television screen.

"My God," he repeated an instant later. "So that's what this is all about—horse racing! I should have guessed. Dad was dead set against it being allowed into the county. He fought hard every election to keep it and what he considered the unsavory element associated with it out of Baywa-ter, right up till his death.

"Dad was the real driving force behind keeping it off the ballot, but I always thought Roger and the others were be-hind him. Now it's clear that they were only biding their time until Dad was out of the way so they could build a racetrack right under our noses—on property belonging to my father." He shot a quick look at Blair. "That means the bill has already been passed."

She nodded, offering tentatively, "The bill allowing pari-mutuel betting was passed the first election year after you and your father...disappeared."

"I guess with Dad gone, everyone else just caved in and gave Prescott and his cronies what they secretly wanted all along."

"It's a billion-dollar-a-year business. Money can make people change their way of thinking."

"Not Dad," Michael said sadly. "If he'd been greedy like the others, he'd probably still be alive."

Blair took a step in his direction. "Michael, I'm sorry."

"So am I," he answered slowly.

Blair didn't know what to say to make him feel better, so she said nothing. The low roar of the television finally penetrated her consciousness, and she moved to switch it off.

All at once Michael straightened and sat drumming his fingers on the arm of the chair, staring at the blank television screen.

"They aren't going to get away with this," he murmured as though to himself. "I may not be able to get the pari-mutuel bill off the books, now that it's on, but I'm going to find a way to stop them. I don't know how—"

"If they killed your father, all we have to do is prove that and send them to prison for the rest of their lives."

"Prison is too good for the likes of them," he muttered fiercely, swinging to his feet.

"It's what they deserve."

"Deserve!" He rounded on her, eyes flashing, nostrils flaring. "They deserve what they gave my father! They deserve to die—just as he did—without any kind of a warning. To lie in a cold, watery grave until their bones are picked clean by scavengers!"

Blair shivered at the picture that provoked. "Michael, don't say that." She lifted her hands as though to reach out to him, saw him back off and lowered them to her sides. "Don't let this turn you into one of *them*. Be like your father. Think about your son."

"Leave him out of this. It has nothing to do with him."

"But it does," she insisted. "Isn't that the reason you came back—so he could have his birthright?"

"I came back to make the guilty party pay. I want to see my father's killers squirm and wriggle when they realize the net is closing around them." Raising a hand, he tightened the fingers into a fist. "I want to watch their eyes when they begin to realize they don't have a hope in hell of getting away from me."

The ferocity of his anger frightened her. "It's justice you should be after, not revenge."

"Justice?" He laughed without humor, the fist raised toward her face as he took a menacing step toward her. "Justice?" he repeated, his voice cracking. "Tell me, where's the justice in what happened to Dad? Where's the justice in what happened to my wife?''

Blair wanted to back away from him, but instead she straightened her shoulders and stood her ground. Her fighting spirit was up. She didn't want him in prison—or dead. How could she have a future with him if he was behind bars or lying in a cold grave?

"What is it you plan to do? Get a gun and go back to Baywater and execute all three of them? And how will you know, even then, that you've gotten the man you're after? It isn't against the law to own a company, or to introduce gambling into a county. Neither of those things makes any of those men a murderer. Aren't you setting yourself up as judge, jury and executioner? Who gave you the right to find them guilty and decide their punishment? Is that the legacy you would leave your son? Do you want him to grow up knowing his father was an assassin?''

Michael gritted his teeth, his nails biting into the palms of both hands as he strained to keep them at his sides instead of reaching for her throat. He didn't like the pictures she painted with her harsh words. His son deserved better than to be known as the son of a murderer.

But he also deserved a grandfather who would have taught him things like fishing, how to throw a baseball, how to sail a boat. A man who could have answered with wisdom the many questions a young boy asked.

"Tell me," he responded noncommittally. "You seem to have all the answers, so where do I go from here?''

"I don't know." Blair shook her head, a little of the tension seeping out of her body. "I think we've probably pieced together most of what happened as far as Roger's concerned, anyway. But I don't know where the others fit in, do you?''

Michael loosened his hands and shook his head.

"As I just said, owning a company and introducing legalized gambling aren't illegal. Nor is turning a patient over to another doctor for treatment," she added, referring to Michael's father's treatment after the poisoning.

"But it *is* a crime to murder someone to get his land!" Michael asserted quickly.

"But we don't have one shred of proof that's what happened. We don't even have a lead—"

"Tom!"

Blair's eyes jumped to Michael's face. "What?"

"Tom," he repeated. "Tom Wallace. You're wrong when you say we don't have a lead. Actually, we have two." He held up one hand with the fingers folded down. "We have Tom's conversation with Dad—" he raised one finger "—and the doctor who treated Dad in the hospital after the poisoning." He raised a second finger, looking from them to Blair's face. "Didn't you say the doctor—"

"Simon Farrell," she supplied.

"—left town right around the time of our disappearance?"

Blair nodded.

"Why? Could he have been paid off because of something he knew, something he might have overheard during a conversation between Dad and Roger?"

"Well, I suppose—"

"Tom's in the hospital in Baywater, right?"

Blair nodded again.

"So let's go talk to him and find out what that last conversation was all about."

"He's in a coma," Blair reminded him.

"That's what *Roger* said," he corrected her.

"You're right," she agreed with a new light in her eyes. "He could have lied."

The stormy weather had disappeared during the night, but dark clouds still hid the sun. It looked as though another rain squall was a possibility at any moment.

Michael's assurance that Tom might know something that would shed light on his father's death filled Blair with a renewed sense of urgency to get to Tom as quickly as possible. And by the time daylight had become a dull memory in the western sky, she couldn't keep the worry to herself any longer.

"Michael, if Tom does know something that can help us prove Roger and the others are responsible for what happened to you and your father, then he's in grave physical danger himself."

"I've thought of that. If what we suspect about Roger is true..." He didn't have to finish the thought; they were both thinking the same thing. It might already be too late; Tom might already be dead.

Michael's foot inched down on the accelerator, causing the speedometer to edge up past sixty-five. It was after seven that evening when they drove past the site where the race park would soon be under construction. The bulldozers and earth-moving equipment were silent now, standing against the evening sky like giant monoliths.

"Are we going straight to the hospital?" Blair asked.

"Yes." He hadn't spoken in over an hour.

As they turned onto the street running alongside the hospital, Michael said, "You're known here and associated in people's minds with Prescott. Maybe it would be better for me to go in and ask to see Tom."

"You're probably right. You get out at the emergency entrance—" she indicated the sliding-glass doors "—and I'll go park the car. You can ask for Tom's room number, and I'll meet you inside, by the elevators on the right."

Michael nodded, climbed out of the car and waited until she'd driven away before walking through the automatic doors. After making his way toward the nurse sitting at the desk to his left, he asked for Tom's room number. The young woman found the number and gave it to him, along with a look of interest and the regretful information that Tom wasn't being allowed visitors just yet, under doctor's orders.

Michael turned away and spotted Blair, who was trying to keep her face turned away from the nurses' desk, standing by the elevator doors. A few seconds later an ambulance arrived with two people who'd been in an accident, tying up the nurse's attention.

While her back was turned, Blair grabbed Michael's arm and drew him into the open elevator.

"Where is he?"

"Third floor," Michael answered. "He isn't supposed to have visitors," he added. "Doctor's orders."

Blair punched the appropriate button. "Then we simply won't stop and ask for permission," she replied blithely.

As the soft bell rang and the doors slid open, she peered cautiously out the door before exiting. Visitors were moving in and out of the rooms along the hallway, and she knew they would have no difficulty blending in with the crowd.

Tom's was the only private room located at the end of the hall, next to the nurses' station. Blair took a deep, fortifying breath and stepped through the door with Michael at her side.

Halfway to their destination, the door to the room directly in front of them opened, and two orderlies, pushing an empty gurney between them, moved into the hallway. Blair automatically stopped, Michael bumped into her, and then they both stepped back against the wall.

At that exact moment the door to the room where they were headed swung open, and Roger Prescott, followed closely by a tall, dark-haired nurse, came into view. Blair grabbed hold of Michael's arm and dodged inside the room directly behind them.

Roger and the nurse passed within a few inches of where they stood with their noses pressed against the crack in the door.

"I want the new medication for Wallace ordered from the pharmacy, stat. The first dose is to be given IV. Is that clear?"

"Yes, Doctor," the woman in white replied dutifully.

"And remember—no visitors. His mental and physical well-being are very delicately balanced at the moment, and I don't want him unnecessarily upset."

"Yes, Doctor."

The two passed on by, leaving Blair and Michael to stare at each other in silence. Blair wondered fearfully what new medicine Roger had ordered for Tom. Michael wondered what was causing Blair to look so apprehensive.

"E-excuse me, but are you in the right room?"

Michael turned toward the elderly man standing next to a bed occupied by a frail-looking woman with skin the color of putty. She had tubes running in all directions, hooked up to various machines at the head of her bed. Michael found himself at a loss for something to say.

"Is this room 310?" Blair spoke up immediately.

"No, it's 306," the old man replied.

"Oh, we've gotten the wrong room. Please excuse us." She smiled at the couple, took Michael's arm in a firm grasp and led him through the door. With every step she took, Blair expected to feel a hand grab her shoulder and hear Roger's deep voice demanding to know where she thought she was going.

"They're all the same," Michael murmured at her side. "Hospitals," he offered by way of an explanation. "They all look and smell the same. The smell is the worst. You can't get it out of your nose, it stays on your skin." His jaw clamped down tight. "I hated it when I was a patient—and I still do."

Blair wanted to ask how he'd managed to stand it, with his wife working in one all those years, but it seemed like too personal a subject to broach in their present predicament.

Once they were safely inside Tom's room, she leaned against the door to catch her breath, and threw the quiet man at her side a questioning glance. His attention was directed toward the center of the room. Blair followed his glance.

Tom Wallace lay silent and unmoving, a narrow mound shrouded beneath white sheets. The side rails on the hospital bed had been raised, and for an instant they reminded Blair of the bars of a jail cell.

An IV bag hung on a stand affixed to one corner of the bed, and a long clear tube stretched from it, feeding a solution into the old man's thin arm. Another tube made of transparent green plastic fed oxygen through a nasal cannula strapped around his head and positioned beneath his nose.

"He's so thin. He looks dead," Michael whispered hoarsely.

"He isn't dead, only sleeping."

They moved closer to the bed. The blinds had been pulled, and the room lay in darkness except for the long, narrow fluorescent light on the wall above the head of the bed.

Blair moved around the end of the bed toward the IV bag and glanced up at the drip.

"What is it?" Michael asked hoarsely. "What are they giving him?"

"Normal saline," she answered in a distracted voice.

The tubing had been set up so another bottle could be piggybacked, added to what he was already getting, through the same IV tubing by the insertion of a needle. She checked to see what medication, if any, had been added to the clear solution in the bag. None had been charted, so perhaps they were in time after all.

Blair pushed a hand through the side rail and touched the cold fingers lying so still on the sheet.

"Tom. Tom, can you hear me?" Closing her own warm fingers around his icy ones, she gave them a light squeeze. "Tom, it's Blair. Can you hear me? If you can, squeeze my hand."

Michael watched silently, listening to Blair's soft yet insistent words. She murmured continually to the old man, talking about things in the past, including Sadie and his job at the marina. Every now and then she would ask him to squeeze her hand if he heard and understood what she was saying.

Michael's glance became riveted on the arthritic fingers lying in Blair's hand, and with everything that was in him, he willed those fingers to move.

"That's it, Tom, that's it!"

Michael's gaze flew to Blair's and found her face filled with suppressed excitement. What had he missed? He glanced back to the old man's hand. Had the gnarled fingers moved just a fraction?

Yes! Tom's fingers quivered ever so slightly and began to move within Blair's light grasp.

"That's it, Tom," she encouraged. "Now, open your eyes. Concentrate, Tom, concentrate on opening your eyes."

Again Michael found his own glance joining hers in studying Tom's face, his will straining to help the old man obey what Blair's gentle voice commanded of him. After a few moments of mounting tension the paper-thin eyelids began to flutter and rise.

Blair leaned over the bed rail and pressed her other hand against the withered cheek, turning his face toward her.

"Hi." She smiled down at him. "It's me, Blair. How are you?"

"Tired . . . very tired," he answered slowly.

"What's been happening to you? What happened at the nursing home? Can you tell me?"

Tom closed his eyes and gave his head a slight shake, then opened his mouth and licked dry, cracked lips. Knowing how dry oxygen could make a person's mouth, Blair anticipated his need for moisture. Turning to the bedside table, she opened a package containing lemon-glycerine swabs and moistened his lips with one.

"Thank . . . you," he croaked.

"Would you like a drink of water?"

He shook his head.

"Tom, did you try to hurt yourself?"

His eyes opened wide, and he began to shake his head back and forth on the pillow. The hand lying in hers tightened spasmodically.

"Didn't . . ." He licked his lips. "Didn't . . ." He seemed to be struggling for the words.

"You didn't try to hurt yourself?" she helped him out. "You didn't take anything—any medicine—at the home?"

"No," he answered. "Sh-shot..." He tried to lift his free hand and reach toward his other arm.

"Are you saying someone gave you a shot?" she asked.

"Y-yes. Sh-shot." He struggled to nod and closed his eyes.

"Michael!" Blair whispered, darting a compelling glance across the bed. "We have to get him out of here. I think they've been keeping him drugged."

She glanced down at the old man's closed eyes and back at Michael. "That isn't good for his heart," she mouthed.

"Can he walk?" Michael asked.

"No."

Michael looked at the pale, lined face of the old man. "Are you certain we should move him? What if he...?" His eyes finished the question.

"Dies?" she asked without sound. Loosening Tom's hold on her hand, she motioned for Michael to follow her to the other side of the room.

"If we leave him here," she told him softly, "there's no question about what will happen to him."

"So it's Roger," Michael commented in a hard voice, his eyes on the still figure in the narrow hospital bed. "He's the one capable of murder."

"It looks that way, and he can't afford to let Tom live. It's only a matter of time before he . . . disposes of him."

A sound from the bed sent Blair scurrying to the old man's side. Tom reached toward her with quivering fingers. "Don't . . . leave me. Please," he begged. He tried to sit up on his own but fell back after only a few seconds' effort.

"Have . . . to . . . tell . . ." he panted, struggling with the words. "Have . . . to . . . tell . . ."

"It's all right, Tom, it's all right." Blair pressed him back against the pillows. "You can tell us later, when we've gotten you out of here safely."

"How do we do that?" Michael asked from close beside her.

"The only way is in a wheelchair. If we use a gurney someone will ask questions, because we aren't in hospital garb. I don't know what Roger has in mind to give him, but whatever it is, he's planning to start it right away, and that doesn't sound good to me."

"Tell me what to do," Michael said.

"See if you can find an unoccupied wheelchair somewhere on the floor, but keep away from the nurses' station and out of Roger's sight. I'll get Tom ready to leave."

Michael nodded and left.

Blair discontinued the IV, checked for any unusual bleeding, then placed a small strip of bandage over the mark from the needle. Next she removed the oxygen, pausing to check for signs of cyanosis in Tom's lips and any difficulty in breathing. Once she was satisfied that at the moment, at least, he appeared to be all right on his own, she went to the closet to look for his clothes.

When she didn't find any, she asked Tom a few questions and realized he'd been transported in his pajamas. She found them in the nightstand and helped him put them on.

By the time Michael returned with a wheelchair, she had Tom sitting up on the side of the bed. Much to Michael's surprise, the old man appeared to be gaining strength with every passing second, and Michael began to believe they just might get away with this after all.

"Did you have any difficulty locating one?" Blair asked Michael, referring to the wheelchair.

"No, I found it sitting down the hall outside one of the rooms."

Blair examined it and discovered it belonged to the X-ray department. That meant someone was going to be looking for it before very long.

"Is something wrong?" Michael asked, watching her face.

"Not if we can get out of here fast enough," she replied.

They transferred Tom to the chair and wrapped a blanket around him, hiding the words across the back of the chair. A few moments later they left the room, walking quickly yet sedately down the hall.

Getting out of the hospital didn't look as if it was going to present a problem. Blair didn't see anyone she recognized who might remember her. All went well until they were standing outside the emergency-room door, waiting for Michael to bring the car around.

When they had passed by the desk where Michael had asked for information, it had been unoccupied, much to her relief. Now, as she glanced back over her shoulder through the glass doors, she saw the young nurse exit a treatment room across the hall from the desk. As she did so, the woman looked directly at Blair, then down at the man sitting in the wheelchair.

The nurse frowned, and Blair's pulse skipped a beat. Her alarm grew when the woman changed directions, moving toward them.

"Come on, Michael," Blair muttered anxiously, taking hold of the wheelchair and pushing it across the walk, toward the driveway.

At that moment a white convertible turned onto the circular drive and rushed toward them. In moments they had made their getaway, but Blair didn't breathe normally until they were a mile from the hospital with Tom lying stretched out safely on the back seat.

Now the question of where to take Tom arose. The best they could come up with was Blair's house. There were no other houses on her street, except for Michael's, and no one was living there.

They considered the motel, but Michael's room had been searched once already, and besides, Michael wasn't equipped to take care of the old man in the same way Blair could. And if Blair stayed at the motel, her presence would raise more than a few eyebrows.

It might become necessary to move him later, but for the time being Blair's house was the best answer to their problem.

Blair kept a close watch on Tom as he dozed on the back seat. He was showing the classical symptoms of having been under heavy sedation. Blair knew the best thing to do was simply let him sleep it off.

When they arrived at her house, once Blair had made certain the coast was clear, Michael carried the old man inside, marveling silently at how light he was. Blair had him put Tom in the guest bedroom beside her own, and then he left her to make the old man comfortable.

Michael was making coffee in the kitchen when she joined him half an hour later. His hair hung damply across his forehead, and his shirt was open down the front.

"I hope you don't mind that I took the opportunity to have a quick shower in the upstairs bathroom," he said, catching her eyes on his chest and beginning to fasten the buttons.

"N-no, of course I don't." She cast her eyes around the familiar kitchen, searching for something on which to focus her attention, something less tantalizing than the tight black curls covering his naked chest.

"What happens, Michael, when this is all over?"

"It is over," he answered simply.

"What about us?" she asked in a voice so low he had to strain to catch her words.

The odor of fresh coffee filled the air. In his mind Michael saw another kitchen, heard another voice asking questions he couldn't answer. Mary had known about Blair from the beginning of their relationship, but she'd hoped his feelings would change after their marriage. When that hadn't happened, she'd confronted him about it. And now, as in the past, he stood silently beneath a woman's searching glance, feeling trapped.

What Blair wanted from him he couldn't give her—he dared not give her. Needing to get out of the room all at once, he pushed past her, moving toward the back door. Outside, he took a deep breath of salt air and gazed up at the diamond-studded sky with desperate eyes.

"Michael!" Blair called softly, stepping up to the screen door. "You can't run away forever."

He whirled to face her; the taut lines of his face were almost hidden in the dark, but his eyes glittered at her. "I can't give you want you want. I'm sorry. I don't want to...hurt you anymore."

"You think you aren't hurting me now?"

"I don't want to. I warned you." Shaking his head, he stalked toward the beach.

Blair watched him go, wishing there was something she could say that would make him realize how much she loved him. She couldn't understand why he fought so hard against loving her. She sensed fear in him, but she didn't understand what lay at the root of it.

Did he think he could live the rest of his life without love? Or was it only with her that he was unwilling to make a commitment?

A little after nine she heard him come back inside. She was looking in on Tom. The old man was resting quietly, and in all likelihood would sleep the entire night away.

Leaving his door partially open, Blair crossed the hall to the door of her own room and reached for the handle just as Michael stepped into view at the end of the hall. She couldn't face him again that night. Twisting the knob, she hurried into her room and closed the door.

"Blair?" Michael rapped lightly on the wood panel.

"Y-yes?" she answered after a slight hesitation. With her hands pressed flat against the door's smooth wooden surface, she could almost feel him on the other side.

"I just wanted to let you know the place is secure," he answered in a gravelly voice, his own body pressed yearningly against the wooden panel. "I don't plan to sleep much tonight. I'll be keeping an eye out in case we have any unexpected visitors. By now I'm sure Prescott must be looking for Tom, and I doubt it will take him long to put two and two together and figure out we had something to do with his disappearance. But don't worry, I'm ready for him. Just go to bed and get some rest."

She felt him move away. Grasping the door handle hastily, she threw the door back. "Michael!"

"Yes?" He halted and looked back over his shoulder.

"Be...careful," she whispered, swallowing back what she really wanted to say.

He nodded, and she closed the door.

Chapter 12

"Blair?" Michael rapped softly against the door. "Blair—are you awake?"

Blair stirred on the bed and slowly opened her eyes. Lifting a hand, she pushed the hair back from her forehead and stretched. She hadn't thought she would be able to sleep after everything that had happened last night, but apparently she had. Her eyes were drawn toward the light coming in around the edges of the curtains, and she realized it must be morning.

"Blair?" Michael rapped more insistently against the wood. "Are you awake in there?"

"Y-yes," she answered, realizing what had awakened her. Throwing back the sheet, she dropped her feet over the edge of the bed and stood. "I'm coming, Michael, just a moment."

She lifted her flowered housecoat from the chair beside the bed and pushed her arms into the sleeves, tying the yellow sash securely at her waist as she hurried toward the door.

"What is it? Tom?" she asked in alarm.

"He's all right, but he's awake and wanting to talk. I thought I'd better come get you. At the moment he thinks he's been kidnapped—and he isn't very pleased about it," he added drolly.

Blair followed Michael as he turned toward the room beside hers. As they drew near, she heard angry muttering coming from inside.

"They won't get away with it—by damn, they won't! This time I'm gonna see to it myself."

Tom broke off in mid-rant as he looked up and spotted Blair in the doorway, with Michael standing slightly behind her. "They got you, too, huh? Let me outta this bed."

He pulled at the blanket and pushed at the sheet in an attempt to free himself, but only bound himself tighter to the bed. The more he pulled, the more agitated he became.

"Tom," Blair said as she came fully into the room and moved to assist him, "it's all right. You haven't been kidnapped." She hesitated, throwing Michael a slightly wry glance. "Well, actually, I guess you have been."

Tom screwed up his face and gave her a penetrating glare. "Well, girlie, which is it? Have I been snatched or not?"

"We—" she gestured from herself to Michael "—are the ones who took you from the hospital. Don't you remember last night?"

Tom shook his head.

"What about this house? It belonged to my parents and now it's mine."

Tom looked around the room, then glanced from her face to the man standing beside her. His eyes narrowed on Michael. "You got a familiar look about you, boy. I know you."

"It's Michael, Tom," Blair informed him, feeling the man at her side stiffen. "Michael Baldwin."

"Well, hell, yes. How's yer dad?"

"Dead," Michael answered shortly, staring into the old man's faded blue eyes.

Tom's eyes widened for an instant before he collapsed slowly back against the pillows, his expression morose. One withered hand felt for the sheet and pulled it up beneath his chin in a protective gesture.

"That's right," he whispered, "I remember now. They got him...."

Blair touched Michael's shoulder warningly as she sensed him preparing to speak. He glanced at her, and with a slight shake of her head she signaled him to remain quiet. Dropping onto the edge of the bed beside Tom, Blair covered the withered hand clutching the sheet to his chest.

"Michael's father was killed in an explosion at sea, Tom. It happened ten years ago. Michael was injured very badly in the accident and had to be hospitalized for a very long time."

Tom's eyes became focused on Michael. "Sorry about yer dad, son. He was a good man."

Again Blair felt Michael tensing to speak, and she touched the leg of his trousers to stop him. Tom's memory was unstable at the best of times, and she didn't want to push him too far. The shock of being reminded about Michael's father was one thing, but Michael was still a stranger, and his sudden intrusion into the conversation could throw the old man into a state of confusion. Tom was comfortable with Blair, used to talking to her and having her ask questions.

"Tom?" She waited for him to look at her before continuing. "Do you remember the night before Michael and his father left on that last fishing trip?"

"Sure I do," he answered after a momentary pause. "Just like it was yesterday. I saw you two kids at the marina that night."

"That's right." Blair smiled encouragingly. "It was a beautiful night, wasn't it?"

Taking his hand from the edge of the sheet, where he'd begun picking at the material, she placed it at his waist, lifted his other hand and placed it on top of the first, then covered them both with her own.

"It was late when you saw us, only a few hours before dawn." Squeezing the trembling hands gently between hers, she held his gaze and asked, "Do you remember talking with Michael's father?"

The hands beneath hers grew suddenly still, and Tom's glance wavered from hers.

"Tom? What is it?"

The old man shook his head and stared across the room at nothing, refusing to answer.

"You can tell us," she assured him steadily. "This is Mark's son—remember? He needs to know everything you can tell him about what happened that night, what his father might have said."

After a moment the obstinate expression on the wrinkled face began to crumble, and Tom's chin started to wobble pathetically. "It's my fault," he whispered brokenly. "I shoulda done somethin'...."

The tension in the room, concentrated mostly around Michael's taut figure, made the air feel alive with static. Blair was afraid that Michael might explode and frighten the old man into forgetting anything he might be able to tell them.

"It isn't your fault, Tom," Blair reassured him, patting his hands, giving the man at her side a cautioning glance. "No one here blames you for anything. We just want to know what happened, anything you know about Mark and his...problems."

"I saw Mark that mornin' when he came down to the boat," Tom said. "I waited for him, 'cause I wanted to know if he'd heard anything from Jake."

"Jake?" Michael asked abruptly, drawing the old man's faded blue eyes.

Tom paused, giving Michael's face a thorough going-over. After a moment he looked back at Blair and explained, "Jake Redmond is a friend of mine. Mark came to me askin' if I knew anybody he could trust to do a little investigating for him. He said he needed someone who could work fast and keep his mouth shut. I told him to go see Jake 'cause we used to work together before he quit the force to go private and I retired."

"You mean Jake is a private investigator?" Blair asked before Michael could.

"That's right...." Tom's voice drifted off, his gaze turning inward, seeing things no one else could see.

Blair was on the brink of reminding him that they were still there when he gave a little shake of his head and said, "Leastways, he *was*," he added sadly. "Ain't nobody seen ol' Jake since before Mark left."

Blair felt her insides coil tightly in anticipation. "How long before, Tom? Can you be more specific?"

"I don't know, mebbe a month or two. Mark said he'd sent Jake to the state capital to get some information for him, and I guess he got what Mark wanted." He shrugged.

"A few days later—in the middle of the night—Jake called Mark and told him he'd learned something else, something that was gonna knock Mark's socks off. He was on the other side of town—said he'd be right over. Only he never made it. When he didn't show up, and nobody seemed to know where he'd gotten off to, after a day or so, Mark had me notify some of my friends on the force." He shook his head, sighing. "They couldn't find nothin'. Jake just up and disappeared, and ain't no one seen him to this day far's I know."

"Didn't they investigate his disappearance?" Blair asked.

"Sure they did, but they didn't find anything. After a while, it got buried beneath more pressing cases," Tom replied.

"Take it easy," Blair said, pushing him gently back against the pillows. "Take your time, okay?" He was getting agitated, and that worried her.

"I'm okay," he whispered after a moment.

"What did Mark do after that?" Blair asked.

"I don't rightly know. When nobody could find hide ner hair of Jake, I got worried about Mark. I told him to be mighty careful. I told him he ought to get somethin' down on paper, somethin' he could use as protection, somethin' to keep the wolves at bay."

Tom shook his grizzled head. "I knew if those fellas Mark was after could get the drop on Jake—well, I didn't figure Mark, bein' what he was, had much chance against 'em. Jake was trained to watch his backside—Mark wasn't."

"Do you think Mark took your advice?" Blair asked. "Do you think he made certain he had some kind of protection?"

"Well..." A secretive expression narrowed Tom's eyes. "That mornin', before he left, I asked if he'd heard anythin' yet from Jake. And when he said no, I warned him again. But he told me not to worry, said he'd taken care of it, said once he got back from his fishin' trip he'd be free to do what he had to do."

"Did he say what the fishing trip had to do with it?" Blair asked carefully.

"Naw." Tom shook his head. "But he mentioned some kinda book, said it was all down in the book." The light began to fade from Tom's eyes, and he began to pick at the sheet again.

"It's my fault..." he muttered staring at nothing. "I was afraid...for Sadie...for myself.... You see—" he met Blair's eyes "—I was all she had...." His eyes pleaded with her. "You understand that, don't you?" But before she could answer, his glance had shifted somewhere else in time. "If only I'd been able to give her what she wanted...babies...."

"Ask him *who!*" Michael muttered fiercely to Blair. "Ask him who Dad was after, and if he knows what he did with the book."

"I don't think—"

"Do it!"

"Tom...Tom..." She captured his fingers and stopped their nervous twitching. "Do you know who Mark wanted Jake to investigate? Or what he found?"

"W-who?" the old man repeated vaguely.

"Yes, who? Did Mark ever mention the name of the person he was having investigated? Or what he was looking for?"

"No." He shook his head. "No, he never said."

Blair glanced up at Michael's grim face and murmured, "I'm sorry."

"But I got my suspicions."

Michael and Blair turned as one toward the old man.

"I seen what's been goin' on right beneath my nose. I ain't stupid." He glanced slyly at the two faces watching him. "I wasn't a cop thirty years fer nothin'."

"And just what did you figure out?" Michael asked harshly.

"I seen my friends take to their beds one by one after a visit from *him*—that's what I seen. One minute they was happy, walkin' and talkin' and actin' fine, then *he* shows up and has 'em sign some papers, and the next I know, the doc gives 'em some medicine and they ain't gettin' outta bed no more."

He looked from Blair to Michael. "Then they're leavin' the place—*in a body bag!*"

"What was he after, this man you're talking about?" Michael asked.

"After? He wanted what belonged to them, their land, their homes, to build shopping centers and them condo-watchamathings. He wants mine, too, but I'm too smart for him. I won't take the medicine. And they can't fool me into takin' it, neither." His mouth twisted into a smirk as he looked from one to the other. "I'm too smart for all of 'em."

"Who is it that brings the papers for your friends to sign?" Blair asked.

"You know him. He's the one always tryin' to get me to sign them papers givin' him power of attorney. Hah! I ain't givin' him nothin' but the rough edge of my tongue."

"Do you mean John Saunders, the lawyer?" Michael asked coldly.

"Yeah." Tom heaved a sigh, sagged back against the pillows, out of breath, and closed his eyes. "He's the one." All of a sudden he reared up and gave Blair a conspiratorial wink. "Don't worry, girlie, I didn't tell 'em nothin'. They can ask all the damned questions they want, and I won't tell 'em what we talked 'bout the other day."

"Did someone ask you about our conversation?" Blair asked quickly.

"They asked, an' I told 'em I was on to 'em, but I didn't mention you." He yawned, and his eyes drifted shut. "Don't get me up for breakfast..." he muttered in a querulous tone of voice. "I don't care what that nurse says. I'm old. I need my rest." A moment later he was snoring softly.

Blair straightened his covers, motioned for Michael to follow her and left the room. In the kitchen she took glasses from the cabinet and poured them both orange juice. Leaning back against the counter near the sink, she drank hers, giving Michael a thoughtful stare.

"Well, it's a little disjointed, but what do you think about Tom's story?" she asked finally.

"I think the same thing I thought before I heard what he had to say. Prescott, Welborn and Saunders murdered my father for the land to build their racetrack. And it looks as though Dad wasn't the last, if Tom's to be believed."

"Do you think they went after your father because he discovered what they were up to and confronted Roger or one of the others with what he knew?"

"Maybe," Michael answered thoughtfully.

"If we could only talk to Jake Redmond—"

"You can forget that," he interrupted, placing his empty glass in the sink beside her. "He's dead."

"Do you think so? Maybe they just . . ." She hesitated.

"Paid him off?"

She nodded.

"I doubt it. If Tom recommended the guy to Dad, I doubt he would have been open to accepting a bribe."

"I suppose you're right." She sighed heavily and set her own glass in the sink beside his. "How do we prove any of this? I seriously doubt the courts would judge Tom capable of giving testimony."

"I don't know." Michael pushed a weary hand through his dark hair and paced around the room like a caged tiger.

"I could try and get the address for Simon Farrell," she suggested. "The doctor who treated your father in the hospital."

Michael stopped his pacing to face her and demand, "And do what? Ask him if he left town ten years ago because Roger Prescott paid him to keep his mouth shut about whatever it is he knows? Do you think he's going to admit anything to you? And what if you can't find him at whatever address the hospital has on file? Are you going to hire a private detective to look for him?

"We don't have much time, Blair. I'm sure the authorities must be looking for Tom. And I'm damned certain Prescott is. After my sudden appearance in town and your less-than-subtle comments at the club the other night, they'll have figured out by now that we know something—something we shouldn't. How long do you think it will take them to come after us? And I certainly hope you realize it's murder they have on their minds, not some kind of payoff," he added harshly.

"But they can't just kill everyone," she insisted. "Someone has to know what they're doing. Someone has to at least be suspicious. Yes, that's it! My friend, Christy, at the nursing home," she explained. "She certainly wouldn't be a party to murder. The other day, when she told me about Tom, there was something in her voice."

Michael made an abrupt move in her direction, startling her into silence. He placed his hands flat against the counter on either side of her, crowding her back against it by leaning over her, and demanded, "Are you trying to get your friend killed?"

Blair shrank away from him, staring into his burning eyes, and shook her head.

"This isn't a game, damn it! These men mean business—and their business is death. And our time is running out. Whatever move we make, it has to be now.

"No." He straightened and moved away from her, shaking his head. "I take that back. Whatever move *I* make has to be now. You and Tom are leaving Baywater as soon as it gets dark."

"No!" Blair pushed her way past him and marched across the room. With a false sense of security created by the space between them she turned and defied him. "I'm not going anywhere. I'm staying right here—whether you like it or not."

"No you are not!" he grated.

"You can't make me go!" She stood her ground, glaring at him despite the fact he was advancing toward her menacingly. "This is *my* town." She pointed a finger at him. "You abandoned it, abandoned all of us, ten years ago."

Michael flinched at that, but she hardened her heart against him and continued inflexibly. "I know they killed your father, and you want them to pay for that, but I want them to pay, too. They're trying to destroy this town and the people in it, and I'm going to stop them."

Michael stopped just short of her, fists clenched at his sides, but his voice was dead calm when he asked, "How?"

"How?" she asked uncertainly. He nodded. "I—" She searched around in her mind for a plan and came up blank. "I don't know...yet! But I'll think of something."

"They'll kill you," he told her flatly, terrifying her with the certainty of it. And though outwardly he appeared calm and in complete control, inside, his emotions were in pandemonium.

He was doing it again. He'd brought Blair to the brink of disaster, just as he had his father and his wife. He had to make her see reason, had to get her out of this alive.

"Have you any idea what we've stumbled into?" He wanted to grab her and shake some sense into her. "This scheme isn't something your employer and his friends just came up with over drinks the other evening. This is something Prescott and the others have been perfecting over a period of years.

"Dad probably found out about it, because he did business with them at the bank, or maybe they wanted to add him to their elite little clan and he refused. And look what *that* got him!"

"God—it's so horrible!" The words burst from Blair's lips. She shivered convulsively and hugged herself tightly. This last week had been like living in a snow globe, the kind you turned upside down and shook to get the snow to fall.

Her world had been turned upside down, starting with Michael's letter. And now friends weren't friends any longer, and the people she thought she knew, had known all her life, appeared to wear two faces, one of kindness and the other evil.

"How can they do it, Michael?" She looked at him for an answer. "How can they calmly set about disposing of their friends—your father, those old people at the nursing home—and for what? *Greed*." She spit the word out angrily.

Michael rubbed a hand behind his neck and shook his head, tearing his eyes from her anguished expression. He didn't have an answer for her. And he couldn't stand calmly by and watch the horror growing in her eyes without touching her—and touching her would be his downfall.

"Don't worry." The words were dragged from him by a need too powerful to resist. "I won't let anything happen to you—I promise you that."

Blair's lower lip began to tremble; she bit down hard to steady it and looked away. Now was not the time to fall apart. She'd just made a grand speech about how she was going to stop three killers; falling to pieces on the tail end of it was definitely not the first step toward that goal.

"If it makes you feel any better," Michael whispered, "I'm finding all this a little hard to deal with myself. I never imagined this much evil living right here in Baywater."

Blair compressed her lips and nodded, focusing her eyes on the wall across the room, seeing the cross-stitch sampler her mother had sewn when she was little more than a child. *Please, God,* she prayed silently, wishing both her parents were still alive, *bless this house, and bless this town, as well.*

Michael closed the distance between them, cupping the cheek nearest him in rough fingers, turning her face gently up to his.

"It's tough living in the grown-up world, isn't it?" he whispered huskily, as though reading her thoughts.

Their glances collided—and fused. She felt the hand at her cheek slide around to the back of her neck and saw his head descend in a blur.

Michael's mouth molded to hers. He clasped her tightly to him, heart kicking against his ribs, and then the phone rang abruptly, causing them to spring apart.

Blair hurried to answer it, murmuring breathlessly into the mouthpiece, "H hello?"

"Blair?"

"Yes?" she answered cautiously, not immediately recognizing the voice at the other end.

"This is Jan Vincent, at the hospital."

"Oh, Jan." She smiled in relief. "How are you?"

"Fine, sweetie, just fine. I know it's awfully early, but I called because I thought I ought to warn you—your boss is on a rampage. It seems one of his patients disappeared from the hospital last night right out from under his nose. The word is out that you were seen on the premises about the time he came up missing—wheeling a man out of the hospital in a wheelchair.

"Now, I don't know what this is all about, or if it has anything to do with you, but I thought you'd like to know."

"Thanks, Jan, I appreciate it." Blair's eyes met Michael's. "Tell me," she spoke quickly before the other woman could hang up, "has Roger heard the rumor about my being there?"

"Oh, yes, he heard it all right," her friend confirmed. "He was signing some patient records in my office when two women from accounting passed by the open door, discussing it."

"What did he say?"

"Say? Not much, but the look on his face . . ."

"I get the picture. Thanks for calling."

"No problem."

"Bye."

"Bye-bye, sweetie."

"So Roger knows we have Tom," Michael stated softly as she turned to replace the receiver. "If we just had some proof!" He slammed the wall in despair.

Blair nodded her agreement. "Why couldn't your father have mailed the information—or whatever it was he had—to himself, or left it with a friend."

"All his friends wanted to kill him."

"Wait a minute!" Blair's eyes widened with excitement as she whipped around to face him. "What are we thinking? Tom said your father kept everything in a book. What book?"

Michael shrugged. He thought about it a moment, then shrugged again. "I don't know. Besides, the way Tom's mind wanders, that could mean anything."

"But what if Tom's right? Did your father ever write things down? Some people keep diaries—"

"No." He started to shake his head, stiffening all at once. "Journal," he muttered. "Dad used to keep a journal when I was a kid. But he stopped doing it just before Mother became really ill—it irritated her. By then her mind had become affected by the alcohol," he explained, "and she was a little paranoid. She kept insisting Dad was writing things down about her, lies, to tell the doctor.''

"I'm sorry, Michael.'' She remembered his mother as a beautiful, vivacious woman who lived on her nerves. Before she began to drink heavily, she'd loved attention and thrived on always being at the center of it.

"It was a long time ago,'' Michael said, rejecting her sympathy.

"Do you think your father could have started keeping the journal again?'' she asked, swallowing back her hurt.

"It's possible, but that's an awfully long shot.''

"I don't think so,'' she disagreed. "Besides, it's all we've got to go on.''

"That's for sure.''

"Do you think Roger and the others suspect there's proof against them?''

"That's a good question. It would explain why they wanted to get rid of Tom so badly.''

"Couldn't that simply be because they want his property?''

"Have you forgotten, Tom said Prescott questioned him about you?''

"But he didn't tell him anything—'' She broke off seeing Michael's look of skepticism. "All right, he could have.''

Michael seated himself at the kitchen table, wondering where his father would have kept a journal. "Where would you keep something like that?'' he asked Blair, "if you didn't want someone to find it?''

"His study?'' Blair suggested, joining him at the table. "The safe? In the vault at the bank? What about another safe-deposit box?''

They were all excellent guesses, and Michael knew any one of them could be correct. But if that was so, then Prescott or one of the others would already be in possession of the journal, because Saunders, as his father's lawyer and executor of his estate, had access to all of those places.

Michael slammed his fist against the table in frustration, clutched his head between both hands and muttered, "Think, damn it—think!''

Blair stared at the top of his dark head, wishing she could say or do something to help him. If only she could find the journal and make him a gift of it.

Knowing his father's killers had been brought to justice would mean everything to him. It would put an end to his ten-year-old nightmare—and he would no doubt feel indebted to her. . . .

What was she thinking? Did she want this man so badly she would be willing to take him under those circumstances?

No way!

But Michael wasn't just any man...and she loved him so very much.

Chapter 13

Blair looked in on Tom and found him sleeping deeply. It looked as though it was going to take longer for his system to rid itself of the drug Roger had given him than she'd first thought.

She paced into the living room and over to the window where she could see the house next door. It was storming again. Torrential rain blew against the window, obscuring her view.

Clasping her hands around her elbows, she stared through the rain at the house next door, wondering where Michael could be. He'd been gone for over three hours now, and she was becoming anxious.

He'd said he was only going across town to park his car in a spot where no one would recognize it. Her own car was sitting in the locked garage. There weren't any windows to peer into, so Michael had seemed satisfied with its location—for now.

But Blair had a feeling the real reason behind Michael's satisfaction at leaving her car on the premises had more to do with his idea of getting her and Tom out of Baywater that night. And though she planned to put up a fuss beforehand, she admitted to herself she would eventually have to give in—if for no other reason than Tom's safety.

All at once the silence was shattered by the ringing of the telephone beside her. She gave a muffled scream and whirled to face it.

This was the fourth time in less than an hour it had rung. She knew it wasn't Michael, because he'd said he would ring on a prearranged signal. He'd also told her not to answer the phone unless she knew it was him.

But what if it was one of her friends calling to warn her—as Jan had done earlier that morning? Maybe she should answer it. . . . No, Michael had said not to.

She found herself unconsciously counting the rings. Fourteen—it had rung fourteen times this time, two more rings than the time before, and four more than the time before that. Someone badly wanted to get through to her.

She considered unplugging it, but she knew she couldn't in case Michael tried to reach her. The muscles in her face and neck ached intolerably; she realized it was because she was clenching her jaws and forced herself to relax.

Where was Michael? She rubbed her hands up and down her arms and found her glance becoming fixed on the pale silver tiles of the roof of the house next door.

What were she and Michael going to do? Their lives were in danger, yet they couldn't go to the police—because they had no proof of everything they suspected. And Michael's story about what had taken place on the boat was over ten years old. The police weren't even likely to believe him. Despite Tom's reputation with the police force, his age and increasing senility would almost certainly render any testimony he gave worthless.

They needed proof! But Michael didn't put much stock in their ever finding any. After talking to Tom, they'd discussed at length the possibility of Michael's father having kept a journal. Michael was of the opinion that if one had existed, his father had probably taken it with him on the *Lazy Daze* for safe keeping. And if that was so, then it was gone, along with the boat and everything on it—including his father.

Blair didn't agree with him. She'd been giving it some thought since he'd left—it was about all she *could* think about. Michael's father hadn't expected to die on that trip, but he might have planned to stage some kind of accident to explain Michael's disappearance. The fishing trip appeared to have been a ploy to get Michael out of Roger's reach without arousing Roger's suspicions.

She had no idea what Mark might have planned for Michael, perhaps an accidental drowning, with Michael's body never being found. Whatever he'd planned, she didn't think Mark would have taken the chance of losing such a valuable item as the journal. It contained information that would back up his accusations against the three men. Taking it on the boat would have meant the chance of losing it, and Mark had been too smart for that.

Her eyes wandered over the second story of the house next door. What if the journal was there—hidden somewhere in the house—waiting for them to find it?

She turned toward the grandfather clock standing against the wall behind her and checked the time. It was just past noon, but looking outside, you would never know it. Dark clouds hid the sun, and rain fell in a sheet.

What if she went next door and conducted a brief, hurried search? Tom was all right, and she would only be gone a few minutes.

No, Michael would be furious! He'd told her in no uncertain terms to stay put, not to answer the phone, and to keep away from the windows and doors. But there weren't any other houses on the street, only hers and Michael's, and it dead-ended on the beach.

Her eyes drifted up over the side of the house toward the attic. A screen had blown off in the storm. Her eyes automatically searched the other windows, looking for more missing screens. At that moment a loud clap of thunder rattled the house, renewing the storm's assault and startling a scream of surprise from Blair.

Her pulse rioted with a burst of adrenaline, and she put a hand to her forehead, feeling dizzy with tension. It was only the storm. She calmed herself with the thought.

After a few moments she returned to scrutinizing the house. Suddenly her attention was caught by the pale flutter of something at one of the downstairs windows.

What in the . . . ? She wiped at the window and squinted through the gray sheet of rain. It was a curtain! Someone, perhaps one of the people who'd conducted the auction, had left a window open in one of the kitchen windows. Rain would ruin the cabinets and hardwood floor. What should she do?

Instinct told her to go close the window. She'd spent a lifetime going in and out of that house. She knew how much Mark Baldwin and his wife had loved it, how much Michael loved it. She loved it, too. How could she let rain ruin what she'd worked so diligently for the past ten years to preserve?

But it could be dangerous. What if her house was being watched? What if Roger, or one of the others, was simply waiting to make certain she was inside before storming the house and taking her and Tom prisoner?

In this weather, that seemed unlikely. Where could they hide? She couldn't see either of the men skulking behind the hill of sand that acted as a dike between the ocean and her backyard.

She made up her mind. All she had to do was make a quick dash across the lawn to the back door of the house, hurry inside, close the window and get back again before Michael came back.

Looking in on Tom, she found him sleeping as peacefully as before and tiptoed from his room. In her bedroom, she changed into jeans, a sweater and boots. From her jewelry box she removed a single key on a small silver chain and clutched it in nervous fingers. It was a duplicate of the key to the back door of Michael's house. She'd had it made after losing the original for a whole week before finding it had slipped through a hole in the lining at the bottom of her purse.

She supposed she should have given it to Marvin, but for some reason she'd pushed it back inside her jewelry box the afternoon he'd come by her house, keeping its existence a secret. And now she was glad she had.

Blair hurried down the hall to the kitchen and into the small pantry to get an umbrella. She found it just as she heard a sound coming from the back door. Her heart leaped. Michael was back! She forgot the umbrella and hurried into the other room.

"Thank God, I was beginning to think—"

"Yes, my dear, what were you beginning to think?" Roger Prescott stepped through the kitchen door, followed closely by Marvin Welborn.

"How—?"

"How did we get in?" Roger asked with a smile. "Marvin has this amazing set of keys. They're very useful in the real estate business—they can unlock anything."

"Get out!"

"I don't think we can do that." Roger shook the water off his umbrella outside the door and folded it, propping it against the wall. "Terrible weather. How about a nice cup of hot coffee?" He stood looking at her calmly.

"No?" he asked, when Blair refused to move or speak. "All right, you sit down right here." He indicated a chair at the table, nodding to Marvin when she still didn't move, watching as the other man took her arm, forcing her to sit. "I'll make the coffee."

"You aren't going to get away with this," Blair told him, wrenching her arm from Marvin's hold. "Michael is at the police station right now telling them everything."

"There," Marvin said in satisfaction. "I told you who it was."

Roger hardly spared the other man a glance as he looked back over his shoulder, his mocking blue eyes on Blair's venomous expression. "Is that right? Well, exactly what is this 'everything' he's telling them?"

"We know all about what you and the others are doing, all about the land—and the murders."

"Where's Tom?" Roger asked abruptly.

"Tom?" she asked, feigning innocence. "I haven't the foggiest idea. I thought he was in the hospital—where you put him."

"You know better than that," Roger replied pleasantly. "You spirited him out of the hospital last night." His blue eyes glittered coldly. "Now, where is he?"

Blair clamped her jaw and glared at him silently. She would be damned if she'd tell him anything more.

"Marvin, go find him. He's got to be here. The old fool's too crazy to be left alone."

"He isn't here!" Blair repeated, half rising from her chair, knowing it was only a matter of a few minutes until they found him—and wishing Michael would appear.

"Sit down!" This time there was no affability in Roger's voice.

"What are you going to do with me?" Blair asked, lowering herself back into the chair, watching him look through the cabinets to find what he needed to make coffee.

The coffee was perking when he turned to ask, "Are you worried?"

"Why did you . . . kill all those people—and you did kill them, didn't you?" she asked.

"I prefer to look on it as euthanasia. I merely put to rest a few people who were too worn out to continue with life."

"Taking what they owned in the process," she muttered in contempt. "What about Mark? He wasn't 'worn out,' as you put it. He was in the prime of life—yet you killed him in cold blood," she accused.

"That's—"

"He isn't here." Marvin entered the room and stood looking from Blair to Roger.

Not there! Blair tried to hide her surprise. Where could he have gone? It couldn't be far; he didn't have the strength.

"Did you search all the rooms?" Roger asked.

Marvin nodded. "Upstairs and down. He isn't here, but two beds have been slept in."

Roger looked at Blair. "You might as well tell us. We'll find him anyway."

"I don't know what you're talking about," she murmured stubbornly.

Marvin moved up behind her, leaning down over her. "I'm going to like the next few hours." He took a deep breath, as though taking a whiff of perfume, and smiled.

"You smell good." He played with the short hair at the back of her neck.

Blair hunched a shoulder and drew away from him. "Keep your disgusting hands off me," she bit out angrily, ready to leap out of the chair.

Marvin raised both hands and backed away. "There's plenty of time for what I have in mind." He darted a glance at Roger. "Plenty of time," he repeated with a smile.

"Maybe not as much time as you think," Blair answered, giving him a shrewd glance.

"What do you mean?" Roger eyed her narrowly.

"I told you—Michael has gone to the police."

"With what? Some story he's concocted about something that took place a decade ago? You know, my dear—" Roger took three cups from the cabinet and lined them up on the sink "—it's very likely the police will wonder why Michael waited so long to come forward with his... story."

"What do you mean?"

"Well," he answered, setting a cup of coffee down before her, "it wouldn't be the first time someone has killed a relative for gain."

"That's a laugh. Michael has taken nothing. You—" she swept both men with contemptuous eyes "—have taken it all."

Roger shrugged and took a sip of coffee. "Nevertheless, who do you think the police are going to believe? Me?" He met her eyes. "Or someone who's been in hiding all these years?"

"Michael hasn't been in hiding. And there's proof...."

"What do you mean?" Roger eyed her sharply.

"I mean there must be proof somewhere of what you've done."

"She's lying," Marvin accused.

Roger moved to the table, set his cup down and reached for her hand. Clutching it in hard fingers, squeezing the bones together painfully, he demanded, "What proof? Tell me, unless you want me to break this pretty little hand."

"No proof," Blair whispered, trying to keep the pain from her voice. She refused to let him see how much he was hurting her.

"That's all right, my dear," Roger returned pleasantly, letting go of her hand. "You'll tell me in the end. Marvin, take another look around the house for Tom, and this time, search it thoroughly. Look in the garage, too. The old man has to be here. And when we find him . . ." He let the sentence trail off, his eyes glued to Blair's face.

Michael pressed himself flat against the brick wall, turning his head a fraction to stare through the tangle of wet rosebushes and into the house across the flagstone patio. It looked as though no one was home, but he couldn't be certain of that. The servants might be there.

He had no idea what time it was, and he figured that by now Blair was one of two things—worried sick, or madder than a wet hornet—because of his prolonged absence. But he had a good reason for it. He felt certain he was on the track of his father's missing journal.

After he'd left Blair's house to drive his car across town, intending to take a taxi to within a few blocks of her house on his return and walk the rest of the way, he'd continued to consider the question of his father's having kept a written account of what he knew about Roger and the others.

His father had a banker's proclivity for keeping meticulous records, and Michael began to revise his earlier opinion. And suddenly, in a flash, it came to him where the journal might be, if it truly existed.

The desk in his father's study! It was a huge antique walnut-and-burr-walnut desk, made in Indianapolis, Indiana. Its construction had been commissioned by Captain Joshua Baldwin, the original owner of the house.

As a child, Michael had at one time or another been shown a number of secret compartments in the desk, any one of which could easily hold something the size of a journal.

The desk, he recalled on his way across town, had been purchased at the auction by none other than John Saunders. Michael remembered Saunders's interest in it over the years and how he'd attempted to purchase it from his father on more than one occasion. Mark had always refused.

When Michael was younger, after overhearing a conversation between the two men about the desk and questioning his father about it, Mark had explained why Saunders, a voracious collector of antiques, was so interested in it. He explained how the desk was all tied up with the colorful history of its original owner.

Piracy in American waters was officially ended by the United States Navy in 1827. However, the United States refused to sign an 1856 international accord banning privateering. And during the Civil War both sides employed privateers.

According to stories handed down through the family, Captain Joshua Baldwin had been a privateer during the Civil War—some said even afterward. Though he apparently ran a legitimate shipping business, it was whispered that his money came mostly from privateering.

Many ships lost at sea in the area were said to be the result of Captain Joshua's dissolute ways. But there was never any proof—at least, none that fell into the hands of the authorities.

But Captain Joshua was said to have kept proof of his own perfidy hidden in the desk. The idea of his having enough information to send himself to the gallows hidden right beneath the very noses of those who would have liked to send him there, and their not knowing about it—or at least being unable to get to it—had apparently added spice to the old man's life.

Michael leaned forward to look into the room once more, brushed the wet hair from his eyes and realized he was looking almost directly at the desk in question. He wondered if the man knew what might lie hidden within its many secret compartments.

Time and time again Saunders had tried to purchase it from his father only to be turned down. Now he owned it, and Michael was furious at the thought. Did it bother him, knowing a man had had to die for him to get it?

Again Michael wondered if the house was indeed empty. He'd spent almost an hour sitting outside, hidden from view, watching the house, with no clear idea of what to do.

The large two-car garage stood open, empty except for a dark red Mercedes. Michael was beginning to think he would have to return to Blair's house without getting a chance to search the desk when June Saunders had entered the garage from the house, climbed into the Mercedes and driven off in a tearing hurry.

Michael had left his car behind the cover of trees, gone around to the back of the house and searched for a way through the thick tangle of jasmine, clematis and honeysuckle forming a natural wall around the back of the patio. He knew there was a possibility that he might run into the servants, but he figured that with the inclement weather, that wouldn't be a problem until he gained entrance to the house.

Fortunately the house appeared little changed from when he'd been a welcome guest in years past. He knew Saunders's study was situated on the same side of the house as the sheltered patio, and that was where he'd headed.

Maybe he should have given some thought to electronic alarms, but in his impatience to search the desk he forgot about them. It wasn't until he twisted the door handle, surprised to find how easily the door opened beneath his hand, that he realized what he could have done—and by then it didn't matter, he was inside.

Michael wasted no time in making directly for the desk. He pulled the double doors open and released the fall-front writing flap, exposing the elaborately fitted interior. One of the many shelves now revealed hid a fake drawer where his father had been fond of hiding things and letting Michael try to find them. The items he'd hidden had always been little presents, he remembered sadly, bought especially for him.

He lowered his weight to the leather chair behind the desk and stared at the rows of choices. Somewhere in the house a phone rang, stopping abruptly after only three rings. Michael tensed, whipping his head toward the door, listening for the sound of voices. There was only silence, but a moment later the sound of heels clattering down the hallway made his heart race in alarm.

Jumping to his feet as the footsteps drew near, he stood in indecision, finally backing toward the French doors he'd left standing ajar in case he needed to make a hasty exit. The steps passed the study and faded into silence.

For a few moments longer Michael remained poised for flight. Finally convinced the threat was gone, he turned back toward the desk. Suddenly, as he stared at the rows of drawers, a picture from the past flashed through his mind and he knew which metal ring to pull.

The fake drawer slid down inside the desk, leaving a square opening large enough to house a book. Michael reached inside, felt around for a small wooden latch, found it and gave it a twist. A wood panel dropped and something—something that looked remarkably like a book—slid into Michael's waiting palm.

Chapter 14

Tom swung himself off the side of the bed and stood on unsteady legs, grabbing hold of the edge of the table to steady himself. He had to find a bathroom.

In the hallway he stopped to lean against the wall for a moment. His head was swimming, and his eyes were slightly out of focus. Closing them, he took a deep breath and held it; after a moment he began to feel stronger.

Keeping his hands against the wall, he moved slowly down the hallway. Where was the danged bathroom? It seemed like he'd been moving down this hall for hours—and where were the nurses?

"Never one around when you need one," he grumbled, coming to the end of the hall.

"Where's Tom?"

Tom stiffened. So *he* was here. Well, in that case, he was leaving.

"Tom?"

The old man heard Blair's voice and hesitated. He listened to the conversation for a moment and knew he was in trouble.

"Got to get to a phone," he muttered beneath his breath. "Got to get to a phone." He stared around at the vaguely familiar room. Where was he, anyway?

His glance found the front door, and there in the corner sat a telephone. Tom made his way slowly toward it. He had to work fast. They were after him!

Lifting the phone cautiously to his ear, praying the wire hadn't been cut, he listened for and heard the reassuring sound of the dial tone. He dialed and listened to it ring.

"Baywater Police Department. Is this an emergency call?" a female voice asked with little inflection.

"Yer damned right it is," Tom answered in a gruff whisper. "I want to report a kidnapping. Is Harry Samson there?"

"If this is an emergency call you need to dial nine, one, one, and can you speak louder, please? I can barely hear you."

"No, I can't speak louder! Get Harry!"

"Hello? Is this an emergency call? If you can't dial nine, one, one, I can do it for you. Do you need me to dial it for you?"

"No, I don't! I need to speak to Harry Samson. Tell him this is Tom Wallace. He'll talk to me."

"I'm sorry—"

"Damn it! I said get Harry!"

"Just a moment, please."

"Damned women!" Tom muttered beneath his breath, casting an eye behind him toward where he'd heard the voices. "Never did think police work was the place for 'em."

"Hello?"

"That you, Harry?"

"No—well, that is, yes. Who's this?"

"It's me, Tom—Tom Wallace. I want to report a kidnapping. They tried to get me in that blasted home, but I was too smart for 'em."

"Mr. Wallace, I have a feeling you want to talk to my dad, but he's retired now."

"Damn it! I told you, I'm—I been—" Tom felt his head begin to spin. "I gotta go—don't feel so good . . ."

"Mr. Wallace, are you all right? Where are you? Wait a minute, did you say Tom Wallace? Weren't you in the hospital? Aren't you the one who's missing?"

"Come an' get me. I feel real bad." The hand holding the telephone began to tremble. He set the phone down on the table and reached for the door. Tom could hear the voice at the other end demanding an address, but he felt too weak to answer. What he needed was a breath of fresh air....

Michael left his car parked three streets from Blair's house and ran down alleys and through yards, dodging fences and piles of debris, through the pouring rain. He couldn't wait to tell her what he'd found. He hadn't taken time to give the journal much more than a cursory examination, but even at that he knew he had the proof he needed against Prescott and the others.

He would take care of them later; his main concern right now was the safety of Blair and Tom. As he threaded his way through a yard one street over, he changed direction and dropped down behind the seawall running along the beach until he reached the back of his own house.

He scanned the area carefully before leaving the natural cover of the seawall at his back, crouching low, to run across the sand to the back of the house.

"You better come in here," Marvin called from the living room.

Roger took Blair by the arm and led her with him to find the other man. "What is it?"

"Look at this." Marvin pointed to the telephone receiver lying on the table, an annoying sound issuing from it, indicating it was off the hook.

"So-o." Roger tightened his hold on Blair's arm. "Who was in the house besides you?"

"No one—"

"Don't lie to me!" His grip tightened painfully. "It was Tom, wasn't it—wasn't it?" He shook her, drawing his hand back to hit her.

"The door was open," Marvin said quickly. "I closed it, because it was raining in, but you can see the floor is wet. Whoever it is, he's gone now."

"Gone!" Roger answered distractedly. "Gone where? Did you look outside for him?"

"Well, no—it's raining—"

"You idiot! Who do you think he called? We have to find him and get out of here right away."

"I thought you weren't worried about the police?" Blair put in mockingly.

"Shut up!" Roger glared murderously at her.

Marvin opened the door and looked outside. "There's no place for anyone to go—least of all that old man you've been pumping full of drugs. If it was him, he's probably lying in the rain somewhere, dead by now."

"*Probably!* Do you think I've built our empire on *probablys?* We have to make sure. Come on."

Michael took up a position behind his former home. He hoped all these precautions weren't necessary, he hoped Prescott assumed they were way out of town by now, but he couldn't take any chances.

The door to Blair's house opened abruptly, and Marvin Welborn and Roger Prescott moved into view, with Blair positioned between them.

Michael stiffened, a black anger descending on him. If they hurt her . . . He was on the point of leaving his cover to go to her rescue when he stopped, realizing how foolhardy that would be. It wouldn't help Blair for him to get himself caught. He had to have a plan.

"He can't have gone very far." Marvin leaned toward Roger to make himself heard about the sound of the rain and the ocean's roar.

Blair's attention was drawn to the curtain hanging out the open window next door. She'd forgotten all about it until now. Poor Tom. If he was out in this rain, he'd probably develop pneumonia.

She wondered where he'd gone, and again her eyes moved toward the open window. Was there more curtain hanging outside than before?

"This isn't getting us anything but soaked," Marvin complained. "Let's go back inside. We can forget about Tom. No one's going to pay any attention to the mutterings of a senile old—"

"Look at that!" Roger pointed toward the Baldwin house. "Do you see what I see?" he asked Marvin.

"It looks like the window is open."

"How astute of you to notice," Roger said sarcastically. "Come on, obviously that's where he's gone."

Blair dug her heels in and refused to move. "I'm not going anywhere with you," she called loudly, hoping to warn Tom if he was inside. "Let go of my arm!" She tried to wrench it from Roger's grasp.

"I have very little patience at the best of times—" Roger pressed his face close to hers "—and you're forcing me to the end. Now, come on!" He twisted her arm up behind her and pushed her along the soggy ground.

"What are you going to do to him?" she asked quickly, referring to Tom. "Don't hurt him, please. He's an old man. I'll go wherever you want, do whatever you want me to do, but please, don't hurt him."

"All I want you to do is shut up," Roger replied angrily.

Marvin already had the key in the lock when they joined him. He was twisting it and rattling the door at the same time. "This damned door, it always sticks," he complained.

"Well, hurry up. As you so aptly pointed out a few minutes ago, we're getting soaked," Roger said.

The floor inside the kitchen had at least an inch of water standing on it, and over in a corner of the room, where he'd managed to drag himself after he'd struggled over the low windowsill, lay Tom.

"Oh, no!" Blair jerked her arm from Roger's grasp and hurried to kneel at the old man's side. It took only a moment to ascertain that it was too late to help him. The excitement, his age, Roger's drugs, all no doubt had combined to bring about his death.

"You did this!" Blair twisted to glare up at Roger accusingly.

"He was an old man," Roger answered coldly. "Did you expect him to live forever?"

Getting to her feet, anger in every line of her face and body, she advanced slowly toward him. "You aren't a young man yourself," she taunted. "One of these days you're going to be in the same boat as Tom—and all those others you've murdered. Will you be so callous about death then?"

Roger reached into his pocket and withdrew a small object. "I think you've gone far enough."

Michael peered through the window and saw the small snub-nosed .38 Smith & Wesson in Roger's hand. He'd been right to be cautious; Prescott was armed.

"What are you going to do with that?" Marvin asked nervously. "You aren't going to—"

"Let's go back next door and wait for her friend," Roger interrupted the other man. "He's bound to be here soon. I want to hear more about this 'proof' she mentioned earlier."

"What are you going to do about Tom?" Blair demanded.

Roger stopped to give her a long, penetrating stare before asking in a soft, even tone, "What do you think?"

"You can't just leave him there."

"Why not? He escaped—left the hospital—and wandered around in a state of confusion until he ended up here. He found the window open and managed to climb inside out of the rain, but, unfortunately, it was too much for his tired heart." Roger shrugged. "End of scenario—end of Tom."

"You cold-blooded bastard."

"Now, really, I don't think there's any need to get nasty. What did you think we were going to do with the two of you? Find out what you knew, swear you to secrecy and let you go on your merry way? You didn't really expect me to let you go so you could ruin a billion-dollar-a-year enterprise, now did you?"

"The racetrack, you mean?" she asked.

"You, my dear, are a very clever young woman. I've always thought so—even when you were a child. It's too bad," Roger added, "you turned out to be nosy, as well."

"Why are you doing this?" Blair asked. "With all the money you already have—"

"No one ever has enough money," Marvin broke in derisively. "Surely you're smart enough to know that."

"Is it true?" Blair demanded of Roger. "Did you kill your best friend? Did you kill Michael's father?"

Roger drew back his hand to slap her, but Marvin stopped him by asking, "Do you think we should mark up the body, in case someone finds her . . . intact. We don't want the authorities questioning their findings."

"You're right." Roger nodded. "Let's get out of here."

"Please," Blair pleaded, "don't leave Tom here like this." She refused to move, despite Roger's stepping forward and prodding her none too gently in the ribs with the gun's solid barrel.

Michael felt his teeth clench in an effort to keep from yelling at Blair not to plead with the bastard for anything. Somehow he had to figure out a way to get the drop on the two men.

He wondered if Saunders was lurking in the vicinity, waiting for him to make a move, but it was only a fleeting thought. He had the journal in his possession—or at least hidden in the gazebo behind Blair's house, where he could easily reach it. His only remaining concern was to get Blair to safety.

"If he'd just reacted like he was supposed to," Roger was talking to Blair, "to the damned medicine I gave him, he never would have regained consciousness, you'd be none the wiser, and none of this would be taking place. You should be angry with him, not me. He's the reason you're in this mess up to your pretty eyebrows."

Blair glared at him. "Tom was an innocent victim—*your* victim. And *you're* the reason I'm in this mess." She swept a contemptuous glance toward Marvin. "You and your greedy friends. You're all nothing but a pack of thieves and murderers."

"I don't look at it in quite the same way," Roger informed her coolly. "Tom outlived his usefulness. He really wanted to be in the grave with his Sadie. I only helped him along."

"Because you want his house."

Marvin laughed. "House? That old eyesore? Not a chance. It's the land we—"

"That's enough, Marvin," Roger commanded with a warning in his voice.

"What are you afraid of?" Blair demanded. "Who am I going to tell? If you're going to kill me, at least explain to me why."

"It's really very simple," Welborn said, obliging her. "We have a very lucrative business, and you could spoil it for us."

"The business of killing people? Mark—Tom—me? How long is the list? Where does it begin? Where does it end? Doesn't either of you have a conscience?"

"We can't afford one," Roger said with a smirk. "Come on, let's move along. We have one more person we need to invite to this little party before we bring it to an end." He motioned toward the door with the gun.

"You first," he told Marvin. "And then you." He pointed to Blair.

Michael held his breath and pressed himself flat against the side of the house, waiting for them as they exited. He threw a punch at Marvin, catching him in the stomach, knocked Blair out of the way, and made a downward chopping motion across Roger's wrist with the edge of his hand, catching the gun before it could touch the ground.

He backed away from the two men, the gun trained on them, reached for Blair and pulled her tight against him.

"I'm sorry, Blair," Michael said, keeping one eye on the two men. "Are you all right?"

"Yes," she answered shakily, rubbing at a small scrape on her arm. "I'm fine." Wrapping her arms around his waist, she hugged him tightly. She had never been so glad to see anyone in her entire life.

Roger Prescott cradled his injured wrist in his other hand and lifted cold blue eyes to Michael's face. "I think you broke it."

"That's too bad," Michael answered without a sign of regret. "Let's move back inside." He motioned for Marvin and Roger to precede him and Blair.

"Michael..." Blair touched his arm to draw his attention. "Tom's inside. He's...dead."

"I know. I'm sorry. I know you loved him. He was a good man."

They followed the other two inside and Michael looked toward the corner of the room where Tom lay and thought about his father. "You—" he pointed the gun at Roger "—take your coat off and put it over him."

"No, it's chilly and damp in here—"

"Do it!"

Roger recognized the deadly gleam in the other man's dark eyes and complied. "I see you didn't come out *totally* unscathed," Roger commented after doing as Michael had instructed, referring to the physical damage from the explosion.

"No thanks to you," Michael answered in a hoarse voice, putting Blair away from him. He directed the small black hole of the barrel of the gun he held at Roger's forehead.

Roger's eyes flicked momentarily toward the gun but showed no sign of fear as he shifted his glance back to Michael's face. "It appears you're as big a fool as your father. I offered him a clean four-way split. All he had to do was launder a little money for us—"

"And he told you to go to hell," Michael finished for him.

Roger raised a well-defined brow and gave a small smile. "Your father used more finesse, but that's basically it. Oh, yes, he did add that he'd see me in hell before he'd allow you to marry into the family."

Michael ignored that to ask, "Which one of you actually wanted to kill my father?"

"Why, all three of us, of course." Roger smiled into Michael's coldly furious eyes.

"Then it looks like *I'm* going to have to kill all three of you," Michael bit out precisely.

"Wait a minute!"

"Shut up!" Roger ordered Marvin fiercely.

"But—"

"I said shut up!"

"Michael?" Blair took a step in his direction, staring into his dark hostile face. What did he have in mind?

"Go on home, Blair."

"But—"

"Go home. This has nothing to do with you."

Michael motioned toward the two men with the gun. "Let's take a little walk out back."

Everyone had been so intent on the unfolding situation that no one had noticed the silent figure enter from the back side of the double stairs.

"Put the gun down, Michael."

"I wondered where you were," Michael commented without moving, his eyes daring the two men he covered with the gun to make a move.

"Do as I said and put the gun down," John Saunders repeated, stepping up and placing the barrel of the gun he held against Michael's spine. "No one has to get hurt here."

"You expect me to believe that?" Michael laughed bitterly. "Your friends have already admitted to killing my father—"

"I didn't admit to anything," Marvin protested quickly.

"Go ahead," Roger said to John, his eyes on Michael's face. "Shoot him."

John spared his associate a brief glance. "You're always eager for bloodshed, aren't you?"

"I only do what's necessary," Roger staunchly maintained.

"Was it necessary to get rid of your own wife?" John asked sadly.

"What?" Blair gasped. Roger had killed his own wife? Cheryl had always believed her mother had a weak heart and that was what had killed her.

"Isn't it a little late in the day to be getting a conscience?" Roger asked mockingly. "You've gotten what you wanted from our little business venture, the desk you coveted for so many years, along with lots of money. And your political clout got us all the permits we needed to start construction without a major delay. I haven't noticed you re-

fusing to get the papers signed before the . . . bloodshed, as
you put it, in the past. You knew what came next, once we
had their power of attorney.''

"I . . . tolerated it. But you enjoy it," John accused with
loathing.

"Admit it. You enjoy the money," Roger charged softly.

"We all enjoy the money," Marvin broke in impatiently.
"Come on, I feel very uncomfortable standing here with a
gun directed at me. Either make him drop the damned thing
or shoot him."

"Michael," John entreated softly.

"Go to hell." Michael's fingers clenched on the handle of
the gun. His index finger drew tighter against the trigger. He
was so close.

After all these years, he was finally standing before the
men who had murdered his father—and tried to murder
him. He couldn't let them go—especially not Roger Prescott.

"I'm sorry, Michael," John said in a voice filled with regret. "But if you don't put the gun down, I'm going to have
to—"

Suddenly everything seemed to happen at once. Roger
made a diving grab toward Blair, intending to use her as a
shield against Michael. At the same time Michael jerked his
head to the left and lifted a shoulder, swinging the gun he
held up and around to smash into John's face.

John wasn't quick enough, nor adept enough to avoid the
blow. He dropped the gun and grabbed at his face.

While all that was going on, Marvin Welborn had used
the opportunity to back toward the door. Michael's voice
reached him at the same instant the older man's hand
reached the door handle.

"I wouldn't do that if I were you," Michael whispered,
the ice in his voice freezing Marvin in his tracks.

"Drop the gun, Michael." Roger had Blair up against
him, an arm around her neck. Obviously his broken wrist
had been a lie to put Michael off guard. "I know just where
to snap her neck with one sharp movement, and if you think
I won't do it—"

But Blair had had enough. Using a trick Michael had taught her when they were growing up, she used the heel of her foot to stomp on Roger's instep, twisted and elbowed him hard in the ribs all at the same time.

Gaining her freedom, she joined Michael, stepping slightly behind him to face the three men.

Roger doubled over from the blow to his solar plexus, folding his arms around his chest against the pain and glaring up at them coldly. "What now?" he asked, each painful breath burning his chest. "Are you planning to shoot all three of us?"

Michael sidestepped to the other gun and kicked it across the floor, making certain it was out of their reach before answering. "I want you to tell me how you killed my father."

"That's the joke, you see," Roger panted, holding his ribs. "We didn't kill your father—he killed himself."

"You're a liar!"

"No, Michael," John spoke up. "Roger's right."

"You expect me to believe you?"

"It's true," John answered. "Your father found out what we were doing. He found out about the racetrack and tried to stop us."

"Dad was against gambling being brought into the county, you knew that," Michael said quickly.

"I know," John answered sadly. "He hired a detective and found out all about Unico and Tri-tran."

"You mean he found out about your land scam and the payoffs?"

John nodded. "Marvin had a close friend on the state planning commission. That gave us an in on what government contracts were coming up—on anything that would require land and lots of it. You see, we'd been acquiring land for a long time.

"Marvin gave Roger the information he got, and Roger gave it to me. I did my best to acquire the property in a legal fashion. If it was something in this area, something involving an elderly client, I used my knowledge of the law to get power of attorney. And if that didn't work, I usually

managed to seize the land for unpaid legal fees or something to that effect. And then it was up to Roger.''

"You mean you handed them over to their executioner,"
Michael said damningly.

Roger smiled. "People in nursing homes are little more
than liabilities to the rest of us. They've outlived their usefulness to their families, to society and to themselves.
They're better off dead. All that most of them want is to lie
next to some friend or family member who's already gone.
In my opinion euthanasia should be a government practice.
Besides, those I helped along the way would have died of
natural causes before long anyway.'' He gave an elegant
shrug. "I merely... anticipated Mother Nature by a few
weeks—that's all.''

"And my father?''

"He threatened to go to the police,'' John replied, "and
that's when Roger pulled his little poisoning stunt. After
that, Mark must have decided to get you safely out of Baywater before he made things... uncomfortable for us. He
must have rigged the explosives to fake some kind of an accident himself, but it backfired. I'm not sure what he had in
mind, but we didn't kill him.''

"I don't believe you.'' But he did. It was exactly what his
father would have done. Now that he'd had time to think
about it, he knew it wouldn't have been enough for his father to send him away; everyone had to believe he was dead.
And what better way than an explosion at sea?

"Do you really expect me to believe you didn't plan to kill
Dad?''

"I didn't say that.'' Roger smiled coldly. "As a matter of
fact, I was going to rig your father's boat to go up. I planned
to wire it the night before your fishing trip. After what I
found, though, I decided to wait and let Mark play out his
little charade before I made my next move.''

"You!'' Blair rubbed her upper arm, rubbed at the spot
that had been aching ever since Roger had grabbed hold of
her the first time. "It was you that night! You're the dark
figure I stumbled into on the beach!''

"That's right. I was on my way to the marina to take care of the boat. I'd tried one last time to reason with Mark, but he still wouldn't listen.

"I hadn't intended for you to be involved," Roger said to Michael. "I would have made sure you missed the boat trip that day. But I bumped into Blair. After that, I didn't dare do anything for fear she had recognized me. You can't imagine how surprised I was—pleasantly, I'll admit—to learn about the accident at sea."

"You're disgusting!" Blair cried in revulsion.

Roger shrugged and directed his glance to Michael's face. "You see, we had to move fast. Your father had just told me that night after dinner that he planned to donate his portion of the land we needed for the race park to the town for a new library. He was going to put that in his will, just in case something—some accident—should befall him. He was a trusting fool. He thought he had everything figured out, so he went to John with what he knew. John acted shocked by what your father said Marvin and I were up to, and your father believed him. He even asked what he could do to legally stop us from getting the land if he died. John told him—then called me.

"I'd already tried to show him a few weeks earlier that his hands were tied. And his words to me were 'Over my dead body.'" Again Roger shrugged. "He made his own choice."

Blair couldn't believe the horror of what she was hearing. She'd been almost as close to this man as Cheryl, his own daughter, and she'd never once suspected him of being a cold-blooded murderer. She shuddered.

"Why didn't Dad try to stop me from getting engaged to Cheryl if he knew all this?" Michael asked.

"Would you have believed him if he'd told you what I just did?"

"Look—what are we going to do?" Marvin asked nervously. "We've been standing around here forever. Listen, Michael, it's too bad about your dad. I liked Mark. We all did. But we can't bring him back. There's plenty of money in this for all of us. All you have to do—"

"Don't waste your breath," John told him. "He doesn't want the money—he wants us dead."

A tense silence followed John's words. The three men stared at Michael, hardly daring to breathe.

"Michael...please," Blair whispered, placing her hand on the rigid muscles of his free arm.

For a long, brittle moment nothing changed in Michael's cold, stony gaze. He wanted to put a bullet right between Roger Prescott's mocking blue eyes. He wanted it so badly he couldn't move, couldn't seem to relax his grip on the gun.

But he was confused. If what John and Roger had said was true, his father had died—however accidentally—by his own hand. Where did that leave him? It didn't absolve the three men of murder; his father had only been one of many. But somehow, though he wasn't quite certain how, it changed things for him personally.

A picture of his son's chubby face, laughing at something Blair had said to him the one and only time she'd met him, came into his mind. They liked each other; that had been plain to see.

Roger cleared his throat, and Michael lifted the gun toward him. Whether the man had been directly responsible for his father's death or not, he didn't deserve to live. What about Tom and all the others? Michael wanted to shoot him.

No, on second thought, Michael decided he didn't want to kill the man. Roger should live. He should live a long, long time—and suffer for what he'd done.

Slowly the rigid control he'd exerted over himself drained away. The muscles in the arm Blair was still touching slackened, and Michael gave her a short, almost imperceptible nod.

A voice came from somewhere in the house. "All right, fella, put down the gun!"

Michael, along with everyone else in the room, froze.

A second voice from the front of the house made itself known. "Take your finger away from the trigger and raise your hands real high! Do it—before I have to shoot you!"

Blair stood back and watched as Michael raised his free hand above his head, kneeled and placed the gun on the floor at his own feet. When the tall, burly man in a dark suit entered the room and told him to kick it away, he did.

One of the four uniformed officers accompanying the man hurried across the room and knelt at Tom's side, feeling for a pulse.

"This one's dead, sir."

Detective Lieutenant Harry Samson made his way toward the spot where the body lay and stood looking down at the old man's still face.

"Would this be Tom Wallace?" he asked, turning his dark gray eyes on Blair's sad face.

Blair nodded, lips trembling.

"I'm Detective Samson, and you are?"

"B-Blair Mallory," she responded.

"Well, Ms. Mallory, can you tell me what's going on here?"

"I certainly can." Roger stepped forward, only to find his way blocked by a uniformed officer, who raised his weapon and motioned him back.

"You," Detective Samson said to him, "be quiet. I was talking to the lady. Now," he turned a gentler look on Blair's white face, "go on, tell me what's happened here."

Blair swallowed, threw a hurried glance toward Michael and began a halting explanation. She had reached the part where Roger had admitted to planning to kill Michael's father when June Saunders's voice sounded from the doorway.

"Let me go, young man," she demanded angrily. "I *will* go inside, whether you like it or not!"

Blair looked across the room at Michael. He was staring at the floor without expression. She ached for him. He'd waited ten long years to confront his father's killer, only to discover his father was responsible for his own death and Michael's disfigurement. What must he be feeling?

She wished everyone would suddenly disappear and leave her alone with him so she could tell him how sorry she was about everything. She knew he needed time to adjust his thinking. Time to heal emotionally from all the pain in his past. He'd filled himself with hate to the exclusion of all else, but now, with the truth out in the open and the three men in custody, the loss of all that passion would leave a great hole inside him.

She could fill that hole. With the help of his son Mark, she could fill it with love. *Please, dear God, make him let me,* she prayed, because this time, if he left her, she didn't think she would live through it.

Chapter 15

"I knew I'd find you here."

Blair felt her heart lurch at the sound of Michael's rough voice. She looked up from her cross-legged position on the sand out of the water's reach. Michael's features were indiscernible in the darkness, but she knew from the tone of his voice that he was grinning wryly.

"Everything taken care of at the police station?" she asked diffidently.

"Yeah, it's all taken care of."

"And June?"

"She's with Rob. She picked him up at the airport this afternoon. That's where she was headed when I went to their house and found the journal."

No one had been more surprised than Blair to find the small nervous woman a part of the barrage of police entering Michael's house a little while ago. It had turned out that June had found the journal while cleaning the desk the day it arrived. Curious, she'd stopped to read parts of it, quickly realizing that it was a thorough account of illegal activities that her husband and the other two men had been involved in for years.

At first she hadn't wanted to believe it, but things that had puzzled her over the years suddenly began to make sense. And that had terrified her. She was a true southern belle, used to being taken care of by her menfolk. She couldn't deal with something so abhorrent as murder and corruption.

In a moment of denial she replaced the journal exactly where she'd found it and pretended nothing had changed. But what she'd read began to nag at the back of her mind, keeping her awake, making her drink far too much and experience bouts of depression.

Finally she'd known she had to tell someone, and when she'd picked up their son Rob, who'd gone to school with Michael and Blair, she couldn't hold back any longer. Crying, she'd told him what she'd discovered. At first he hadn't wanted to believe it any more than she had, but being a lawyer himself, he knew there was only one thing to do. He'd driven his mother to the police station and held her hand while she told Detective Harry Samson about the journal.

Harry had just finished his strange conversation with Tom Wallace, and they'd managed to get a trace on the call before the receiver was replaced. He'd been on his way out to track down the address when June arrived with her son. He'd dispatched a patrol car in his place and waited to hear what she had to say.

When Harry had heard it all, he'd assured her that they would look into the matter and left. But June wasn't satisfied with that; she'd insisted that Rob follow him. It came as no surprise to her when they headed toward Blair's house, and even less of a surprise to find her husband, Prescott and Welborn there when she arrived.

Michael eventually had his say, explaining all about his surveillance of the Saunders's house and what he'd found in the desk. Technically he was guilty of breaking and entering, but June Saunders didn't press charges.

Once Michael's innocence had been established, Prescott, Saunders and Welborn had been taken into custody. Michael had retrieved his father's journal from Blair's gazebo and handed it over to Detective Samson.

Blair's statement had been taken on the premises, and she'd been asked to come to the station in the morning to sign a copy of it. But Michael had been asked to go to the police station to give them the details of what he knew.

Blair had offered to stay with June, but the other woman had thanked her and told her no, she would be fine with Rob. When they'd left, Blair had stayed and helped the ambulance attendants get Tom in the ambulance. She'd been sorry to tell her old friend goodbye, but realized he was finally at peace.

She'd been sitting on the beach for the past two hours, watching the ocean, letting the fresh wind blow the cobwebs from her brain. The storms they'd been having for the past week appeared to have passed on, and a bright moon shone overhead. Whether she admitted it to herself or not, she'd been waiting for Michael, hoping he would come back to her, if only for a brief time.

Now he pulled his hands from the pockets of his jeans, pulled the legs up a little and hunkered down beside her. "I'm sorry about Tom."

"Don't be. Roger was right about one thing at least—it's what Tom wanted, to be reunited with Sadie."

"That's the only thing he was right about," Michael answered in an unforgiving voice.

Blair shifted her eyes from Michael's face to stare out over the undulating water. She'd begun to find a small measure of peace, but now she felt unsettled again. "I thought I knew Roger—poor Cheryl. How is she going to react to all this?"

"Her husband will see her through it."

"You're right, he will—but everything has changed. The town won't be the same."

"I'm sorry." A note of irritation crept into Michael's voice. "Would you rather I hadn't come back, that I'd left you to your little idyll of how you *thought* things were instead of waking you up to reality?"

Blair cringed. "I didn't mean it that way."

Michael pushed a hand through his hair and let his breath out in a long sigh. "I know. I'm sorry."

"This has been a very strange day."

"What's strange is the way June Saunders turned in her own husband because of his part in all this. I never would have thought her capable of it."

"I know." She sounded saddened by it. "It must have been the hardest thing she's ever had to do in her entire life, but she did it."

"She didn't do it immediately," Michael reminded her shortly. "She waited three days."

"Oh, but, Michael, think what it must have cost her to face the fact the man she loved was a criminal, involved in murder and grand larceny. June's a gentle person, I've never heard her say a harsh word to anyone in my whole life. What she did took a great deal of love on her part as well as courage."

"I doubt John is feeling very loved at the moment."

Blair surprised him by answering, "I think you're wrong. I think John is feeling very lucky, and very relieved."

"You're a funny person...."

Stung, Blair climbed abruptly to her feet and stalked down the beach. He thought she was silly!

"Hey, wait up." Michael dusted the sand off his jeans and hurried after her. But she gave no sign of having heard him. He dropped back after following for a short distance and let her go on alone. He could take a hint—obviously she didn't want his company.

But Blair didn't go far, and in a short while she was sitting in the same spot as before, digging her fingers into the sand, letting it slide off them and drift back to the beach.

"What did I say?" Michael asked softly, coming up behind her.

"Nothing." She shrugged and gave a short laugh. "I don't know what to do. For the first time in my life I feel as though I've been cast adrift. I don't even have a job—my boss is in jail." She tried to make it sound humorous, but her voice rose and ended on a choked sob.

"Maybe it would have been better if I hadn't come back." He wanted to hold her, but he didn't dare.

"Don't say that!" Blair stared up at him. "I didn't want you to leave in the first place." Her glance softened. "I don't want you to leave now." She shouldn't have said that—she'd promised herself she wouldn't. He knew how she felt about him; she wouldn't beg.

"Blair..." He knelt beside her.

"No, it's all right. I won't try to change your mind." After what they'd been through together, if he couldn't admit that he loved and needed her, then he was right. They should be parted. "I remember what you said. You said there was nothing inside you, nothing but hate—"

"I know what I said," he cut her off in exasperation. He didn't like being reminded. Things had changed. He no longer felt responsible for his father's death. It had been an accident. Knowing that didn't change anything that had happened over the past ten years, but it made it easier for him to cast aside some of the guilt he'd been carrying around inside all that time.

"No, damn it, it isn't all right," Blair abruptly refuted what she'd just said. "Your wife is dead, and I understand that you loved her very much, but does that mean there is never going to be another woman in your life—not ever?"

"It isn't just me," Michael began with difficulty. "There's Mark to consider. He misses his mother."

"Oh." All the fight went out of her. She couldn't come between a child and his love for his mother.

"He wasn't much more than a baby when she died," Michael continued, "but he misses her. He needs a woman in his life, someone to cuddle him. Elaine and her husband want to adopt him."

"Oh, Michael! You aren't going to let them? You can't! You love him—I know you do."

"Well, of course I love him—he's my son. But—"

"But nothing! That boy needs you—and you need him."

"I need you."

Blair couldn't breathe. The softly spoken words had sucked the air right out of her lungs. She licked her dry lips, trying to form a reply, but even that was impossible.

"Did you hear what I said? I'm not planning to let anyone adopt my son. When I said Mark needed a woman in his life...I meant you. I know he's only seen you one time, but Elaine says you're all he talks about." He wished he could see her face, read the expression in her eyes, but her face was turned away. Why wasn't she saying anything?

"I see," she answered blankly.

The words rang hollowly in Michael's ears. It seemed he'd been wrong in thinking she still loved him. He must have misunderstood the things she'd said in the past few days, that certain look in her eyes, the depth of her lovemaking.

Or maybe, after the way he'd acted toward her, all the crazy things he'd said, she'd decided she didn't want anything more to do with him.

He had changed a great deal from the youth she'd known. He was a man now, no longer the gentle companion of her childhood. But he'd attained his manhood at a price, and he wouldn't apologize for it—not even to Blair.

"I guess you want something more than a ready-made family," Michael said distantly. "I can understand that, but I don't think we can continue to see each other."

Blair turned to him. "See each other? What are you talking about? Aren't you leaving Baywater?"

"No." He shook his head. A sudden gust of wind blew the dark hair across his forehead and into his eyes. Blair wanted to reach over and smooth it back, but Michael reached up and pushed it out of the way with impatient fingers. "I thought I'd stick around, see if I could straighten out some of this mess I've helped make."

"What happened to your father isn't your fault!" Blair jumped to his defense. "So don't try to shoulder the blame for that, too."

"Too? What do you mean?"

She debated whether or not to answer. His marriage was really none of her business.

"Don't you blame yourself for your wife's death because you didn't use the money your father put in the safe-deposit box to make her life easier?" She felt him stiffen, and thought for a moment he was going to get to his feet and stalk off.

"I blame myself for marrying her. I loved her," he assured Blair quietly, "but not enough. I'll carry the burden of that knowledge with me to the grave," he said bleakly.

"Perhaps she never knew," Blair responded softly.

"Oh, she knew," he contradicted her. "How could she not—when I spent months in the hospital calling out one name?"

Blair's fingers curled in the damp sand. She felt as though a tight band had closed around her chest, squeezing the breath from her lungs, stopping the flow of blood from her heart. She couldn't face him with the question raging through her mind.

"I..." She licked her lips. "I'm sorry."

"Are you?" He turned accusing eyes on her face. "Well, you should be," he said, shocking her. "It was your name—your face—I couldn't get out of my head."

Blair gasped at the raw emotion in his voice. "Then why didn't you send for me?"

"Do you have any idea what I looked like right after the accident?" He saw her shake her head. "It was so bad that everyone had orders from the doctors—once I'd regained consciousness—not to let me get my hands on a mirror."

"I wouldn't have cared," she murmured softly, yearningly.

"I cared."

"But you didn't mind Mary seeing you?" she asked faintly.

"It wasn't the same."

"She must have loved you very much."

Michael didn't contradict her. He pushed the picture of Mary's face—the unguarded looks of distaste she'd tried so hard to hide when they were first married and he was still undergoing plastic surgery—out of his mind.

He hadn't blamed her for them then, and he didn't blame her for them now. She'd been his salvation at a time when he'd been lost in hell. And if he hadn't loved her as much as she deserved, he'd loved her as much as he could.

"I made her happy," Michael said. "As happy as possible, under the circumstances."

Blair reached down inside her and found the courage to ask, "What is it you want from me? A mother for your son? Or a companion for you—one who doesn't mind the scars?"

Michael twisted toward her, scooted closer and took one of her small hands in both of his. Gently, without speaking, he pried open the fingers, dusting the sand from them and laying them against his cheek, holding them there beneath his own hand.

"I want all those things and more. Look at me. Look at me, Blair!"

Turning his face up to the moonlight, his eyes on her, he asked, "Is this a face you can live with—stand to see across the breakfast table every morning for the rest of your life? A face you can introduce to your friends?" He choked. "A face you can love?"

Dropping his head, he pressed her palm against his trembling lips, holding it there with both hands.

"Oh, Michael!" There were tears in her eyes. "I love you! I've always loved you! I'll love you till the day we both die— and beyond.

"It wouldn't matter to me what you looked like. You could have two heads and I'd still love you, because it wouldn't change who you are inside. But there's no reason for you to think you look different than anyone else."

"And Mark?" he asked, his warm lips moving against her fingers. "Can you love him—another woman's child?"

Blair captured his face between both hands, turning his eyes up to hers. "Can I love the boy any less than I love the man? He's you all over again. How lucky can I get in one lifetime? I'll be able to introduce Mark to all the childhood pleasures his father introduced me to so long ago."

"He isn't totally my child," Michael warned. "He has some of his mother in him, too."

"All the better. From what I know about Mary, she was a good, kind person."

"God! Are you sure?" His eyes probed her face, searching it closely.

"Do you doubt me?"

He took her shoulders in trembling hands and held her, studying her face. "I don't want to," he answered slowly.

"Then don't. Believe me," she whispered, leaning forward to put her lips against his, "I love you."

His hands were at her cheeks, holding the kiss. "I love you, too," he murmured against her mouth.

"Oh, Michael, I thought you were never going to say it."

Lips inches from hers, he grinned. "You're probably going to get tired of hearing it over the next fifty years or so, 'cause I plan to say it every day for the rest of our lives. Are you up to that?"

Blair looked beyond the teasing and recognized the deepseated fear lurking in the depths of his dark eyes. She knew he was asking for more than his words implied.

"I'll be there for you, Michael, for you and Mark, always, for as long as you need me—for as long as you want me."

In a quick move he had her on his lap, cuddled tightly in his arms, his lips moving hungrily over hers. The moon rose and set, the tide came in, forcing them to move farther up the beach, the sky went from pitch-black to a luminescent gray, while they talked, made love, made plans—and made love again.

It must have been somewhere near five in the morning when Blair put her head against his shoulder and asked, "What about Mark?"

"What about him?" Michael asked languidly, eyes closed, satiated with love.

"Will he accept me? Or will he resent my usurping his mother's place?"

Michael grinned. "I think if he could, he'd adopt you. Elaine said you've taken the place of Pudge, her dachshund, in my son's affections."

Blair had to think about that. She wasn't certain replacing a dog in someone's affections was an encouraging sign for a prospective new mother. And then she caught the look Michael was slanting in her direction from beneath halfclosed eyes.

He was teasing her, just as he had when they were young. "Oh, you...!" She pulled away from him, drew her fist back to punch him—and he grabbed it, pulling her over on top of him.

"I love it when you get feisty," he murmured, nuzzling her neck. His kisses started a chain reaction that quickly spread through her whole body.

"I..." She shivered as his lips left hers and moved down the underside of her chin, down toward the neck of her blouse. "Oh, I love it, too...."

Michael held her suddenly away from him. "This does mean you're planning to make an honest man of me, doesn't it?"

Blair calculated busily in her head. Three weeks, that was plenty of time to plan a wedding. "I've always dreamed of being a June bride," she replied, throwing her arms around his neck and knocking him back in the sand, planting kisses all over his face.

"So have I," he agreed, more interested in what she was doing than in what he was saying. "So have I!"

* * * * *

SILHOUETTE·INTIMATE·MOMENTS®

COMING NEXT MONTH

#437 SOMEBODY'S LADY—Marilyn Pappano

Zachary Adams and Beth Gibson were as different as chalk and cheese. Zach knew the beautiful attorney could never be interested in a country lawyer like himself. But when an important case forced him to seek Beth's help, he took advantage of the opportunity and pleaded *his* case. After all, what better place for a courtship than a courtroom?

#438 ECHOES OF ROSES—Mary Anne Wilson

Music was everything to Sam Boone Patton—until he met Leigh Buchanan. Sam thought Leigh was the perfect woman. She was beautiful, sensitive and creative. But then he learned that she was also deaf. Sam cared for Leigh, but he couldn't imagine life without sound. Until he realized that life without love was even worse....

#439 WHOSE CHILD IS THIS?—Sally Tyler Hayes

Kate Randolph was a woman with a secret—J. D. Satterly knew that much. What he *didn't* know was whether her foster child was the baby he was searching for—his baby. He'd already had his share of dishonest women, and he didn't want another. Unfortunately, his body kept telling him otherwise....

#440 PAROLED!—Paula Detmer Riggs

Dr. Tyler McClane had lost so much—his medical license, his daughter, his freedom. And the one person he'd thought would help him had been instrumental in convicting him. Now Caitlin Fielding was back, asking for forgiveness. True, they had once shared something special. But as much as he wanted Cait, could he ever learn to trust her again?

AVAILABLE THIS MONTH:

#433 UNFINISHED BUSINESS
Nora Roberts

#435 TRUE TO THE FIRE
Suzanne Carey

#434 WAKE TO DARKNESS
Blythe Stephens

#436 WITHOUT WARNING
Ann Williams

"GET AWAY FROM IT ALL" SWEEPSTAKES

HERE'S HOW THE SWEEPSTAKES WORKS

NO PURCHASE NECESSARY

To enter each drawing, complete the appropriate Official Entry Form or a 3" by 5" index card by hand-printing your name, address and phone number and the trip destination that the entry is being submitted for (i.e., Caneel Bay, Canyon Ranch or London and the English Countryside) and mailing it to: Get Away From It All Sweepstakes, P.O. Box 1397, Buffalo, New York 14269-1397.

No responsibility is assumed for lost, late or misdirected mail. Entries must be sent separately with first class postage affixed, and be received by: 4/15/92 for the Caneel Bay Vacation Drawing, 5/15/92 for the Canyon Ranch Vacation Drawing and 6/15/92 for the London and the English Countryside Vacation Drawing. Sweepstakes is open to residents of the U.S. (except Puerto Rico) and Canada, 21 years of age or older as of 5/31/92.

For complete rules send a self-addressed, stamped (WA residents need not affix return postage) envelope to: Get Away From It All Sweepstakes, P.O. Box 4892, Blair, NE 68009.

© 1992 HARLEQUIN ENTERPRISES LTD.   SWP-RLS

"GET AWAY FROM IT ALL" SWEEPSTAKES

HERE'S HOW THE SWEEPSTAKES WORKS

NO PURCHASE NECESSARY

To enter each drawing, complete the appropriate Official Entry Form or a 3" by 5" index card by hand-printing your name, address and phone number and the trip destination that the entry is being submitted for (i.e., Caneel Bay, Canyon Ranch or London and the English Countryside) and mailing it to: Get Away From It All Sweepstakes, P.O. Box 1397, Buffalo, New York 14269-1397.

No responsibility is assumed for lost, late or misdirected mail. Entries must be sent separately with first class postage affixed, and be received by: 4/15/92 for the Caneel Bay Vacation Drawing, 5/15/92 for the Canyon Ranch Vacation Drawing and 6/15/92 for the London and the English Countryside Vacation Drawing. Sweepstakes is open to residents of the U.S. (except Puerto Rico) and Canada, 21 years of age or older as of 5/31/92.

For complete rules send a self-addressed, stamped (WA residents need not affix return postage) envelope to: Get Away From It All Sweepstakes, P.O. Box 4892, Blair, NE 68009.

© 1992 HARLEQUIN ENTERPRISES LTD.   SWP-RLS

"GET AWAY FROM IT ALL"

Brand-new Subscribers-Only Sweepstakes

OFFICIAL ENTRY FORM

This entry must be received by: June 15, 1992
This month's winner will be notified by: June 30, 1992
Trip must be taken between: July 31, 1992—July 31, 1993

YES, I want to win the vacation for two to England. I understand the prize includes round-trip airfare and the two additional prizes revealed in the BONUS PRIZES insert.

Name _____

Address _____

City _____

State/Prov._____ Zip/Postal Code _____

Daytime phone number _____
(Area Code)

Return entries with invoice in envelope provided. Each book in this shipment has two entry coupons — and the more coupons you enter, the better your chances of winning!
© 1992 HARLEQUIN ENTERPRISES LTD.   3M-CPN

"GET AWAY FROM IT ALL"

Brand-new Subscribers-Only Sweepstakes

OFFICIAL ENTRY FORM

This entry must be received by: June 15, 1992
This month's winner will be notified by: June 30, 1992
Trip must be taken between: July 31, 1992—July 31, 1993

YES, I want to win the vacation for two to England. I understand the prize includes round-trip airfare and the two additional prizes revealed in the BONUS PRIZES insert.

Name _____

Address _____

City _____

State/Prov._____ Zip/Postal Code _____

Daytime phone number _____
(Area Code)

Return entries with invoice in envelope provided. Each book in this shipment has two entry coupons — and the more coupons you enter, the better your chances of winning!
© 1992 HARLEQUIN ENTERPRISES LTD.   3M-CPN